Praise for

FILLET OF MURDER

"Quirky characters, a darling small-town New England setting, and a plucky heroine. I thoroughly enjoyed this puzzler of a mystery. Reilly cooks up a perfect recipe of murder and mayhem in this charming cozy."

—Jenn McKinlay, *New York Times* bestselling author of *Copy Cap Murder*

"You had me at deep-fried haddock and malt vinegar. This is a terrific book—smart, sassy, and a little bit scary. Everything a good cozy should be!"

—Laura Childs, *New York Times* bestselling author of *Devonshire Scream*

More praise for Linda Reilly

"Reilly's debut uses her expertise in title searches to create a pleasing mystery with some interesting twists."

—*Kirkus Reviews*

"Sure to attract cozy fans."   —*Library Journal*

"I had the pages turning so fast that I was almost afraid of setting the book on fire. I loved the characters and can't wait to see them again very soon."   —Myshelf.com

Berkley Prime Crime titles by Linda Reilly

FILLET OF MURDER
OUT OF THE DYING PAN

OUT
OF THE
DYING
PAN

LINDA REILLY

BERKLEY PRIME CRIME, NEW YORK

BERKLEY PRIME CRIME

An imprint of Penguin Random House LLC
375 Hudson Street, New York, New York 10014

OUT OF THE DYING PAN

A Berkley Prime Crime Book / published by arrangement with the author

ISBN: 978-0-425-27414-9

PUBLISHING HISTORY
Berkley Prime Crime mass-market edition / March 2016

PRINTED IN THE UNITED STATES OF AMERICA

10 9 8 7 6 5 4 3 2 1

Cover illustration by Dan Craig.
Interior text design by Laura K. Corless.

Penguin
Random
House

Mom and Dad,
this one is for you

ACKNOWLEDGMENTS

A gigantic thank-you goes to Jessica Faust, my extraordinary agent, for always being there with the right answers. Jessica, you are a gem.

Michelle Vega, you are the editor every writer dreams of having. Thank you, once again, for making all my wishes come true and for embracing the personalities of my characters.

I am deeply grateful to the folks at Berkley Prime Crime for all their contributions, and for the gorgeous cover design.

To all those readers who expressed their enjoyment of *Fillet of Murder*, I can't thank you enough. You've made the journey both inspiring and rewarding, and that's really what it's all about.

To Angela Sanders, a tip of the hat for your expert advice on choosing a scent for Talia.

I owe my friend and fellow animal lover Kelsey Dakoulas a big hug for lending me her name. Kelsey, I hope you'll enjoy your role in this story!

A huge tribute goes to Martha Hoelscher, who left this earthly realm far too soon. Her spirit lives on in the hearts and the minds of those lucky enough to have known her. Peace, Martha.

And to the anonymous young man in the doughnut shop

across from Pittsfield High School—thanks for the great tip about the skateboard wheels! You helped make the story better.

Lastly, I would be remiss if I didn't thank my husband, Bernie, for his infinite patience and for cheerfully whipping up his own meals while I pounded away at the keyboard.

Talia Marby watched with a lump in her throat as the sign that read LAMBERT'S FISH & CHIPS was lowered carefully to the ground. The technician stepped down from his ladder, one large hand steadying the sign. "You want us to take this back to the shop, ma'am, or do you want to keep it?"

Keep it? Talia had been so excited when she ordered her new sign that she hadn't given a thought to disposing of the old one. She bit her lip and with her gloved hand reached out to caress the toothy blue fish engraved below the eatery's former name. A larger lump filled her throat, this time accompanied by tears pricking at her eyelids. She swallowed. "Do I have to decide now? I . . . I'd like to keep it, but I don't really have room for it."

The technician's long-lashed hazel eyes flashed with understanding. "Hard to part with things, isn't it? Lots of folks get real nostalgic about this stuff."

Nodding, Talia looked away, instead sweeping her gaze over the Wrensdale Arcade, the cozy shopping plaza in her hometown of Wrensdale. Nestled in the heart of the Berkshires, the arcade had been designed to resemble a sixteenth-century English village. Boasting Tudor storefronts and a cobblestone plaza, the shopping arcade had seven shops that formed a U-pattern around the plaza.

Talia rubbed the early December chill from her arms, recalling the day she'd first walked into the eatery looking for a part-time job. She was a teenager then, with a home life that had grown somewhat chaotic. The Lamberts, Bea and Howie, had taken to her immediately and hired her on the spot.

That was half a lifetime ago. It seemed almost surreal to Talia that she was now the proprietor of this quaint eatery. At Bea Lambert's urging, she'd expanded the original fish and chips theme to include other deep-fried delights. She renamed it Fry Me a Sliver—hence the need for the new sign.

"Ma'am?" The sign technician cleared his throat. "You wanna keep the old sign?"

"Sorry, I was daydreaming." She heaved a quiet sigh. "I'd love to keep it, but I don't have a place to store it. I guess you can take it back to your shop and recycle what you can from it. Do you know when my new sign will be ready?"

"Uh, yeah, we had a little glitch with that. We ordered the color paint you wanted, but when it came in, it was the wrong shade. Gonna be at another week or so. Sorry," he said.

Talia nodded her understanding, but a wave of disappointment washed through her. Without a sign, would people think she was closed?

The tech was striding off toward his truck when a crash from behind Talia rattled her ears. *Oh, no. Not again.*

"Sorry about that." The voice rose from the cobblestone, where Lucas Bartolini, Talia's nineteen-year-old employee, had fallen from his skateboard for the umpteenth time.

"Lucas, one of these days you're going to crack your head open," she scolded, feeling more like his mom than his employer.

In one smooth move, Lucas hoisted himself up and scooped his skateboard into his hands. He brushed off the knees of his jeans, a tuft of blond hair drooping over one twinkling blue eye. He grinned as if to say, *No worries. I'm cool.* He patted his jacket with his large hand. "Yup. iPad's okay, too. And my mom made zippers for my shirt pockets so my cell won't fall out."

Lucas lived with his folks only three blocks from the bustling downtown where the Wrensdale Arcade jutted off from the main drag. He was determined to conquer the cobblestone surface with his skateboard, even if he broke both knees and his neck in the process.

"When's our new sign getting here?" Lucas asked. He glanced across the plaza at the new shop that had opened a week earlier.

Our new sign. Talia loved his enthusiasm. "It won't be ready for at least another week," she said. "But I can't wait to see it hanging there. The designer did a great job creating a whimsical blue haddock juggling a handful of deep-fried goodies."

"Cool," Lucas said.

Talia glanced at her watch, pleased to note that Lucas was always punctual. He was also smart and personable, and had taken on the task of creating a Facebook page for the eatery—something she'd been meaning to do but could never squeeze into her busy days. The only flaw she could see in her new employee was his propensity for clumsiness, even when he wasn't trying to skim the cobblestones on his skateboard.

"Why don't you go ahead inside and get started on the potatoes," she told Lucas. "The new shop across the way opened at ten, and I'm anxious to take a peek and welcome my fellow proprietor. I'll only be a few minutes."

"Sure thing, Ms. Marby. Okay if I grab a cup of java?"

"Of course," Talia said and squelched a smile. He asked the same question every day, and every day she gave him the same response.

Talia hurried across the plaza to the new boutique. Vintage clothing, she'd heard. She couldn't help admiring the fancy new sign, the words ONCE OR TWICE engraved on it in copper-colored script. Beside the shop's name was the painted image of a 1920s flapper, beautifully drawn in shades of blood red and coal black.

She peeked inside first, through the pane of the leaded-glass door. Vintage dresses and jackets hung on painted, cast-iron racks placed strategically throughout the store. In one corner rested an antique hat stand graced with old-style hats and scarves. Behind a glass display counter, a young woman with long, dark hair and a slender form frowned as she removed from a cardboard box what appeared to be antique brooches. Eager to investigate and to meet the new owner, Talia swung open the door. "Hello there," she said brightly.

The sales clerk jerked her head up and planted a quick smile on her face. "Hi," she said shyly, shoving the box aside. "We only opened last week, so let me know if you're looking for anything in particular. Everything's a little jumbled right now."

"That's fine," Talia said. "I'm Talia Marby. I own the fish and chips shop across the way. I wanted to stop in to welcome you to the arcade."

The clerk sidled around from behind the glass counter. "I'm Kelsey Dakoulas," she said, offering a slender hand. "Like I said, we've only been here a—"

A brocade curtain behind the counter suddenly whooshed aside. From a back room appeared a stunning, thirty-something woman, her lush, ginger-colored curls pulled loosely over the front of one shoulder and fastened with a feathered barrette. A smattering of pale freckles dusted her prominent cheekbones. Unsmiling, the woman crossed her arms and glared at Talia.

"This is Ria, my boss," Kelsey said, her cheeks flushing slightly. "Ria, this is Talia from the fish and chips place."

"Happy to meet you, Ria," Talia said, offering her hand.

Ria's azure eyes hardened into twin glaciers. She turned to Kelsey and snapped, "Haven't you put those things away yet? This is the holiday season, remember? People are going to want to *buy*, and they can't *buy* if we don't display the goods."

Yikes, Talia thought. *Someone's having a bad day.*

Kelsey blinked. "Sorry," she murmured, sliding her gaze sideways. "I'll have it done in a jif."

Feeling about as welcome as a hailstorm, Talia moved toward the door. "I can see I'm interrupting. I'll stop back another time. Your shop looks beautiful, by the way."

Talia rushed back to her eatery, the sting of Ria's rebuff sharp in her mind. What was that about anyway? Before today she'd never even met the woman!

The moment she'd entered Fry Me a Sliver, the annoying scent of lingering tobacco had irritated her senses. Martha Hoelscher, Talia's other new employee, was tying a cerulean blue apron around her sturdy form, while Lucas was busy scooping up the Idaho potato he'd dropped on the tile floor. Talia pulled in a calming breath. "Good morning, Martha."

"Morning. I'll get started on the Parmesan batter, if that's okay with you. I love making that stuff. It smells so good."

The Parmesan batter was used to prepare the deep-fried meatballs, a new side that was already a hit with customers. The meatballs were a variation on one of the recipes Talia remembered her grandmother making. Nana had died that past spring, leaving a hole in Talia's heart, and Talia now lived in her charming bungalow.

Talia couldn't resist shooting a glance at Martha's scarf. Brown and ratty-looking, it was draped over Martha's wool peacoat, which hung on a hook on the kitchen's back door. It wasn't the scarf itself that bothered Talia—it was the stale, smoky odor that emanated from it. She'd been trying to come up with a solution, short of ordering Martha not to wear it, but so far she hadn't thought of anything that wouldn't send Martha into a snit.

"You need to get started on the dining room first, Martha. The chairs need to be wiped down, and the tables scrubbed."

Martha glowered, her helmet of straight gray hair swinging sideways as she bent to retrieve a spray bottle from beneath the counter. "Yeah, yeah, I know," she huffed. "It's not like I don't do it every day. Freakin' kids make such a mess in there. You'd think their parents could teach them to eat without splattering tartar sauce and ketchup all over the place."

"Children are messy, Martha. You might as well get used to it." Talia grinned. "Don't they have kids where you come from?" She wedged herself past Martha and removed a large bag of sliced cabbage from the commercial fridge.

"Yeah, they have kids where I come from," Martha grumbled, "but I always stayed as far away from them as possible."

A transplant from New Hampshire, Martha had settled in Wrensdale several months earlier. Her past was a bit hazy.

According to her résumé, she'd worked for more than a decade for a national insurance company, but was abruptly let go for reasons Martha couldn't adequately explain. When she applied for the job at the eatery, Talia saw right away that she was wildly overqualified. But the woman's obvious intelligence, along with a sense of mild desperation, persuaded Talia to give her a chance.

Talia busied herself preparing the eatery's piquant coleslaw. A healthy dose of chipotle sauce gave it the *zing* customers loved. Bea Lambert had created the recipe herself, and the side dish was a long-time favorite.

Lucas dropped only three more potatoes in the peeling process—a new record for him—and was now stocking the napkin holders and refilling salt and pepper shakers.

By eleven thirty the phone orders began streaming in. With the holidays only a few weeks away, Talia predicted a busy Saturday. She hoped that her lack of a sign didn't deter diners. The regulars, for sure, knew she was open for business.

"Um, Ms. Marby?" Lucas, phone in hand, put a caller on hold. "The guys at the firehouse want to know if we do delivery now."

Talia slid two slabs of flour-coated haddock through a tray of batter. "Tell them no, sorry." It was the second time that week someone had asked about delivery.

Lucas conveyed the message and then scribbled out a huge takeout order. He hung up and said, "Um, they wanted me to tell you that if you delivered their order instead of forcing them to send someone to pick it up, it would make it easier for them to keep the town safe from raging fires."

Talia lowered the haddock slices into the deep fryer. "I hope they were kidding."

Lucas grinned. "I think so, but they really did want delivery."

Business remained brisk, and by seven o'clock Talia was beat. Lucas's shift had ended at four, so she and Martha handled the dinner orders on their own.

Talia slid her arms into the sleeves of her flared jacket. "We're still on for tomorrow, right?" she asked Martha.

Martha sighed and tucked her ugly scarf around her neck. "Yeah, I guess so."

On the first Sunday of every December, the Wrensdale Community Center held its annual Santa fund-raiser. It was a fun-packed event at which local merchants filled the gymnasium and peddled their goods. The proceeds went to local families who had fallen on tough times. Santa would be there, too. Perched in an elaborate velveteen chair, he'd be entertaining kids and handing out small gifts.

"You don't sound thrilled," Talia said. "Is it because of all the kids?"

Martha waved a stout hand. "Nah. I just like my days off. On Sundays I can read all day and tell the rest of the world to take a flying—"

"Martha."

"I was going to say a flying flapjack," she said testily.

"I wouldn't have imposed on you, except that Mom has to work, Ryan spends Sunday afternoons with his dad, and Rachel has some family affair she can't get out of. Besides, as a fairly new resident, I thought you might enjoy meeting some of the locals."

Martha shrugged. "Yeah, sure, whatever," She shoved the handle of her plastic chartreuse handbag over her arm. Talia locked up, and together they crossed the cobblestone plaza and headed in the direction of the town parking lot.

All along Main Street, glimmering white snowflakes hung from the light poles. Wrapped diagonally around each pole was a garland of fake evergreen. Many of the storefronts boasted blinking lights. In the window of Peggy's Bakery, a string of blue mini-lights illuminated a beaming fake Santa, one outstretched arm bearing a tray of red and green frosted cookies.

"Isn't the downtown lovely," Talia said. "So festive and cheery. I love Halloween, but Christmas has always been my favorite time of year in Wrensdale."

Martha kept her head down, navigating the sidewalk in her sensible shoes as if there were landmines beneath the pavement. "Yup," she said. "Pretty."

Talia wanted to question Martha about her own hometown, but sensed she wasn't in a chatty mood. The woman was definitely an enigma.

They came to the lighted parking lot, and Talia watched as Martha lowered herself onto the front seat of her olive green Chrysler. The car was a monstrosity that seemed to take up half the lot. The little silver tag identifying the model had fallen off, so Talia wasn't even sure what it was.

Martha revved the engine and waved a halfhearted good-bye. Talia slipped inside her own car, a turquoise Fiat, and locked the doors.

She looked over to give Martha one final wave, but the green metal beast had already torn out of the lot as if a demon were riding its tail.

2

"See, Martha, doesn't this look like fun?" Talia said.

The gymnasium was chockablock with vendors setting up their tables. On the opposite side of the gym a charming Santa's village had been created. An oversized chair covered in dark green velveteen served as Santa's chair. Next to the chair was a bulging burlap sack stuffed with small wrapped gifts. Against the wall, above a faux fireplace, was a mantel wide enough to hold the items donated by the vendors for the annual raffle. Talia had donated a gift certificate for two free fish-and-chips dinners at Fry Me a Sliver.

Martha stuck her chartreuse bag under their assigned table and peeled off her coat. She shoved that underneath, too, on top of the purse. Talia was grateful to see she'd left that horrendous scarf at home.

"Yeah, well, first off, I had to park a block away," Martha

griped. "By the time I got here, all the spots were taken. Well, there was *one* spot, but my car couldn't fit into it."

Maybe that's because it's the size of aircraft carrier, Talia was tempted to say, but then instantly scolded herself. The rattletrap Martha drove might be the only thing she could afford.

"I'm glad you offered to help me today," Talia said kindly. "I really think you'll enjoy yourself." She straightened the red plastic table cover that Martha had dislodged when she'd roughly stuck her belongings under it.

"I didn't offer, I agreed," Martha pointed out. "There's a difference."

Talia breathed in slowly, determined not to let Martha get to her today. "Yes, and I appreciate it more than you know."

Talia had been one of the first to arrive, and for the most part had her corner booth all set up for business. A smaller table rested behind the larger one, since she needed a safe place to set up the portable fryer. She didn't want any curious fingers straying toward the sizzling hot oil.

She glanced over at the empty table catty-corner to her own. So far, the vendor hadn't shown up, but as it was only nine fifteen, there was still plenty of time.

Talia was featuring only one item today—deep-fried marble cake with raspberry sauce. She'd already sliced three large sheets of marble cake—compliments of Peggy's Bakery—into serving-sized squares. They were stacked inside a covered plastic container, next to the cooler that held the sweetened batter and the raspberry sauce.

"I'll need some help getting the portable fryer out of my car," Talia told Martha. "Wanna make a trip to the parking lot with me?"

"No need to trouble the lady, miss. I'll help."

Talia turned abruptly. The voice came from a seriously attractive man with wavy blond hair and a muscular build, who seemed to have materialized out of nowhere. Late forties, early fifties, Talia guessed. Worked out a lot, for sure.

"Oh, um, thanks," Talia stammered. "But—"

He stuck out his hand and grinned. "Scott Pollard, at your service. I own Pollard Home Renovations."

Talia smiled and accepted his handshake. "Talia Marby. I'm the new owner of Fry Me a Sliver, in the Wrensdale Arcade."

"Ah, my kind of comfort food," he said, his dark brown eyes twinkling. "I've been meaning to check it out. Hey, look, if you'll show me where your car's parked, I'll grab that fryer for you."

"Well, thank you, um, Scott. I believe I'll take you up on that."

"Excellent."

Talia threw on her jacket and accompanied him toward the community center's back entrance. He opened the door and they strode outside. "December's been unseasonably warm, hasn't it?" she said.

"Yeah, too warm if you ask me. The cold weather suits me much better."

"That's me. The blue Fiat," Talia said. "I parked as close to the building as I could." She popped the hatch, and Scott instantly leaned over and lifted the box holding the fryer. The left sleeve of his forest green sweater slid up slightly, and Talia spied part of a tattoo. She stifled a giggle. Was that the feathered tip of a pirate's hat engraved into his skin? Ugh, she couldn't imagine getting a tattoo. Just the thought of the needle piercing her skin was enough to give her the willies.

Scott hefted the box with ease, while Talia lugged the

half-gallon container of vegetable oil she'd brought along. Inside, Scott set the box down on the table Talia indicated. He studied the fryer, frowning as he peered at the electrical cord. "This won't stretch to the wall," he said. "I'm going to hunt down a power strip for you. I don't like the looks of this table, either. You need something sturdier. Be back in a flash."

Martha ambled over. "Well, isn't he helpful?" she said slyly, a rare twinkle in her soft gray eyes. "A real knight in golden armor."

"Seems like a nice man," Talia said. Was Martha implying that Scott was interested in her? Even if he were, it wouldn't matter. Not a man on earth compared to Talia's current squeeze, Ryan Collins. They'd only been seeing each other for a number of weeks, but just thinking about him made her feel all warm and tingly. She pushed Ryan temporarily from her thoughts. For the next five hours, her focus had to stay on deep-frying slabs of cake for the masses.

Vendors began arriving in clusters. The ambient noise level rose. Holiday music pumped from the speakers, and Talia caught herself humming to the cheery tune of "Jingle Bells."

At the edge of her vision, she saw a gorgeous woman marching in her direction trailing a wheeled suitcase behind her and carrying a tote bag on her shoulder. Eyes swiveled and gaped as the woman passed. Her thick mane of ginger-colored hair hung loose around her shoulders, and her blue-eyed gaze skimmed the room as if looking for someone.

Oh no, it was that Ria woman! The one who'd treated Talia so rudely.

When Ria saw that her assigned table was in the corner adjacent to Talia's, her face went taut. Her plump lips morphed into a thin line. She slammed the wheels of her luggage on the floor and shot lasers at Talia with her blue eyes.

"This is unacceptable," Ria said. "I'm going to demand a different table."

At that moment, Scott reappeared clutching a power strip and two wooden pallets. Ria whirled on him. "Are you in charge here?"

For a moment Scott looked stunned. "I'm helping out, but I'm not in charge. What can I do for you?"

"This table will *not* work for me. I'll have no visibility in this corner." She aimed a blood red fingernail at Talia's fryer. "And I'm not going to spend my entire day smelling that greasy excuse for food. I need to relocate, preferably to a table near the entrance."

Scott's jaw tightened. "Miss, I'd love to help, but the tables near the entrance are reserved for the hospital volunteers. They're big supporters of this fund-raiser, and they bring in lots of *do-re-mi*, if you catch my drift."

"Then find me another spot."

Talia stepped forward. "Ria, have I done something to offend you?" she asked quietly. "You seemed perfectly fine until you saw me."

"I'm *offended*," she said, "by being placed next to a fry cook."

Talia felt her temper bubble to the surface. "I'll confess that I'm a fry cook, but I'm here to raise money for needy families, just as you are. Why don't we try to work together, at least for the next five hours?"

Ria's face reddened. Attracted by the raised voices, a few curious faces gathered to gawk.

"Oh, never mind," she sputtered at Scott and waved a

dismissive hand at him. "I'll set up here." Ria turned an evil eye on the gawkers, and they scattered like frightened mice.

Scott nodded, winked at Talia, and went over to the portable fryer. "I found a nine-foot power strip, but tables are at a premium. Luckily I had two clean pallets in my truck. I'm going to set this up so it'll be good and secure. I don't want anyone getting burned by hot oil if they accidentally bump the table."

"That's nice of you, Scott. Thank you."

He worked for the next few minutes setting up the fryer so that it was safe from wobbles and bumps. When he was through, the pallets rested neatly atop each other, and precisely parallel to the edge of the table. He gave Talia a two-fingered salute. "Let me know if you need anything else. Now I gotta go help Santa move his Christmas tree. He says it's blocking his view, and he's worried that the kids won't see him there."

She laughed. "Sounds like you're the good deed doer of the day. Thanks, Scott."

Ria had tossed a black velvet runner over her table and was setting out pieces of antique jewelry. When she saw Scott start to stride off, she called out, "Wait a minute. I'd like some help."

He turned, and she tossed her car keys at him. "Red Camry," she said. "I need you to bring in my tall rack. It's in the trunk."

Scott stared at her for a moment, his hand gripping the keys so hard Talia thought the metal was going to liquefy. "I'll be right back," he said softly.

Her gaze aimed at her thick leather shoes, Martha tapped Talia on the shoulder. "I'm going for another coffee," she said. "Want one?"

"No thanks, but I'd like you to set out the napkins and paper plates when you get back. Oh, and the plastic forks."

Martha nodded and trudged off, passing Kelsey Dakoulas on the way.

"Hey, Kelsey." Talia smiled at the young woman, who looked as if she'd just swallowed a lump of coal. "That sweater is adorable."

Kelsey looked down at the whimsical cat wearing an elfin hat that graced the front of her maroon fleece top. "Oh, hi, um . . . Talia. Thanks." She turned to Ria. "I need to talk to you," she said through clenched teeth.

Ria reached into her suitcase for another box. "Sorry, don't have time," she said, avoiding Kelsey's stare. "My *employee* chose not to help me today, so I have to do everything myself."

"I told you, Ria, I do children's face painting every year at this event, and I'm not going to disappoint the kids. And for the record," Kelsey added in a lowered voice, "what you did to me was despicable. I'm not going to forget this."

Ria's smile was devious. "Whatever do you mean?" she piped innocently.

Kelsey glanced at Talia and then turned back to face Ria. She lowered her voice to a furious whisper, and the rest of the conversation melded into the surrounding din.

Talia hated to be nosy, but with Ria treating Talia as if she carried the plague, she was more than anxious to learn what the woman had done to infuriate Kelsey. She unsealed the container of vegetable oil she'd carried in and slowly began filling the fryer. Ears perked, she leaned her head toward Ria's table, but only a few snatches of conversation sifted through the growing clamor.

"You're . . . nasty woman . . . why I ever liked you."

". . . over it. Cats are a dime a dozen."

Kelsey pounded her small fist on Ria's table. "You are not going to get away with this," she said, and stormed off.

Whoa. What was that about?

Ria dug a small folding table rack from her suitcase, stuck it on the corner of her table, and began setting out tree ornaments that had a vintage look. Talia stole a quick peek. The ornaments appeared to be tiny angels made of embossed foil. She itched to get a better look, but didn't dare approach Ria's table.

And where was Martha? She'd been gone for over ten minutes. Talia was getting a bad feeling that the woman was going to be more of a hindrance today than a help.

Scott returned carrying a tall stainless steel rack. He set it down between Ria's table and Talia's, plopped the car keys atop the velvet runner, and strode off.

Well, isn't this day starting with a bang, Talia thought to herself.

Ria snagged her keys, stuffed them inside her purse, and then stalked off in the direction of the restrooms at the opposite corner of the gym. Talia was setting out plastic forks when she noticed a plump, white-haired senior wearing a bright gold sweater emblazoned with dachshunds leaning over Ria's table.

"Hello, there," Talia greeted her.

The woman jumped slightly, and her cheeks flushed. "Oh, golly, you startled me. I'm Vivian Lavoie. You must be the new fish lady," she said. "I heard all about your restaurant."

Fish lady? Okay, the name did fit, sort of. In fact, Talia liked it.

"Nice to meet you, Vivian." Talia introduced herself. "We still serve fish and chips, but we've added some new dishes to the menu. I hope you'll stop in sometime."

"Oh, I intend to. My friend Ethel told me about your scrumptious deep-fried meatballs, and I'm dying to try them." Vivian's gaze slid back to Ria's table, and from her expression Talia saw that she was clearly perturbed about something.

Talia shot a look at the wall clock. She still had twenty minutes before the official start of the event, and her internal engine needed a jolt of caffeine. Excusing herself, she began threading her way across the room, the luscious scent of fresh-brewed coffee drawing her to the table where a coffee urn and boxes of doughnuts had been set out. A thin, bespectacled man dressed in a Santa getup was struggling to fill a cardboard cup without staining the fuzzy sleeves of his outfit.

"Need some help with that?" Talia asked.

Santa turned abruptly. When he saw Talia, a fierce blush colored his sallow cheeks. "Oh, thank you. The coffee sputters all over the place every time I pull the lever."

Talia took his cup and filled it carefully. "I see what you mean. The spout's a bit temperamental." She handed him the cup of steaming coffee. "There. Mission accomplished."

Santa took the cup, staring at Talia through thick, round-ish glasses that were clearly not a prop. "Thank you. You're very sweet. May I ask your name?"

"Talia Marby," she said, filling a cup for herself. "I'm the new owner of Fry Me a Sliver, on the arcade."

Santa's pale blue eyes lit up at the name. "Marby, huh?" He grinned and stuck out his free hand. "Andy Nash. You related to Pete?"

Talia accepted his white-gloved handshake and then grabbed a cardboard cup for herself. She filled it with coffee and plopped in a creamer packet. "Sure am. Peter is my dad."

Andy nodded thoughtfully. "You're a lucky girl, then. A lucky girl."

Interesting response, but Talia didn't have time to pursue it. It wouldn't be long before hungry customers might start flowing toward her table.

"I'm the director of the community center," Andy offered, just as Talia's foot was poised to make her escape. "Hence the yearly Santa gig. But I have a second job at my dad's Ford place out on the Pittsfield-Lenox Road, so if you ever need a new set of wheels, stop in on a weekend and see me." He winked at her. "Give you a great deal."

"Thanks, Andy. Right now I'm not looking, but I'll keep you in mind."

His face fell. "Oh, okay. Anyway, it was nice meeting you. Hey, if you get a chance later, pop over to Santa's village."

Talia breathed a sigh of relief after Andy strolled off. Coffee cup in hand, she wound her way back toward her table, anxious to get the fryer started. She was ten feet or so from her table when she realized that someone was crouched beneath it. Then a head popped up, ginger hair askew, her face a mask of fury.

"What did you do with my angel ornaments?" Ria hissed. "They were right here five minutes ago, and now they're missing. I know you took them."

Talia set her cup down. This was really too much. "All right, Ria. I've had enough. Get out from under there now. Martha and I left our personal things there, and you have no right to paw through them."

Ria crawled out from under the table and rose. "Then give me back my ornaments before I call the cops!"

"I didn't take your ornaments and you know it," Talia said, squashing the urge to stamp her foot. "Did you check your car? Maybe you decided not to sell them and brought them out there for safekeeping?"

Ria jabbed a finger at Talia's nose. "Maybe I'll check *your* car, because that's where they are."

What was wrong with this woman? Talia threw up her hands. "I went to my car once, with Scott, to get the fryer and the vegetable oil. I'm not a thief, Ria."

At the word *thief* Ria paled. She stumbled backward a step and sent Talia a look blistering enough to melt the North Pole. "You won't get away with this. Mark my words."

Mark my words? Was that a threat?

Talia watched Ria stomp back behind her own table. She took three deep breaths to calm herself. The deep breaths did nothing, so she slugged back a mouthful of coffee from her paper cup. Not bad considering it was brewed in an ancient commercial urn.

The rack Scott had fetched from Ria's car had been moved to the other side of the table. Draped over its arms were scarves of every style and color. Most were knitted, but some appeared to be designer scarves from another era. One of the scarves suddenly caught Talia's eye. Thick and woolly, it was a shimmering shade of cornflower blue with knotted tassels at the ends.

Talia's heart leaped into her gullet. She knew that scarf. She'd *knitted* that scarf.

She felt her pulse pound as she stepped over to Ria's table. "Where did you get that?" she demanded, pointing at the blue scarf. "That is my Nana's scarf!"

3

For one scary moment, Ria stared at Talia through eyes that would freeze steam. "You're a real piece of work, you know that? First you filch my ornaments. Then you accuse me of stealing your granny's scarf. I'm warning you now, *Ms.* Marby, you'd better stay away from my stuff, or else."

Talia gripped her own hands to keep them from shaking. "Where did you get the scarf, Ria?" she said, hating the tremor in her voice. "I made that for my grandmother when I was sixteen. It was my gift to her for teaching me how to knit. You can't even buy that kind of yarn anymore. It's a specialty silk-wool blend, and the manufacturer went out of business years ago."

Ria swung her lush hair behind her and turned her back on Talia. She bent and started rummaging through her suitcase, muttering under her breath as she hunted for the missing ornaments.

"All right, I'll pay you for it," Talia said. "How much do you want?"

Ria swerved and yanked the blue scarf off the rack. She pretended to read an imaginary price tag. "Let's see. Oh yes—this one is a bargain at four hundred and ninety-five dollars." With a smirk, she tossed the scarf back on the rack.

This battle was going nowhere. Talia glanced again at the clock. It was a few minutes before ten, and the room was beginning to fill. She'd have to figure out a way to get the scarf back later.

Now where was Martha? Hadn't she only gone for coffee? With an exasperated sigh, Talia turned on the fryer and set two covered bowls beside it on the table. On the opposite side of the fryer she placed the container of sliced cake squares, just as two grade-schoolers, followed by a red-cheeked woman, trotted over to Talia's table. "Are you open yet?" the woman warbled. "Ever since my kids saw your restaurant on the list of vendors, deep-fried raspberry cake is all they've talked about!"

"Give me one minute," Talia said with a smile. "It's actually deep-fried marble cake with raspberry sauce, and you're my first customers of the day!"

The kids, a gap-toothed boy with a cowlick and a little girl with a dark cluster of curls, grinned eagerly at her. Using her metal tongs, Talia dredged a slab of marble cake through the sweetened batter, then lowered it carefully into the fryer. The temperature was perfect—350 degrees—and the oil began to gently sizzle. She did the same with a second piece of cake, and within two minutes they were fried to a golden hue. Talia lifted the basket to let them drain for a few seconds.

Martha still hadn't set out the paper plates, so Talia dug them out from beneath the table and set a small stack next to the fryer. She placed each fried treat on a plate and drizzled a hefty spoonful of raspberry sauce over each one. "There you go," she said, giving them napkins and plastic forks. "They're hot, so be careful, okay?"

The kids nodded, and the little girl blew on her cake. She forked up a tiny bite and popped it into her mouth. "Mommy, this is yummy!" she declared, while her brother bobbed his head in agreement.

Talia collected three dollars from their mother, who beamed as if she had the most brilliant children in the world. "Thanks," the mom said. "From the way they're gobbling these, we may be back later for a second helping."

They scooted away, and out of the corner of Talia's eye she saw Martha slink in behind their table. At least she was pretty sure it was Martha. Her gray hair was tucked into a lime green crocheted hat from which two long braids dangled, one on either side. At the top of the hat, two ears had been sewn on, each with a plastic google-eye glued into the center. She was either a frog or a creature from a distant planet.

"Martha," Talia said in a low voice. "What on earth are you wearing?"

"A hat," she said. "What do you think I'm wearing?"

Talia counted to ten in her head. "Don't you think it's more of a children's hat?" she said, instead of what she really wanted to say, which was, *Don't you think it looks ridiculous on a grown woman?*

Martha shrugged. "It's an adult size, and the lady who sold it to me said they're all the rage."

"It's already quite warm in here," Talia pointed out. "With all the activity, it'll probably be stifling before the day is out. By noon you'll be ripping it off your head, I guarantee."

"I like it warm," Martha countered. "Besides, old people are supposed to keep their heads toasty."

Talia squeezed the bridge of her nose with two fingers. Could the woman be any more contrary?

"Martha, I'm really going to need your help today," Talia pleaded, hearing her voice inch toward whiny. "It's hard for one person to do the frying and take care of the cash box at the same time. I already sold two cakes and had to juggle the money."

"So I'm here," Martha said. "Tell me what to do and I'll do it."

What an opening that was, Talia thought wryly. No, she had to be nice. She was raised to be polite, and polite she would be. If it killed her.

"Smile at the customers. Keep the table stocked with forks and napkins, and be sure I've always got a stack of plates next to the fryer. And most important, handle the money."

Martha cocked a finger at her. "Gotcha," she said with an exaggerated wink.

Talia sensed a touch of sarcasm in Martha's response, but decided to ignore it. Who knew? Maybe that silly hat would actually attract customers. Anything was possible.

Before long people began streaming toward the table, and at one point there was a line four deep. Within an hour they sold about four dozen servings. Talia was glad she'd prepared for a deluge. Although she was still pretty well stocked, she'd left a second container of sliced marble cake squares in her car. And in the community center's commercial kitchen she'd tucked a backup bowl of batter.

Twice Martha had ducked off to the restroom, leaving Talia to cope on her own. Most people were giving her exact change, which helped tremendously.

And she had to admit—Martha's goofy hat was definitely attracting attention. Kids giggled as they approached, and a few asked her if she was Kermit. Martha only smiled mysteriously at the question and wiggled her gray eyebrows.

"Wish we could take a coffee break," Martha grumbled, as the noon hour approached.

On top of the two bathroom breaks you've already taken? Talia was tempted to blurt out. But that wasn't fair, was it? After all, people *did* need to use the bathroom. In fact, she wouldn't mind a mini-break herself. Could she trust Martha alone for ten minutes?

Talia waited for a lull, then said to Martha, "Do you mind if I—"

"Go ahead." Martha waved a chunky hand at her. "I was wondering when you were going to ask."

Talia smiled. "Thanks. I won't be long."

Talia snagged her purse from beneath the table. She'd ignored Ria all morning, but it looked as if the annoying woman was doing a brisk business of her own. Talia prayed someone wouldn't buy the blue scarf before she could figure out a way to buy it for herself.

After a fast trip to the restroom, Talia strolled along the perimeter of the gym. She spied Kelsey Dakoulas at her face-painting table. Biting her lip in concentration, Kelsey was putting the finishing touches on the face of a darling brown-haired little girl who'd been transformed into a striped tiger—complete with whiskers and a round black nose.

Talia gave her a thumbs-up and mouthed, *Nice job.*

Kelsey set her brush down and handed the child a mirror. "There you go, Samantha. Now you're a baby tiger."

The little girl's eyes widened and she broke into a grin. "Thank you," she said softly.

Kelsey smiled, but her eyes looked tense. The child went off with an older woman, no doubt her doting grandmother, bouncing and making growly sounds as if she were a real tiger.

"You're very talented," Talia told Kelsey.

"Thanks. Unfortunately, I'm not much in the mood to paint today. That horrid, evil woman spoiled everything."

"You mean Ria?"

Kelsey nodded and stuck her brush in a plastic cup filled with cloudy gray water.

"Anything I can do to help?" Talia asked.

"No. Not unless you want to kill her for me."

Talia itched to know what Ria had done to Kelsey to make her so angry. "That bad, huh?"

"You have no idea," Kelsey said, her brown eyes glittering with fury. Then her face softened. "I'm sorry. I shouldn't talk about her that way. After all, she *is* my boss. Unless she fires me tomorrow, which is a definite possibility."

"Have you known her long?" Talia asked.

"About eight months," Kelsey said. "Until a few months ago, we both worked at the Wiltshire Inn in Stockbridge. I want to study to be an animal care technician, and my mom suggested I work for a year first to save up some tuition money. Mom has MS and can't work anymore, so she depends on me a lot."

"I'm sorry to hear that," Talia said.

"Anyway, I was waiting tables at the inn when Ria got the hostess job. Even though she's quite a bit older, we ended up becoming pretty good friends, and started doing lots of stuff together. You know, shopping, movies . . . girl stuff."

Talia was anxious to hear more, but didn't dare leave Martha alone much longer. "Kelsey, I'm sorry, but I have to get back to my table. Please drop in and see me anytime you want to talk, okay? Even if you come by before opening, just knock on the front door and I'll let you in."

Kelsey's face fell, but then she quirked up one side of her lips in a halfhearted smile. "Thanks for the offer, Talia. I might just do that."

Talia headed back to her table by a different route, slowing when she neared Santa's village. Partially hidden behind a portable divider wall, the "village" had a cozy look. A cardboard sign capped with fake snow made from cotton balls had been propped up, announcing, SANTA IS FEEDING HIS REINDEER. COME BACK SOON.

Talia peeked around the divider wall and paused to admire the tree. Standing about six feet tall, it glittered with tinsel and blue mini-lights. Now that she was living permanently in Nana's bungalow, she'd have to think about putting up her own tree.

A clipped voice suddenly filtered into earshot from the other side of the tree. It sounded a lot like *freaking witch*, except Talia was sure the "freaking" was a slightly different word, and the "witch" was really the *B* word.

Talia peered between the tree branches and saw a swatch of bright red. Oh no, was that Santa Claus cursing like an escapee from a prison movie?

She ambled away, but couldn't resist turning around for another look once she had a better angle. Yes, it was Santa all right. Huddled behind the tree, he was stabbing furiously at his cell phone with both thumbs, his mouth twitching.

Santa, aka Andy Nash.

Wow. That was an eye-opener. Why was everyone so angry today?

Talia felt a tap on her shoulder and jumped. She turned

to see a round face framed by silver curls beaming at her like a burst of sunshine.

"Hi," Vivian Lavoie said. "I saw you standing there, and wanted to ask if you had a minute to check out my hand-crafted ornaments."

"Oh . . . um, of course." The woman looked so hopeful Talia couldn't bear to say no. "I'd love to see them."

Vivian rubbed her fingers together with glee. "Follow me, then."

Talia trailed Vivian to a table in the center aisle that was covered with a faded red tablecloth. A slew of balsa wood ornaments had been carefully set out. Some were small. Others were far too oversized for Talia's taste. Snowflakes, reindeer, candy canes, and even a few elves were included in the mix. Hand-painted with a not-too-steady hand, they had a definite amateur look about them. It was clear from Vivian's bubbly smile that she was proud of her handiwork, and was keen on having Talia admire it.

Talia's heart went out to the woman. "These are . . . really sweet, and quite interesting, Vivian. How much are they?"

Vivian's lips puckered. "Well, they started out being four dollars each, but I had to lower the price because nobody was biting." She sighed. "It's the economy, I guess. Anyway, I'm selling them for two bucks apiece. Is that too much for you?"

"Not at all," Talia said with a big smile. She chose five different ornaments and paid Vivian.

"Thank you!" Vivian said, sticking the cash into her pocket. She seemed so excited that Talia wondered if it was the first sale she'd made all day. Poor woman.

Talia eased the ornaments into her purse and hustled back to her table. She'd only been gone about twelve minutes, but what she saw when she approached her table shocked her.

Martha the Frog was frying up cake squares as if she'd done it all her life. And the expression on her face! In spite of the dab of raspberry sauce clinging to one corner of her mouth, she actually looked . . . pleasant. She was going about it so efficiently that Talia wondered who was handling the money.

"Excuse me." Talia squeezed past the row of kids and their moms who were waiting patiently for the line to move forward.

"There you go." Martha handed a fried cake smeared with raspberry sauce to a towheaded little boy. "Fresh out of the fryer for one of Santa's favorite helpers!"

The little boy giggled and his mom thanked Martha profusely. "Is this the donation can?" the woman asked.

Donation can?

"Yes, ma'am." Martha nodded and winked at her, grinning when the woman deposited a ten-dollar bill in the can. Ten dollars for one fried cake.

Talia shook her head in disbelief and slipped behind the table. "What's going on?" she said to Martha.

"Isn't it obvious? I'm frying me up some marble cake. And since you weren't here to handle the cash, I set up a donation can. A buck fifty is too low when you're selling for charity anyway, so I'm letting people decide for themselves what to pay."

Talia graced the waiting customers with a frozen smile and peeked into the can. It was stuffed halfway to the top with tens and fives!

Before she could ask Martha where she'd scrounged up the can, Martha said, "Hand me another stack of plates, will you? I'm running low."

Still baffled, Talia did as instructed. For the next two hours they worked in tandem, keeping the steady line of hungry customers moving along quickly. It was after one when the line dwindled to a trickle and Martha said, "These creaky old legs need a rest. Plus I gotta pee."

"Take a nice long break, Martha." Talia grinned. "You deserve it."

Talia still couldn't believe how much cash they'd collected. She did a quick count of the money in the donation can. They'd made over a hundred dollars!

Still wearing the silly frog hat, Martha fetched her chartreuse purse and moseyed off toward the restrooms. It wasn't until a prickle ran up Talia's spine that she noticed someone observing Martha's receding form with a critical eye.

Ria.

She was staring intently at Martha's back with a quizzical expression. Almost as if she was trying to remember where she'd seen her before.

Not good, Talia thought. Did Martha have some history with Ria? Is that why she bought the frog hat, as a disguise?

Talia didn't have time to ponder it, because a well-dressed man somewhere in his fifties was approaching her table. He had a full head of salt-and-pepper hair, the ends of which curled softly over his Burberry wool scarf. Everything about the man's classic style screamed *money*, but there was a gentleness in his emerald green eyes that made Talia feel instantly at ease.

He nodded with a friendly smile as he passed Talia's table. For a moment Talia thought maybe he knew her from somewhere. Then he spotted Ria, and his eyes brightened like twin stars.

Ria broke into a schoolgirl grin when he strolled into her line of vision. She moved around her table and ran to him.

He swept her into his arms and the two embraced, right in front of Talia's table.

"I got your text a few minutes ago," Ria whispered, a catch in her voice. "Oh, sweetie, I am so glad you're here."

"Me, too," he rasped, burying his face in her hair. "There's no place I'd rather be, my love."

After that, their words were lost in hushed whispers and secretive smiles. Ria took his right hand and rubbed her fingers over the chunky ring that graced his ring finger. Talia sensed they were making plans for later. She only wished they'd move their love fest a little farther away from her table.

But the man, whoever he was, didn't linger. After a flurry of butterfly kisses, he promised to see her later and then left. Ria waltzed back to her table, a dreamy expression floating in her eyes. Her bliss faded when she saw two female customers fumbling through her antique brooches as if they were cheap doodads.

"May I help you ladies?" Ria said tersely.

Both women ignored her and continued fingering Ria's jewelry. Then one of them—a thin blonde with a crooked nose—looked up at Ria and gasped. "Oh my God," she shrieked, "I just realized who you are. You're Oriana Butterforth, aren't you?"

Talia felt her jaw drop, and suddenly it all made sense.

Oriana Butterforth.

The rabbit thief.

Talia was only seven or eight the summer Oriana stole the rabbit out of its cage. The bunny belonged to Noah Ostrowski, the little brother of Talia's best friend, Rachel. When Talia spotted Oriana in the local variety store clutching a basket of carrots and lettuce, she was immediately suspicious. She looked up Oriana's address in the phone book and pedaled her bike over to the two-family house where Oriana lived with her mom. The rabbit was there, in a makeshift cage Oriana had constructed from cardboard boxes.

The look on Oriana's face that day still tore at Talia. Heartbroken, there was no other way to put it. It seemed the rabbit was the girl's only friend in the world. Oriana gave the rabbit back, but only because she'd been caught.

Talia glanced over at Ria, but the woman was pointedly ignoring her. At least Talia now knew why Ria hated her. But wasn't the better part of three decades a long time to nurse a childhood grudge?

"I'll have two, please," piped a pimply teenaged girl with a pierced eyebrow, snapping Talia out of her musings. "But I only need one plate."

Talia smiled at her. "Coming right up!"

She battered and fried two chunks of marble cake, swirled extra raspberry sauce over them, and gave the plate to the girl. The teenager shoved five dollars into the can and shuffled away with her cakes. Martha still hadn't returned, but the donation can was working overtime, doing a jolly job raking in cash for the event. Talia had to hand it to Martha—the can had been a clever idea.

Still, where was the woman? How long was she going to be gone *this* time?

By two thirty it looked as if Martha wasn't going to return. Talia was torn between annoyance and concern. Had something happened to her? She realized that she didn't even have Martha's cell number. In fact, did Martha even own a mobile phone? Talia had never seen her use one.

Talia snuck a peek over at the standing rack beside Ria's

table. The cornflower blue scarf was still hanging in plain sight, almost as if it was taunting her. Since she didn't have any customers at the moment, Talia decided to make one last stab at buying it. She sidled over to Ria's table.

"Ria," Talia said softly. "I would really love to buy that scarf. I understand now why you're mad at me, but that was a long time ago." A *very* long time ago, she was tempted to add.

Ria refused to meet her gaze. Instead, she went over to the rack and snatched the scarf.

"Thanks," Talia said gratefully. "Just tell me how much—"

Ria tossed the scarf around her own neck, tucked it under her hair, and made a loose knot in the front. Without a word, she turned her back on Talia and began packing up whatever vintage jewelry she hadn't sold.

Talia blew out a sigh. "Okay, I get it. You hate me. But will you at least tell me where you got the scarf?"

"Sure," Ria said, her voice dripping with poison. "When you give me back my ornaments."

"I didn't take your ornaments, Ria."

"Liar!" She sent a withering glance at Talia. "Let me tell you something, *Ms*. Marby. You'll get this scarf over my dead body."

With a shake of her head, Talia slipped back behind her own table. In a way she felt sorry for Ria. It had to be a mental drain to lug around a vendetta for so many years.

Talia glanced around the gym. The crowd had thinned considerably. Most of the vendors had already shut down early and left, unwilling to wait for three o'clock to roll around.

It was ten to three when Talia saw Scott Pollard advancing in her direction. He came over and stood, hands fisted on his slender hips, between Talia's table and Ria's. "Either of you gals need any help packing things up?" he asked, but his gaze was directed at Talia.

Talia had barely opened her mouth to speak when Ria blurted out, "Yes, I need help. Start taking those scarves off the tall rack and hand them to me, one at a time. I'll pack them and you can make a trip to the car with me. You can carry both racks."

Scott's mouth opened slightly. "Yes, *ma'am*," he said, with a click of his sneakered heels and a sly wink at Talia. "I'll be back to help you with that fryer, Talia. Just sit tight, okay?"

"Will do," Talia said. "Thanks, Scott."

He rolled up the sleeves of his sweater and began yanking scarves off the taller rack. Talia half expected Ria to reprimand him about his rough handling of the merchandise, but for once she remained silent.

Talia turned back to her own tasks. She hadn't had any customers since the teenager with the pierced eyebrow. She might as well close up shop. She turned off the portable fryer and unplugged it from the power strip, which she then unplugged from the wall. While the vegetable oil cooled, she shoved her other supplies into the cardboard box she'd carried them in.

Looking around, she saw that the room had pretty much emptied out. Ria and Scott were already headed for the rear exit, Scott toting a display rack in each of his hands.

Talia continued packing up her supplies. Martha could've helped a lot if she hadn't vanished. What was it with that woman?

Minutes later, Ria stormed back to her table, Andy Nash trailing in her wake. Andy's Santa hat was gone, revealing a balding scalp and a wide forehead.

"We had a date," he said hotly. "I was looking forward to it. It was really mean of you to cancel."

Ria's face was milky pale, and her gaze was jumpy. "It wasn't a date, it was only a drink," she said testily, "and I only agreed to it so you'd stop bugging me. We'll do it another time, okay?"

Andy pouted, and in a childish gesture stuck out his lower lip. "Promise?"

Ria placed both hands over her face and shook her head slightly. "Yes, I promise. Now please, just go away."

"I don't believe you."

Sensing that he was about to create a scene, Talia waved her arm at him. "Um, Andy? Do you know if they held the raffle yet?"

He glared at Talia for a moment, but then his face relaxed. "Yeah, we did. Didn't you hear the announcement?"

Actually, she had, but she decided to play Dora the Dunce. She gave him a disarming smile. "I heard something come over the loud speaker, but I guess I didn't pay much attention. Dopey me."

"It was at least an hour ago," he said crossly. "I thought everybody heard it."

Andy started to turn back to Ria when a scrawny, sixtyish woman in a worn ski jacket scooted around him and stepped directly in his path. The woman went over to Ria's table. "Hey," she said, without much interest. "You sell much?"

Ria pouted. "Yes, and I thought you were going to be here to help. Bad enough Kelsey bailed on me. You couldn't even be bothered to show up."

The woman shrugged. "Sorry, honey. Got talking to Ralphie after my shift ended, and we decided to grab a beer at the diner."

"You're always sorry." Ria grabbed the woman's arm. "Mom, listen to me. I saw the dragon today."

The woman's lined face stiffened. "What are you talking about?"

"The *dragon*," Ria repeated in a brittle voice. "I saw it today. The dragon is back."

The woman jabbed a yellowed fingernail at Ria. "Now you listen to me, Ria. I had enough of that dragon crap when you were a kid, so don't even go there, okay? I don't know what you're trying to pull, but your drama queen act isn't going to work on me anymore. Can it, or I'll do it for you." She pulled her arm roughly out of Ria's grasp.

Ria stuttered backward as if she'd been slapped. For a moment Talia thought she might burst into tears. Andy, who'd been watching the interchange with an odd expression, spun on his Santa boot and scurried off.

Talia snapped the covers onto her food containers. The woman was obviously Ria's mother, but what was the dragon? Talia glanced over at Ria, and immediately felt sorry for her. Whatever her "dragon" issue was about, she clearly didn't have a sympathetic mom.

Ria's mother twitched her hands nervously, and she ran her bony fingers through her head of dishwater blond frizz. "You need help getting the rest of this junk in the car?" she said, a touch of apology in her tone.

Ria shook her head.

"Great. Then I'm leaving. You eating home tonight?"

Again, Ria shook her head.

"Okay, well, good, 'cuz Ralphie and me might go see a movie at the mall in Lanesboro."

"What about Princess?" Ria sniped. "You're leaving her alone again?"

"Princess?" Her mother gawked at her. "It's a cat, for criminy's sake. She's fine on her own. Besides, you're the one who brought her home. Who said I wanted a cat anyway?"

Ria gathered up her velvet runner, including a few stray brooches, and stuffed the whole thing inside her suitcase. Her mother shot a nervous smile at Talia, as if she'd just realized that their squabble hadn't exactly been private.

Ria's mother softened her tone. "I'll make sure she has plenty of food and water before I go, okay? I s'ppose you have plans."

"Yes, I have plans."

"Okay, well, um, I'll see you later then, honey."

The woman hurried off as if her shoes had jet packs. Still wearing the blue scarf, Ria zipped her suitcase with a loud *zing*. She smacked the wheels on the floor and trounced off, heading in the direction of the exit.

Talia let out a long breath. A fun adventure, this day was *not*. At least she'd made a few hundred dollars for the Santa fund. She was happy about that. She continued gathering her supplies, stacking her two covered bowls atop one another. Even with Scott's help, she'd need to make two trips to her car, so she decided to make the first by herself with the two big bowls.

Talia reached under the table to collect her purse and jacket, and then groaned. Martha's peacoat was still there! Argggh. She'd have to fetch it later, when her arms weren't so loaded.

By the time she trudged out to her Fiat, she felt as if she'd done two days of hard labor. She stacked the bowls on one side of the back storage area and slammed the hatch shut. She tossed her purse onto her front seat and clicked the locks.

Martha's behemoth vehicle was nowhere in sight, but on her way back inside the building Talia spotted an older-model red Camry. She wondered if it was Ria's, but then dismissed the thought. Camrys were fairly common, and Ria had seemed pretty anxious to blast out of there after she left.

Back inside, two volunteers were folding up the abandoned tables and emptying oversized waste cans. The canned music was gone.

Talia glanced over at Santa's village. The divider wall was still up, blocking her view of what was behind it. It almost looked as if the wall had been pulled around to keep anyone from seeing beyond it.

She traipsed over to her table. The oil was now cool enough to transport, so she secured the lid. Luckily, her new portable fryer was pretty much spill-proof. As long as she rested it securely in the back of her Fiat, she should be able to get it home without too much difficulty.

Talia looked up to see Scott striding toward her, his face slightly red. He grinned when he spotted her, and that's when she noticed Andy Nash scuttling along in his wake. Andy's Santa getup was gone, replaced by brown chinos that sagged in the rear and a gray crew-neck sweater.

Scott rubbed his hands together in a playful fashion and grinned. "Okay, Santa sent his helpers to get you packed up and outta here."

Scott hoisted the fryer off the table, and Andy propped the pallets against the wall. Talia grabbed her box stuffed with the remaining marble cake squares, along with the bag of napkins, plates, and forks.

Andy flashed a lukewarm smile. "What can I carry for you?"

"My helper ditched me without taking her coat. Can you

nab it for me, Andy? It's under the table. Oh, and if you could take the container of vegetable oil, that would be great."

With a halfhearted nod, Andy did as instructed. He grimaced when he tossed Martha's peacoat over his arm. "Yuck. This lady loves her cigarettes, doesn't she?"

Scott wrinkled his nose and sniffed. "Oh, wow, I hear you, man. Once you've kicked the habit, nothing smells worse than stale cigarette smoke. I gave 'em up eons ago and never looked back."

Their comments made Talia wonder if Martha *did* smoke in secret. Martha had led her to believe she'd quit a long time ago.

Talia slipped on her jacket, and the trio trotted out to the parking lot and got everything loaded into the Fiat. "I appreciate your help, both of you," Talia said. The role of helpless female didn't suit her at all, but today she was desperate enough to welcome the assistance.

Scott bowed and flashed a wide grin. "At your service, miss. Anytime you need help, just call on the dynamic duo." He clapped Andy on the shoulder.

Andy issued a flat smile. "Always glad to help," he said without much enthusiasm. "Uh, look, guys, I gotta run. After this little gig, I got a ton of paperwork to do."

"Thanks again, Andy," Talia said. "I'll drop off a check to you sometime this week, as soon as I figure out what's in my donation can."

Andy hustled back inside the building, while Scott helped Talia secure all her supplies in the back of the Fiat to ensure that nothing would roll around. "There, you're all set," he said. "Snug as a bug in a rug."

"I'm not sure I want that," Talia joked. "But thanks for everything, Scott. You've been a huge help."

Talia started her car, flicked on the heat, and then pulled out of the parking lot at the rear exit. A right turn at the cross street brought her back to the busy main drag. Holiday shoppers clogged the sidewalks, their arms laden with bags. She prayed she'd find enough time to do some shopping herself. The eatery had been keeping her so busy that she didn't have much downtime anymore.

She'd driven only a block before she remembered something. Her backup bowl of sweet batter was still in the commercial fridge at the gym. Talia groaned to herself. It wasn't the batter she was concerned about—it was her covered stainless steel bowl. Not that she thought anyone would steal it, but it would be a pain to have to retrieve tomorrow.

With a sigh, she made two more right turns and swung back into the community center's parking lot. Only a few vehicles remained. The red Camry was still there, so it must not be Ria's. Talia hustled inside, anxious to grab her bowl and head home.

Without all the chatter and bustle, the building gave her an eerie feeling. When she reached the corridor that led to the gym and to the kitchen, she broke into a near jog. Her Keds made slapping sounds on the linoleum floor. She passed a closed door labeled OFFICE from which the low murmur of a male voice drifted. No doubt it was Andy's office, since he claimed he had loads of paperwork to do. Talia wondered briefly if he was still trying to contact Ria.

The kitchen was on the side of the hallway opposite the gymnasium. Fortunately, no one had locked it yet. She pushed through the swinging metal door and went to the fridge. Her batter bowl had gotten pushed back, and she had to relocate several cans of soda to retrieve it.

On her way out she took one last wistful peek into the gym.

It really could have been fun, if Martha hadn't gone rogue on her, and if Ria hadn't been so combative.

All at once she spied a slender figure leaving through the front entrance of the gym. Talia narrowed her gaze and saw that it was Kelsey Dakoulas. Wasn't it late for her to be hanging around? She was sure she'd seen Kelsey leave the gym around two fifteen, carrying her painting supplies in a carryall.

Talia was turning to retrace her steps to the rear exit when something else caught her eye. In the area where Santa's village had been, the faux furnishings sat abandoned. The folding divider had been pushed flat against the gymnasium wall. A swatch of blue peeked out from beneath it. From the texture and color, Talia would have sworn it was Nana's scarf!

How could that be? It didn't make sense.

She shifted her feet into second gear and hurried over for a closer look. Cornflower blue tassels jutted out from beneath the divider wall. Had Ria tossed the scarf over the divider to get rid of it? Talia bent and set her batter bowl on the floor. She went over to the divider and pushed it to the right. Despite being on wheels, it was not easy to move. After several tries, she managed to shove it far enough over to get a better look at the tassels.

She was surprised to see that behind the divider was a closet of some sort. When she looked down, her heartbeat spiked. That was definitely Nana's scarf peeking out from under the door of the closet. She couldn't mistake those tassels—she'd hand-knotted each one herself!

Talia turned the knob and opened the door. The inside of the closet was dark, but enough light dribbled in from the gym to illuminate the form slumped at her feet. She squeaked and jumped backward a step. Her legs wobbled and she stared in horror, not wanting to acknowledge the sight that met her eyes.

A woman lay face up, her face pale and bloated, the blue scarf tied tightly around her neck. Talia could never mistake those lush, ginger-colored curls or those azure eyes.

Talia turned and stumbled over her batter bowl. And then she screamed like a baby.

4

Sergeant Liam O'Donnell sauntered into the interview room at the Wrensdale Police Department, slapped a manila folder on the table, and slung his toned form into a chair. "Ms. Marby, we meet again."

Talia blew out a slow breath and rubbed her icy hands together. In her mind she kept seeing Ria's face, and that scarf— She choked back a sob and said, "Yes, I'm afraid we do, Sergeant. Not by choice, I assure you."

A few months earlier Talia had stumbled upon a body in one of the shops in the Wrensdale Arcade. Until today, it had been the worst experience of her life. It was just her luck that the same scary investigator from the Berkshire Detective Unit of the Massachusetts State Police was now working Ria's murder.

"You're aware that you're being filmed and recorded, correct?"

Talia nodded. "Correct," she said softly.

"Do you want a cup of coffee? A cola?"

Sure, pump her with caffeine to keep her jittery.

"No, thank you." She'd barely kept down the water they gave her when they took her initial statement at the community center.

"Then let's start from the beginning," he said.

Talia told him everything, from the time she returned to the building for her batter bowl, to the moment she opened the door to the supply closet and discovered Ria's body.

"And you didn't touch anything?" he said sharply.

"No. Nothing." She took a deep breath. "It was obvious there was nothing I could do. Her face . . ." Tears poked at her eyelids. She grabbed a tissue from the box on the scarred wooden table and blotted her eyes.

"I understand you knew the victim."

"I knew her, but not very well. Before yesterday I hadn't seen her since I was in grade school."

His smile was flat. "But there *was* some bad blood between you, am I right?"

"I wouldn't call it that exactly." How could she explain the childhood grudge Ria had nurtured for almost thirty years? "You're right about one thing—Ria definitely didn't like me."

O'Donnell opened his folder and narrowed his gaze, but at what, Talia couldn't see. For all she knew, it could have been his grocery list. Then he went back to the beginning and started over, asking her the same questions again and again.

Talia's head felt as if someone was bashing it with a hammer. She'd give anything for a couple of ibuprofen.

O'Donnell sat back and folded his arms over his chest.

"Tell me something, Ms. Marby. How do you suppose Ms. Butterforth got hold of your grandmother's scarf?"

"I have no idea, Sergeant. I asked her, but she refused to tell me. And I've told you that at least four times." She was tempted to ask if he had a hearing problem, but decided not to test fate.

"How well do you know Kelsey Dakoulas?"

"Not well at all. I only met her yesterday." In her initial interview with Derek Westlake, Wrensdale's chief of police, she'd blurted out that she spotted Kelsey leaving the gym right before she found Ria's body. She hadn't meant to incriminate Kelsey—she was only trying to state the facts as best she could.

She almost wished she could take it back, except . . . what had Kelsey said to her earlier when she was spouting off about Ria?

Not unless you want to kill her for me.

Talia shifted on her chair, which felt as comfy as a slab of iron.

"You look chagrined, Ms. Marby. Did you just recall something?" O'Donnell stared at her, hard.

"I—no," she said, feeling unnerved. "I was just thinking that someone Kelsey's size could never have overpowered Ria long enough to . . . you know, strangle her."

"So you've already entertained the notion that Ms. Dakoulas might have murdered her employer?"

"No! That's not what I meant."

O'Donnell smiled, but it was more like a smirk. "Did you know, Ms. Marby, that it only takes about three pounds of pressure to strangle someone? A young woman in good health could accomplish it with ease." He focused his gaze on hers like a heat-seeking missile.

Talia rubbed her fingers over her eyes. Was he implying that *she* could accomplish it with ease?

He pummeled her with more questions for another hour or so. Around the time Talia felt her head was going to split open, he stood abruptly and said, "I think we're done here. For now."

Talia pushed her chair back and slipped her jacket on. "Aren't you going to tell me not to leave town?" she said, more testily than she'd intended.

O'Donnell tapped the edge of the folder onto the palm of one large hand. "I don't have to, do I? You just did it for me."

Rachel Ostrowski, her BFF, was waiting for her in the lobby. "Oh, honey." Rachel threw her arms around Talia and hugged her close. "I can't believe this is happening to you again!"

Talia returned the hug, and then stood back and looked at her friend. As always, Rachel looked spectacular in her black cashmere jacket and gray suede boots. More important than her outer beauty was the kind and generous soul housed within.

"Those earrings," Talia said, smiling at the glittery, over-sized reindeer dangling from Rachel's ears. "They're *so* not you."

"I know. But aren't they a hoot? Derek got them at—" Her face flushed. "Oh, never mind. It doesn't matter where they came from."

"Rach, you don't have to be afraid to say Derek's name just because he's the chief of police."

Rachel's face grew somber. "Derek's removing himself from the case because of our . . . you know, relationship. Did he tell you?"

"No, he didn't. So he won't be working with O'Donnell then?" Talia didn't know whether to be worried or relieved. What was that old saying about the devil you know?

Rachel bit her lip and frowned.

"What is it? What aren't you saying?" Talia asked her.

"It's nothing. It's just that the detective who's going to work with the state police is a real go-getter. Type A personality. Works practically around the clock. In other words, a royal pain in the—"

"I get the picture," Talia said.

"Never mind that now. You didn't do anything wrong." Rachel looped her arm through Talia's. "Come on, I'll drive you home. They've cordoned off the community center, so you won't be able to get to your Fiat until tomorrow."

Talia groaned. "I hadn't even thought of that."

Rachel's Jeep Cherokee occupied a prime spot directly in front of the police station on Wrensdale's busy main street. They jumped inside, and Rachel started the ignition and flicked on the heat.

"It's all so surreal, isn't it?" Rachel said quietly, shaking her head. "Oriana Butterforth. I can't stop picturing her as that lonely little schoolgirl who stole my brother's rabbit."

"I know. Me, too. It was so awful, Rach. If you could've seen her, lying there . . ." Talia swallowed back the lump in her throat. "We've got to figure out who did this to her."

5

Bojangles, Talia's calico cat, issued a plaintive meow the moment Talia stepped inside her bungalow.

"Oh, Bo, sweetie. I'm sorry I didn't get home sooner!" Talia flipped on the nearest lamp and tossed her purse onto the sagging tweed chair her grandfather had been so attached to. She lifted the cat into her arms. Bo rubbed her silky head against Talia's face and began chewing on her hair.

"Come on, let's get you some real food. Do you want turkey medley or fancy shrimp tonight?" She kissed the cat's whiskers, and Bo made a *brrrrup* sound in her ear. "Okay, turkey it is."

The sight of her cozy kitchen was so welcome that it almost made her weep. She'd kept everything the way her nana had left it, right down to the old white Zenith AM radio that had the worst reception on the planet. Nana had died earlier that year, and Talia still missed her horribly. She always would, she realized, but Nana was always alive in her memory.

After feeding Bo, Talia raced into the bathroom and took a quick shower. She felt like staying under the hot spray forever, but Ryan would be arriving in half an hour.

She thought about Ria again and tears streamed down her cheeks. Ria should be home right now, getting herself all gussied up to meet that handsome stranger. It was obvious the man had been smitten with Ria. He couldn't stop drinking her in with his eyes. Talia wondered if he'd heard about her death.

Talia fluffed her short blond hair with a brush, then threw on a pair of good jeans and a perky green holiday sweater. Still blotchy from the crying jag she'd had in the shower, she dabbed on a bit of blush and a hint of eye shadow. The doorbell rang and she scurried to the front door.

"Hey," Talia said weakly, her stomach already roiling at the aroma of chicken lo mein and egg rolls.

Ryan Collins dropped his brown bag on the floor and enveloped her in his arms. Talia pressed herself against his chest, relishing the lingering scent of his citrusy soap.

After a long moment he cupped her cheeks in his hands, one dark curl brushing the top of his rimless glasses. "You holding up okay?" He kissed her lightly on the forehead.

Talia covered his hands with her own. Tears threatened again, but she forced them back. "Of course I am. Come on into the kitchen. You're probably starving." She grabbed the brown bag while Ryan shed his lined nylon jacket and folded it over the arm of the old green sofa. He scooped up Bo, who'd been wrapping herself around his legs in a pathetic plea for attention.

"Hey, Bobo, you taking good care of my gal for me?" Ryan cradled the kitty in his arms and ferried her into the kitchen.

My gal. Talia knew it sounded old-fashioned and maybe even sexist, but she loved it when Ryan called her that. Her almost-fiancé, Chet, who'd strung her along for years, had always called her *babe*, which she'd hated.

Ryan set Bo down and looked at Talia with concern. He pulled out a chair for her. "You sit while I set the table. You feeling okay to eat?"

Talia took another whiff of the spicy food. "I wasn't sure a minute ago, but I'm starting to get my appetite back, at least a little." Very little.

Ryan set out two pink-flowered plates, along with napkins, silverware, and glasses of ice water. While they ate, she gave him a play-by-play of her day, ending with her "interview" with Sergeant Liam O'Donnell.

Ryan shoveled a forkful of fried rice into his mouth and followed it with a swig of ice water. "That name, Oriana Butterforth—it sounds so familiar. I think she might have been in my class in grade school."

"She was a few years ahead of me, so that's possible," Talia said, feeling her eyes well up again.

"Have you talked to your folks?" Ryan asked gently.

"I talked to Mom while Rachel drove me home. She freaked when she heard what happened, of course. She was a little calmer by the time we hung up. Dad's off skiing in Colorado with a couple of his college buds. He got sick of waiting for it to snow in the Berkshires." She took a tiny bite of her egg roll, which she'd barely touched.

"Tal, the police will find the killer. They're pros. They know what they're doing."

Talia gave him a faint smile. "Is there a message buried in there somewhere?"

"I just . . . I don't want you getting hurt. Remember what happened a few months ago?"

Remember? How could she forget her confrontation with a vicious killer?

"How is Arthur?" Talia said, changing the subject. Ryan's father, who suffered from early-onset Alzheimer's, lived at the Wrensdale Pines, the assisted-living facility where Talia's mom, Natalie, was the assistant director.

"Okay." Ryan blinked. "He was a little off today. Maybe he sensed that you were having a rough day. I distracted him by reading him some Dickens. He's always loved *The Pickwick Papers*."

"You're such a good son." Talia beamed at Ryan. "I'll go with you next Sunday to visit, if that's okay."

If I'm not being held on a murder charge, she thought glumly.

Ryan brushed her fingers with his. "It's more than okay. Dad will love it. Hey, before I forget, I have a treat for you." He slid off his chair and fished a plastic container out of the brown carryout bag Talia had left on the counter. He gave it to her, and she popped the lid.

"Oh, glory be," Talia said, staring at what looked like a puffed-up fortune cookie. "Let me guess. This is from Tina, right?"

Ryan grinned. "It's a lemon *mad-e-leine*." He pronounced it with an impeccable French accent. "Tina heard what happened and wanted to send you a treat. She said to let her know if you wanted some ideas for deep-frying it."

Tina Franchette was an acquaintance of Talia's from high

school. She was also the head chef at the Wrensdale Pines. "Share it with me?"

Ryan shook his head. "Not a chance. It's not that big, and you barely ate a thing tonight. That, my love, is all yours."

Talia felt heat flood her face. Ryan had never addressed her that way before.

As if he realized he'd let his feelings slip through, Ryan reddened and made a production out of clearing the dishes from the table.

"Oh, this is scrumptious," Talia said after she'd swallowed a bite. "Buttery, lemony, and downright heavenly." She had to remember to call Tina and thank her for the madeleine.

"Hey, I almost forgot," Ryan said. "If you're interested, I can get tickets for *A Christmas Carol* at the Colonial Theatre in Pittsfield."

"Really? I thought that was last weekend."

Ryan sat down next to her and grinned. "It was, but they're giving a command performance next Sunday at four in the afternoon."

"What about your dad?" Talia touched his arm.

Ryan's eyes danced. "That's the best part. I can get three tickets. We can all go."

Talia leaned over and hugged him. "That's great. Arthur will love it."

After the kitchen was tidied up, they watched television for a while. With Ria's murder running laps around Talia's mind, she couldn't really concentrate on anything. It was almost ten when Ryan yawned, encased her in a long hug, and kissed her good-bye. "Long day tomorrow," he said. "I'm working on a project for a new facility in Waltham, and we have a tight deadline to meet." Ryan, a software engineer, worked for a company that designed programs for medical offices.

Another ten minutes elapsed before he was finally out the door. Talia stood in the doorway of her adorable bungalow, watching the taillights of his Honda recede in the distance. A wave of longing fell over her. She sensed Ryan had wanted to stay, that he was ready for the next step in their relationship.

The problem was, she wasn't. Not yet.

She wasn't sure she would be for a very long time.

6

Monday morning dawned with a crisp December chill in the air. Clouds crowded out the sun, and Talia wondered if the first snow of the season would finally arrive.

She was almost ready to leave when she remembered that her Fiat was still parked behind the community center. She called her mom and begged a ride to the restaurant, a task Natalie Marby was happy to perform.

"You look exhausted!" her mom exclaimed when Talia plunked herself onto the front seat of the toasty warm Buick. Talia hugged her, assured her she was fine, and the two headed toward the eatery.

Traffic was sluggish. As they drove past the town lot, Talia was shocked to see Martha's gargantuan Chrysler parked at an angle in a spot close to the sidewalk. Was that white streak a new scratch on the side? It was hard to tell with all the dents and dings that covered the monstrous thing.

Talia had never given Martha a key to Fry Me a Sliver. She wondered if her employee was prowling the busy downtown in search of a strong cup of coffee.

"I wish I could help you today, honey," her mom said, pulling up in front of the arcade. "I've got meetings scheduled nearly all day long."

"I'll be fine, Mom. Honestly. I'm dragging a little, but work will keep me occupied. The day will be over before I know it."

Her mom, dark blond hair perfectly coiffed and sprayed into place, bit down on her glossed lip. "I suppose," she said. "Call me if you need a ride later, okay?"

They hugged again and Talia unlocked the door to Fry Me a Sliver. She thought about what she would say to Martha—*if* the woman showed up, that is. Early that morning she'd discovered a garbled message from Martha on her cell phone, apparently left late the night before. A supposed "GI" attack had sent Martha scurrying home from the fund-raiser. She'd spent the remainder of Sunday in her apartment, running in and out of the bathroom.

Way more than Talia wanted to know.

Inside the eatery, Talia made a pot of French roast coffee for herself and then started on food prep for the day. She shredded cabbage and carrots for coleslaw and set it all to drain in a massive colander. Next she whipped up a batch of meatballs, using her slightly revised version of Nana's original recipe. To Talia's delight, the deep-fried meatballs had been a surprising hit. The drawback was that they were time-consuming, especially since she served them with a homemade marinara sauce.

The fish delivery truck arrived, and she signed for two boxes of kitchen-ready haddock. She was slicing a large dill pickle when a knock on the door startled her.

Talia wiped her hands on her blue apron, and when she opened the door, there stood Martha.

"Okay if I start work early?" Martha said in a sheepish voice. Her face was pale. The ever-present scarf was wrapped around her neck, and her peacoat—this one a ghastly shade of orangey-gold that reeked of mothballs—was buttoned right to the top.

"Well . . . sure," Talia said. "Of course you can, Martha. Why don't we sit and talk for a minute and have some coffee. Did you know you left without your coat yesterday?"

"Yeah, I know. Lucky thing I had a backup."

Martha slung her backup coat and the scarf over the hook on the back of the kitchen door. "I'm sorry I left you hanging in the breeze yesterday. In between customers, I kept sneaking some of that marble cake and raspberry sauce. Didn't even bother to fry it. I didn't realize how much I'd eaten till it landed in my stomach all at once and started rumbling around."

In that instant, Talia felt terrible. She'd asked Martha to volunteer her day off for a local event she probably had no interest in. How selfish was that?

They sat at the tiny table in the alcove behind the commercial fridge. Talia poured Martha a cup of coffee and refilled her own mug. "Martha, I'm the one who should apologize, asking you to work on your day off. I'm going to pay you for the time you put in yesterday."

Martha took a loud slurp of her coffee and set her mug back down. "Nah, you don't have to. It's not like I ever have anything special to do."

Talia's heart twisted. Was Martha truly that alone?

"Does any of your family live close by?" Talia asked her. Martha shook her head and gulped back the rest of her coffee. "I'll get started sprucing up the dining room. You ever notice how much space those clunky wooden chairs take up? I bet the dining area would look a lot roomier with different chairs."

Talia sighed. It wasn't the first time Martha had hinted that the eatery was too cluttered, and the kitchen too small. And she had to admit, the captain's chairs were a bit oversized. Still, that was no reason to ditch perfectly good chairs.

"By the way," Martha said when Talia didn't respond. "I went over to Queenie's Variety for a coffee and a jelly doughnut this morning. Seemed like everyone in there was yammering about the murder." She grabbed the lime spray cleaner from beneath the counter.

Talia's senses went on red alert. "What are they saying?"

"Well, I overheard this one guy saying he wondered why the same person found two dead bodies in such a short span of time."

That would be me.

"I know it seems crazy, Martha, but it really was a coincidence."

Martha grinned. "Ah, so it's true what they were saying. You *did* find the first body."

"It wasn't anything to smile about." Talia shook her head. "It was one of the worst days of my life."

"Sorry," she said. "I can dig that."

A crash, followed by a yelp, exploded from the cobblestone plaza.

"He's gonna kill himself, you know that?" Martha bleated with a shake of her gray bob.

Talia ran to the front door and whipped it open. "Lucas, are you all right?"

"Yup. No worries. I'm cool." Lucas flashed a thumbs-up and leaped to his feet, wincing as he rubbed his left knee.

He limped into the eatery, his skateboard tucked under his arm. He propped it against the back wall in the kitchen and then scrubbed his hands in the sink. "Okay if I grab a cup of java, Ms. Marby?"

Talia smiled. "Of course it's okay. And from this point on, you never have to ask, okay?"

Lucas dried his hands on a paper towel. "Oh, okay. Cool. Want me to get started on potato duty?"

"If you would," Talia said. "That would be great."

"I, um . . ." Lucas stammered. He swallowed, and his blue eyes clouded. "I almost wasn't able to come to work today. My mom's really freaked about the murder. She's afraid the killer might come in here looking for witnesses and blow everyone away."

"Well, she's your mom," Talia said, although she didn't agree with her. "She has a right to worry."

Lucas shrugged. "Anyway, it was no prob. I convinced her it was highly unlikely I'd be in any danger. Razzle-dazzled her with all kinds of complicated stats I knew she wouldn't take the time to unravel."

"What kind of stats? Real ones?"

"Well, yeah . . . they were, but I was actually comparing the Patriots' third down conversions this season to their fourth down conversions, only I didn't use the words *Patriots* or *football*, and I changed the word *conversions* to *assault*. Plus, like I pointed out, I'm nineteen. Technically I'm an adult."

Technically being the operative word, Talia thought, although she couldn't help admiring his ingenuity.

Martha chuckled and pointed her spray bottle at him. "I

like you, kid. You think for yourself. What you did to your mom was a little sneaky, though. You ever think about going into politics?"

Lucas flushed. "Um, no. I don't like politics. I'm into computers and sports. And skateboarding."

The threesome went about their assigned tasks, and at eleven thirty, Talia officially opened for business. By twelve, they'd served only one customer in the dining room. The day wore on with only three more sit-down customers, and take-out orders at an all-time low.

By two thirty, Talia knew it wasn't simply the usual Monday lull taking hold. Customers were staying away, in droves. It clearly had something to do with Ria's murder, but what? Were people afraid that Talia was the killer and might poison them with tainted food? Or were they just wary of tumbling into Talia's sticky web of excruciatingly bad luck?

With glum faces, they all sat at the tiny table for a quickie lunch. Lucas munched on a slab of deep-fried haddock. A napkin scrunched in his hand, he swiped his long fingers over his phone.

"Um, Ms. Marby? Did you look at our Facebook page today?"

"No." Talia's stomach tumbled. "Why?"

Lucas frowned. "Um, someone posted a really bad review a couple days ago. Listen to this: *If you value your stomach, stay away from the old fish and chips joint in the Wrensdale Arcade. The chef, if you can call her that, serves bad fish, soggy coleslaw, and fries that have been floating in rancid oil for a year. Health department, take note! Shut this dive down before the chef*—she put chef in quotes—*sends someone to the morgue with her revolting food.*"

Talia felt the blood drain from her face. None of that was true. Who would write such things?

"Oh, my. That *is* a bad review. I know every restaurant gets them, but . . . wait a minute. Who wrote that?"

Lucas squinted at his phone. "Um, it says OB Cottontail." He made a face. "What a weird name."

OB. Oriana Butterforth. Cottontail obviously meant *rabbit*.

"Well, I guess that explains our dismal lack of business today." Talia's voice shook. "What day was that posted?"

"Let's see. Um, it says forty-one hours ago."

Of course. That was Saturday, the same day Ria had snubbed her when Talia went into the vintage clothing shop to introduce herself. Had Ria created the Facebook profile just so she could torment Talia?

Lucas's face fell. "Ms. Marby, I feel like I'm responsible for this. I'm the one who asked if I could create a Facebook page for the restaurant."

"You are not responsible," Talia assured him. "The Facebook page was an excellent idea. You did a great job with it, too." She lowered her voice. "Besides, I'm pretty sure I know who posted that."

Light suddenly dawned on Lucas. "It was that lady who was murdered, wasn't it?" His eyes went wide. "I saw it on the news last night. Her name was Oriana Butterball. OB."

"Butterforth," Martha corrected, focusing her gaze at a spot on the table. "Look, kid, that's the risk you take with social media. I read this article once that said there are all sorts of trolls out there looking to trash people just for the perverse thrill they get."

Lucas looked unconvinced. "Yeah, but—"

"Lucas, even if she hadn't posted her vile comments on our Facebook page," Talia said gently, "she'd have done it on one of those review sites. I don't want you blaming your-self, okay? You can delete the post, right?"

Lucas nodded. "I can, but . . ."

"But what?" Talia said, feeling her stomach curdle.

"What if the cops already saw it?" he said. "If we delete it now, they'll probably think you're trying to hide your motive for killing OB."

"What I want to know is," Martha piped in, "why OB hated you so much."

Lucas left at his normal four o'clock, still stressing over the Facebook page.

"Why don't you leave, too, Martha," Talia said with a sigh. She slid the near full container of coleslaw into the commercial fridge. "There's not much point in your staying if we're not going to have any more customers. You might as well go home and read, or whatever you like to do. And don't worry about the lost hours. I'll pay you for the full day."

Martha angled her gray eyebrows toward the door. "You might want to rethink that. Looks like we got ourselves a customer."

Talia turned and saw a man step through the door and into the dining area. She instantly recognized the Burberry scarf and the full head of salt-and-pepper hair. It was the same elegantly dressed man who'd swept Ria into his arms at the fund-raiser.

Smoothing her blue apron, she stepped around the side of the speckled turquoise counter and into the dining area to greet him. Something told her she needed to find out more about this dapper gent. "Hello, again," she said, extending her hand. "I'm Talia Marby, the proprietor."

The man smiled and accepted her handshake. His eyes looked puffy, as if he'd been crying, but his tone was kind and gracious. "Yes, my dear, I know. You are Howie and Bea's successor, are you not?"

"I took over the lease, yes," Talia said. "May I ask how you know?"

Despite the pain etched into his face, his emerald eyes twinkled a bit. "Allow me to introduce myself. I am Will Claiborne, your landlord."

Talia's eyes popped wide. "Oh my Lord, you're . . . you're Claiborne Properties? I sent my first rent check to you a few weeks ago! I wanted to be sure it got there by the first."

"Oh, good," he said with a touch of humor. "I love tenants who pay on time."

Bea Lambert had always told Talia that the owner of the Wrensdale Arcade was a mystery man. If the eatery experienced a problem or needed a repair that was covered by the lease, she simply sent an e-mail to Claiborne Properties and the matter was fixed the next day—and to perfection.

"I understand," he said, "that you are the young woman who solved the murder of one of my tenants not too long ago. I was out of the country at the time. I didn't realize what had happened until I got back."

"I didn't really solve it," Talia said. "I just happened to be at the right place at the right time. Or the wrong place at the wrong time, I guess you could say."

"With a deadly killer," he emphasized. "You are most brave, Talia. I commend you." Claiborne glanced around the eatery and his face brightened. "This is the same charming place I remember."

Talia opened her mouth in surprise. "Wait a minute. You've eaten here before?"

"Oh my, yes, more than a few times. Bea and Howie didn't know who I was, of course, and I didn't enlighten them. I was afraid they'd give me special treatment, and I didn't want that."

The more Will Claiborne spoke, the more Talia liked him.

"This project was my first love, you know," he said wistfully. "I designed it after a charming village in England, in the county of Hertfordshire. I wanted people to experience the allure of an earlier era."

"I've always loved the cobblestone plaza," Talia said. "Though I have to say, it's not the easiest surface to walk on."

Will Claiborne's emerald eyes sparkled with a hint of mischief. "Yes, it slows you down, doesn't it? Forces you to take time to savor the beauty."

Talia smiled and said, "Mr. Claiborne, may I get you something? No special treatment. I promise."

"Thank you for the offer, Talia, and please call me Will." His eyes grew watery. "Normally I would relish a hearty fish and chips meal, but I'm afraid I'm not myself today."

"You loved Ria, didn't you?" she said quietly, prodding him a little.

Will removed a linen hankie from his pocket and dabbed his eyes. "I adored Ria. I knew from the moment I met her that I wanted to marry her. I believe she loved me, too, though perhaps not with the same passion I felt for her."

Talia remembered the way Ria's hard edges had softened the moment she saw him, how she'd thrown herself into his arms. "From what I saw, Will, I'd say she loved you very much."

"Thank you," he croaked. He blotted his eyes again, and that's when Talia noticed his right hand. His ring finger was graced with a large jade ring set in gold.

He smiled sadly when he caught her glance. "Do you like

it?" he said, holding out his hand to give her a closer look. "I had it hand-crafted for me right here in Wrensdale, at LaFleur Jewelers. I picked it up yesterday, right before I saw . . ." His eyes grew moist again. He closed them and tipped his head back to stanch the flow of tears.

Talia attempted to distract him by studying the ring. An unusual figure or animal of some sort was engraved into the jade, but Talia wasn't sure what it was. "Is that a . . . snake?" she asked, peering at the design.

He sniffed. "Yes, a two-headed snake wrapped around the stem of a tulip. It's my family crest—it goes back to the fifteen hundreds. Before this I had a different ring with the same design, but the jeweler who created it didn't have the artistic talent this fellow at LaFleur has."

Talia couldn't exactly say she admired it. Even the suggestion of a snake made her skin break out into goose bumps. A two-headed one doubled the horror. "It's intriguing," was all she could say with any honesty.

Will smoothed the forefinger of his left hand over the jade. "I was going to have a pendant made for my Ria with the same design. I planned to give it to her as . . . as an engagement gift." His eyes grew moist again.

"Will, I'm so sorry for your loss. Are you sure I can't get you a coffee or anything?"

"You're so kind, but no," he said. "I'm headed over to Ria's shop. I want to be sure everything is secure."

"I understand."

"It was at my urging, you know, that she opened the vintage clothing shop. I wanted something more for her than being a hostess at a restaurant." His handsome face clouded. "She was so smart, so beautiful. One of the few women I've met who could truly embrace the finer accoutrements of an earlier era. I even gave her six months' free rent to give her a leg up, as it were." His smile was weary, and hopelessly sad. "Not that it would've mattered. If she agreed to marry me, everything I have would have been hers, as well."

Talia turned to see if Martha was lurking in the kitchen so that she could introduce her to Will, but she didn't see her anywhere.

"I'll stop in again, when things are more . . . settled," he promised. "I want to be sure Ria has a proper memorial service and burial. I know her mother must also be devastated."

Talia thought about the skinny woman with the yellowed fingernails who'd had the tiff with Ria the afternoon of the fund-raiser. How awful she must feel, knowing her last conversation with her daughter had been a kerfuffle. Talia made a mental note to pay her respects to Ria's mom when the time was right.

After Will left, Martha reappeared. "Martha, are you okay?" Talia asked her. She didn't add the obvious, that she'd been in the bathroom a long time.

"Yeah, I'm fine. Feeling my age, I guess."

With Martha it was always about her age—it was her standing excuse for everything. Yet she seemed strong as an ox, and in the kitchen she churned out meals quickly and efficiently.

"Really, Martha, I wouldn't mind if you left early. The way things are going, I'm sure I won't be too overwhelmed."

Martha shrugged. "Well, so long as you don't mind." Within seconds she had her coat and smelly scarf on, and was out the door.

Talia spent the next few hours tidying and cleaning. Only

a few orders trickled in, all takeouts. By six thirty she was worn to a frazzle, but the eatery sparkled.

She was looking forward to closing when a tall, dark-skinned woman with close-cropped curls and exquisite cheekbones stepped into the eatery. Wearing a navy overcoat and black slacks, she glanced all around and then strode up to the counter. "Talia Marby?" Her expression was serious, but a glint of humor shone in her nutmeg-colored eyes.

Talia wiped her hands on a towel and smiled at her. "That's me. What can I get for you?"

The woman pulled a notepad from her pocket and peered at it. "Let's see. I'd like an order of bad fish, soggy coleslaw, and fries that have been floating in rancid oil for a year."

Talia froze for a moment. "I . . . I'm sorry, *what* did you say?"

The woman reached into her jacket and flashed a silver badge. "Detective Patti Prescott, Wrensdale Police."

Talia felt her legs wobble. "Oh." The woman had to be the investigator Rachel had warned her about. Talia forced back a lump of dread and held her chin high. "Our food is fresh, crisp, and delicious, Detective Prescott. I'd be pleased to prepare something for you. If that's why you're here."

"And if it isn't?"

"Then maybe you should tell me why you *are* here. You . . . obviously saw the post on our Facebook page. A post written by someone who had never eaten here," she added quietly.

Prescott moved a tad closer. She studied Talia with shrewd eyes. If she smiled, she'd be lovely. Talia suspected she didn't smile much. At least not while she was on duty.

"Why do you suppose she did that?"

Talia debated whether to tell her the rabbit story. So far, she hadn't told any of the investigators. It had nothing to do with Ria's murder. Then she sighed. Maybe now was the time to tell all.

She gave Prescott a brief summation of the ages-old tale of the stolen rabbit.

Prescott looked dubious. She scribbled something on her notepad. "So you're saying that Ms. Butterforth was carrying a thirty-year-old grudge against you? All because of a rabbit?"

Talia nodded. "Almost thirty years, yes. It's the only reason I can think of for why she seemed to despise me."

More scribbling on the notepad. "Ms. Marby, you spoke at length yesterday with Sergeant O'Donnell of the state police. Although they're officially in charge, I'm going to be working behind the scenes as the local liaison." She pronounced *liaison* with a French flair.

"I see." Talia peeked at the detective's note pad. She would have sworn she saw a rough drawing of a rabbit on it.

"Earlier today I listened to the interview you had with him. I don't recall you giving an adequate explanation of how Ms. Butterforth got possession of your grandmother's scarf."

She had to be kidding.

"Detective Prescott, I think I said, at least three times, that I have no idea how Ria ended up with my nana's scarf. I was shocked to see it hanging on her rack."

"Shocked in an angry way?"

Talia gripped the turquoise counter. "No! Shocked in a baffled way." Of course she *had* been seriously miffed, but that was between her and the deep fryer.

Prescott narrowed her eyes. "Prior to the fund-raiser, when was the last time you saw the scarf?"

"I . . . I'm not sure. Nana died this past spring. I guess it was some time before then."

"I'm sorry for your loss."

"Thank you. Anyway, I probably hadn't seen it since last winter." Her voice lowered, and she felt a lump forming. "I knitted it for Nana many years ago. She wore it all the time in cold weather." Talia glanced at the wall clock. Twelve minutes to closing.

"I won't keep you, Ms. Marby, at least for now. It's almost time for my supper break anyway." Talia detected a touch of humor in her tone.

Prescott closed her notebook. "But I urge you to give serious thought to the last time you saw that scarf. Since we believe it was the murder weapon, it's important that we determine its provenance." Another perfect French pronunciation.

"What do you mean, *believe* it was the murder weapon?"

"ME's report still isn't in," Prescott said. "And you know what they say about assuming." Her nutmeg-colored eyes twinkled.

Talia forced a smile, but she was sure it came out like a grimace. "I'll check with my mom about the scarf. If I learn anything useful, I'll let you know right away."

Prescott pulled out a business card and dropped it on the counter. "There's all my contact info. I check my cell messages nearly twenty-four/seven, so feel free to call anytime."

Talia took the card, wondering if the detective ever slept. *Detective Patti Prescott*, the card read, along with the Wrensdale Police Department number, her cell number, and two e-mail addresses. Talia smiled. "I take it you don't like the name *Patricia*."

Prescott flashed a shark-like grin. "You're right. I don't. Fortunately it's not my name."

Oh, boy. Open mouth. Insert runaway brain.

"Have a good evening, Ms. Marby." Prescott turned to leave.

"Detective," Talia said quickly. "Since it's your break time, I'd be happy to stay a few minutes and whip up a meal for you. It wouldn't take long." She hoped it didn't sound like a bribe. She truly did enjoy preparing meals for people.

Prescott hesitated, but only for a moment. "Thanks. I have a sandwich and a root beer in my car. Maybe another time."

Moments later, the detective was gone. Talia grabbed her cell from her purse and called her mother.

"Mom," she said urgently when she heard her mother's voice. Talia's own words caught in her throat. "What did you do with Nana's scarf?"

7

Talia dreaded calling Detective Prescott to tell her what she'd learned. Not that it was bad—it wasn't. It simply wouldn't do anything to further the investigation.

After Nana's death, Talia's mom and the twins—Talia's aunts Jennie and Josie—had spent an entire day sorting through Nana's belongings. Some things they couldn't bear to part with, like the tattered sewing box Nana's mother had brought with her from Italy. Other items, including the blue scarf, they'd donated to Goodwill.

"Aunt Josie feels terrible about it," Natalie Marby said when she called Talia back. "It was the end of the day, and we were all so tired and so sad. We had two piles—a "throw-out" pile and a "keep" pile. Your aunt apparently tossed the scarf in the wrong pile. She really had meant to keep it."

Talia choked back a sob. "It's no one's fault," she said. "I should have been there to help you."

At the time, Talia had still been working as a commercial

real estate broker in Boston. It was a grueling job, one she'd never really enjoyed. Using her heavy workload as an excuse, she'd begged off the task of helping them go through Nana's things. The real truth was that she couldn't bear the thought of tossing out any of Nana's belongings. She'd have made them keep everything.

She opted for e-mailing Detective Prescott instead of calling her, but she'd do it once she got home. She begged another ride from her mom, who happily picked her up and delivered her to her charming bungalow.

After a quick shower and a bowl of Cheerios and bananas, she snuggled on the old green sofa with Bo and her laptop. Curled in Talia's lap, the little calico touched one mottled paw to the keyboard. "Would you like to write the e-mail?" Talia asked her. She kissed the cat's silky head.

Bo curled her paw beneath her. She looked up at Talia with big gold eyes as if to say, *No, that's really your job, isn't it? Mine is to be a furry ball of lap candy, and I'm doing quite well at it.*

"All right, if you insist. You know what I think about Detective Patti Prescott? I think she puts on a tough act, but inside she's a big ole marshmallow."

Talia shot off a quick e-mail to the detective, explaining how the scarf had ended up at Goodwill. Then she shut her laptop down, watched a few inane sitcoms, and texted with Ryan for a while.

After that, she tumbled into bed, too exhausted to read even one page of her romance novel.

By Tuesday morning the state police had released the crime scene. Talia was free to reclaim her vehicle.

Talia's mom gave her a ride to her car, begging her to be careful when she dropped her off. Talia thought she spied a news van heading toward the community center. She popped into her Fiat as quickly as she could and zipped out of the parking lot.

Lucas had taken the day off to study for exams, so she and Martha would be on their own. Right before opening time, Talia left Martha in charge and dashed next door to Sage & Seaweed.

As always, the specialty bath and body shop smelled like a fragrant slice of heaven. The scent of peppermint filled the air, blended with a hint of pine. Talia got a sudden craving for a heaping bowl of candy cane ice cream.

The owner, Suzy Sato, was busy at the checkout area, searching the shelves behind the counter for a particular brand of lotion. "Is that Talia?" she warbled, swinging around.

Talia laughed. "In the flesh. You obviously have ESP."

Suzy scooted around the counter and greeted her with a squishy hug, her tummy protruding a bit. "How are you doing?" she said, her springy red curls bobbing around her face. She rubbed Talia's arms. "I can't believe you stumbled over another body!"

Suzy had a bent for the dramatic, but she was a kind soul. Five months pregnant with her first child, she wore a glittery red tunic over black stretch slacks. Her sky blue eyes hadn't stopped glowing since the day she found out she was having a girl.

"I'm fine, Suzy. How are you feeling?"

"Great. Better than ever. Morning sickness gone. On to the next stage." She laughed, and her face beamed.

Talia glanced around. Two women browsed at one of the shelves of scented bath oils. Another poked at a rotating display of lip glosses near the counter.

"We had almost no business at the eatery yesterday," Talia confessed to Suzy. "Has it been slow here?"

"Lordy, no," Suzy said. "This is my busiest season. I did over a thousand dollars of business on Saturday alone. Yesterday was pretty decent, too. Especially for a Monday."

"I'm glad your shop is doing so well," Talia said, a bit wistfully. "When I have a free minute or two, I'm coming in here to load up on Christmas gifts."

"Good. That's what I like to hear. Oh! I'm raffling off a gift basket once a week until Christmas. Only fifty cents a ticket, and each prize is gorgeous. I'm giving the proceeds to the women's shelter in Pittsfield." Her blue eyes filled.

Talia hugged her. "That's such a sweet thing to do. Save me a bunch of tickets and I'll run over to pay you later!"

She left, feeling happy for Suzy's success. During her college days, Suzy had gotten involved in a sorority prank that resulted in the death of a young pledge. Talia knew she was still tormented by guilt and was trying hard to make up for it.

By noon, four takeout orders had been called in, all from local businesses. Martha was really getting the hang of preparing fried food quickly and efficiently. Talia wondered if she'd been a short-order chef in a past life.

Around twelve thirty, a harried-looking woman with two kindergartners in tow plopped onto a chair in the dining room. Plunking an oversized red shopping bag onto the floor, she instructed the kids to each take a chair and sit quietly.

Talia greeted her with a big smile, a coffeepot, and a mug. "You look like you could use a coffee."

"I could use a martini, but I'll settle for coffee." She ran her fingers through her frizzy brunette curls. "It's crazy out there with all the shoppers! Wyatt, please do not poke your sister.

Amelia, please stop putting gummy worms in your brother's hair. Thank you." Her gaze tender, she plucked one off his head and caressed his cheek.

Wyatt giggled softly, and another gummy worm rolled off his head.

The kids were adorable—a pair of lookalike teddy bears with huge brown eyes and plump, pink cheeks. Dressed in lined jackets and red rubber boots, they reminded Talia of two little elves from the North Pole.

"The kids won't eat fish," the woman said with a sigh. "But I'll have an order of fish and chips with slaw. What's on the menu that the kids might like?"

"Hmmm. Do you like meatballs?" Talia asked the pair.

Wyatt made a face. Amelia looked into her lap and nodded eagerly.

"Wyatt, I'm figuring you for a hot dog man." Talia winked at him. "How about a deep-fried meatball for Amelia, and a deep-fried mini hot dog for Wyatt? With a side of mushy peas and a glass of milk."

Both children nodded. For kids, they were awfully silent.

"Bless you," the woman said, lowering her gaze at her charges. "This will be such a treat for them."

"I'll start the order," Martha said when Talia returned to the kitchen. She'd obviously been listening to the conversation. She stared hard at the kids for a moment, then turned and began prepping the fish.

Talia removed a mini hot dog and one meatball from the fridge. She swirled each of them in batter and lowered them into the fryer reserved for the meats. Expanding her menu had meant adding an extra fryer in the kitchen, as well as a convection oven. Space was getting tight, but so far they'd managed.

When Martha had everything ready, Talia stared in awe at the children's plates. Using the eatery's tangy mustard sauce, Martha had drawn eyes, floppy ears, and a nose above the hot dog to make it look like a grinning pup. On Amelia's plate, she'd turned the meatball into the face of a cat and used marinara sauce to form the ears, eyes, and whiskers. A mound of mushy peas graced each plate.

"Martha, that's . . . really clever," Talia said, wondering what had gotten into her employee. The one who couldn't stand to be around kids.

Martha shrugged. "Don't forget the milk."

Talia delivered the plates, along with two glasses of milk, to the table. "I'll bring yours right along," she said to the mom.

Amelia's face brightened when she saw the faux cat on her plate. "Look, Mommy," she said in a tiny voice.

"Oh, honey, that's darling," the woman said, her eyes welling up.

Wyatt stared at his plate. He said nothing, but a sweet smile lit up his face.

When Talia returned with the woman's fish and chips, Wyatt and Amelia were slowly digging into their meals.

The woman clasped her hands in delight when Talia set her order on the table. A chunk of crispy fried haddock, along with a slew of fries, was tucked into a lined cone forged from swirls of black stainless steel. "Oh, what a charming way to serve the fish," the woman crooned. "The liner's supposed to look like newsprint, right?"

Talia grinned. "Yes, just like the old days. Only a lot more sanitary."

A few more diners trickled in. Talia hoped it was a good sign. Lucas had successfully deleted Ria's vicious post from the eatery's Facebook page. Another customer had posted a glowing review, which gave Talia a breath of relief.

The mom and kids finished up and Talia delivered the bill to their table. Both kids had polished off their lunches, right down to the last drop of mushy peas. "The kids' meals are my treat," Talia said quietly. She smiled at Wyatt and Amelia. "Please visit again, okay?"

The mom's eyes grew misty again. "You bet we will. Are you getting a sign for the front? I'm not sure people realize you're open."

"It's coming, hopefully by the weekend," Talia said. "There was a glitch with the paint color."

The woman rose. She cupped Talia's elbow and nudged her slightly to one side. "Thank you so much for your kindness," she murmured. "My husband and I are in the process of adopting Wyatt and Amelia. We took them in as foster kids a little over a year ago. They came from a very ugly home life. It was a rough adjustment, but they're doing wonderfully now."

Talia hugged her. "It's obvious you adore them both. Good luck."

"We'll be back, I promise," the woman said.

After they left, Talia ducked back into the kitchen to answer the phone.

"That was a big takeout order from the fire station. They're becoming one of our best customers!" Talia stuck the order on a metal clip in front of the work area.

Martha squinted at the slip. "Cripes—they want six large orders of fried pickles."

"Yup, and they asked for delivery again. I felt bad having to say no." Talia grabbed eight chunky dill pickles from the fridge and began slicing away.

"Delivery might be something to think about," Martha pointed out. She squeezed past Talia with an exaggerated *oomph* sound. "Lucas is young and strong. He could do some deliveries during the busy patches. Like, say, from eleven thirty to one thirty. You and I could handle the orders, easy." She extracted five slabs of haddock from the box in the fridge.

Talia had to admit, when she and Martha got into a rhythm, they worked together very efficiently. If only the woman could smile a bit more, maybe complain a bit less.

"He doesn't have his own car," Talia said. "He uses his mom's when he has to go to his classes. Plus, I'd have to look into the insurance. It would probably be more trouble than it's worth."

Martha scowled. "Yeah, I forgot about the insurance."

Together they whipped up five orders of fish and chips— three with mushy peas and two with slaw. Added to that were the six large orders of fried pickles, two double orders of deep-fried meatballs, and an order of the mini hot dogs.

The door flew open. In rushed a red-faced young fireman with spiky blond hair and the body of weight lifter. "Man, I hope our food is ready," he said. "We're, like, starving over at the firehouse."

Grinning, Talia set two large brown bags on the counter. "You're all set. But I always thought fireman made their own meals!" she teased.

The young fireman laughed. He dredged a handful of currency from his pocket and shoved it across the counter. "Yeah, back in the day they did. Problem is, old Walt Angley retired last month, and the rest of us can't boil water." He hoisted the bags off the counter and called out, "Keep the change!"

After he left, Talia thought about her new sign. The space

where the Lambert's sign used to be sure did look bare. Did customers think she hadn't opened yet?

She didn't have long to mull it over. A fresh wave of customers came in, keeping her and Martha hopping for the next hour and a half. A gaggle of twenty-somethings had no sooner left when Vivian Lavoie stepped inside. Cheeks rosy, her arms laden with shopping bags, she toddled into the dining area. "I've been shopping all day, and I am ready for lunch!"

Talia greeted her warmly and gave her a menu. "It's good to see you again, Vivian."

"Oh, I'm glad to be here. It's a zoo out there! I spotted one of those tour buses from the outlet shops headed this way. Don't be surprised if you get a new flock of customers pretty soon!" She asked for a table close to the restroom, just in case she had to "make a run for it."

Twenty minutes later, Vivian was finishing up her deep-fried meatballs and wiping her mouth with a napkin. It was after two, and the dining area had emptied out. Talia ambled over and offered her a coffee warm-up.

"Yes, please," Vivian said. She leaned across the table. "Terrible about that poor woman being killed, wasn't it?"

Talia nodded, but said nothing. Did Vivian know she was the one who'd found Ria? Was she fishing for information?

Vivian's eyes sparked with a touch of glee. "I suppose the police will be checking out that poor Andy Nash fellow," she said, lowering her voice. "You know, what with his background and all."

Talia didn't know, and normally she disliked a gossipy type. But with Ria's murder so fresh, and the police breathing down her neck, she decided to hear what Vivian had to say.

"What do you mean?" Talia said, sliding into a chair opposite her.

"Well, there was an incident a while back with a young girl who worked at the town clerk's office. She accused Andy of stalking her. The girl's father was furious. Positively livid! The girl finally ended up getting a restraining order." Vivian tsked and took a loud slurp of her coffee. "If you ask me, it was all a big to-do about nothing."

Okay, now Talia's curiosity was piqued. "What do you mean by stalking? Did he follow her?"

"Yes, once or twice, but he didn't mean any real harm. The silly girl had fits over him sending her a dozen roses! She told him to leave her alone, but poor Andy had already been struck by Cupid's arrow. He doesn't seem to have much luck with the ladies, if you get my meaning." She gave Talia a bland smile. "Anyway, a few days after the roses incident he tucked a love poem under her windshield wiper. Wrote it himself, poor devil. The girl went nuts and called the cops. Can you believe it? Why, if a man did that to me, I'd be flattered!"

Talia couldn't believe her ears. Was Vivian that naïve about the dangers of stalking?

"Vivian, unwanted attention can be very scary," Talia pointed out. "I don't blame her for being so upset. I would've been creeped out!"

Vivian sighed. "Yes, well, that's what everyone said. Anyway, it was humiliating for the poor fellow. He truly never meant her any harm."

Oh, wow, she really didn't get it. "Did he ever do that to anyone else?"

"Oh, no. Not that I know of anyway. Like I said, it was only that one girl he fancied. Plus, it was about ten years ago.

No one really holds it against him anymore. Everyone's pretty much forgotten about it."

Talia thought about Andy, how furious he'd seemed when Ria canceled their so-called date. Had he been angry enough to kill her?

Vivian looked around, and then leaned closer to Talia. "I'll tell you someone who's *not* the sweet fairy princess she pretends to be. It's that Kelsey Dakoulas girl." She gave a sharp little nod to emphasize her point.

"What do you mean?" Talia said.

Vivian gave her a smug smile. "It's not common knowledge, but that girl was arrested a few years ago. Arrested!"

"Are you sure, Vivian?"

Vivian nodded, a glint in her eye. "The way I heard it, she was visiting an aunt in Maine when it happened. Got into a spat with a neighbor lady and bopped her over the head with a heavy weapon."

"What kind of weapon?"

"A chair is what I heard. Now, Lord knows I'm not one to spread gossip, but I also heard she had to go before a judge. The woman she attacked had to get stitches. The Dakoulas girl should've gotten a jail sentence, but apparently the judge was lenient with her. No doubt because of her pretty face and that Betty Boop figure," she added in a snippy tone.

Talia thought the whole story sounded bizarre. Not that she knew Kelsey all that well. It just didn't seem like the kind of thing she would do.

"Vivian, are you sure about all this?" Talia said carefully.

"As sure as I can be." Vivian sat back with a knowing look. "You know that Ria girl who was murdered? Well, her mom, Anita, clerks at the dry cleaner's where my cousin Ralphie works. Anita told him the whole story."

"But how would Ria—"

"Ria and Kelsey used to be real good friends," she said, anticipating Talia's question. "Then something happened about a month ago to split the two of them up. Ralphie wasn't sure what it was. Probably squabbled over a man, would be my take on it." She shook her gray curls in disgust.

All of that made zero sense, Talia thought. If Kelsey was on the outs with Ria, why did she agree to work in the vintage clothing shop?

And then something Kelsey had said on Sunday popped into Talia's head. Something about a cat . . .

Cats are a dime a dozen. Those words from Ria.

Then Kelsey had shot back, *You are not going to get away with this.*

"Vivian, did Ralphie mention anything about a cat?"

Vivian's gray eyebrows dipped toward her nose. "A cat? No, I don't think so. What would a cat have to do with the price of apples in China?"

Not a thing, Talia thought. *Much like this conversation.*

Still, she couldn't completely dismiss some of the bombshells Vivian had dropped.

Andy a stalker.

Kelsey assaulting someone with a chair.

"Well, I'm full up to my eyeballs," Vivian said, pushing back her chair. She darted a glance at the corner where the door to the restroom was located.

"I hope you enjoyed everything," Talia said. "I'll get your bill."

By the time Vivian shuffled out of the eatery with her bags, Talia's head felt like a whirlybird. She wasn't sure what bothered her more—the idea of Andy stalking a woman, or the thought that Kelsey attacked someone with a chair. She simply couldn't picture Kelsey doing something like that! Andy, however, was a different story. He'd seemed to be an odd duck from the get-go.

Although the police hadn't said as much, Talia knew they considered her a "person of interest" in Ria's death. While Vivian's tales might be more fiction than truth, Talia would definitely have to put some feelers out to see what she could find out.

The eatery was in its usual midday lull. Talia dug a small notepad out of her handbag. She sat at the corner table in the kitchen, pencil in hand. Her first thought was to list all the suspects that came to mind, devoting a separate page to each one.

She had just written Andy's name on the first page when Martha set a plate in front of her. "You look frazzled," she said gruffly. "Have a hot dog."

Talia couldn't help smiling at the plate. Martha had used the mustard sauce to draw a kitty's face over a downturned deep-fried hot dog.

"Thank you, Martha. You're quite the *artiste*."

Martha raised one thick eyebrow. "Me? I can barely draw a stick figure."

Talia swirled one end of the hot dog in the mustard sauce and took a cautious bite. Tangy with a bit of heat, it tantalized her taste buds. No wonder the deep-fried mini-dogs were fast becoming a customer favorite. She swallowed. "You sure made those little munchkins happy today with your artistic skills. It was a very nice thing to do."

Martha lifted her broad shoulders in a shrug. "I was just practicing, in case I decide to take an art class one of these days."

Talia grinned. "You're a fibber, Martha, and you know it. You wanted to make those kids smile, didn't you?"

Martha looked thoughtful, her gaze far away. "They were just too quiet. Kids ought to be giggling and squirming and jumping and—" She stopped short, as if she realized she'd said too much. "Never mind."

Talia decided not to push. Martha was a puzzle. Maybe one day Talia would put all the pieces together. For now she was grateful to have a hardworking employee who seemed to enjoy her job.

She turned to a fresh page in her notebook. With the eatery now offering a variety of deep-fried goodies, she would have to keep innovating, adding new items to the menu. For some reason, seeing Wyatt and Amelia today made her think of veggies.

A lot of kids resisted healthy foods. Almost every kid hated at least one vegetable. For Talia it was beets. She loved the color, but couldn't stand the smell.

"Martha, what's your favorite vegetable?"

Martha soaped and rinsed the last of the stainless steel cones and set it to dry on the overhead rack. "Veggies don't thrill me in general, but I like Brussels sprouts. They have kind of a nutty taste."

A nutty taste. Hmmm . . .

"Could you picture deep-fried Brussels sprouts with a light peanut sauce?"

A rare smile split Martha's face. "Yeah. Yeah I could." Her smile faded instantly. "But remember, some people are allergic to peanuts. You're opening a whole can of worms if you do that."

"You're right." Talia scribbled it in her notebook. What other veggies could be deep-fried? Broccoli florets? Cherry tomatoes? Maybe those kalamata olives her dad loved?

She groaned. How could she concentrate on experimenting with recipes while she was a suspect in Ria's death? Thoughts of being arrested clogged her mind, leaving little room for creative endeavors. If anything felt fried right now, it was her brain. Closing her notebook, she rose. She snagged two large potatoes from the supply closet and set them on the worktable.

"Need help?" Martha said, clearly a bit curious.

"Nope. An idea just struck me, and I want to test it out. But after I'm done, I'll need your opinion, okay?"

Martha hesitated for a moment. "Okay, but only if it's food related." She grabbed the spray cleaner and a cloth from underneath the counter. "Since we're in a lull, I might as well clean off the tables. I'll bet those two kids made a big freakin' mess out there."

Talia pressed her lips into a smile, but said nothing. She knew Wyatt and Amelia hadn't left even a tiny spill on the table.

While Martha puttered around the dining room grunting to herself, Talia peeled, sliced, and boiled the potatoes. After she drained them, she dumped them into a large bowl. From the fridge she extracted a bag of shredded cheddar. She plopped a full cup into the potato mixture, and added a few hefty shakes from the salt and pepper shakers. The mixture still had to cool, but in the meantime she mashed it with her potato masher.

Martha meandered back into the kitchen and stuck the spray bottle and cloth under the counter.

"Was it a big mess out there?" Talia said innocently.

Martha avoided Talia's gaze. "Not too bad. What'cha doing?"

Talia grinned. "Something I saw on TV a few nights ago. Grab me an egg, please, will you? And some milk?"

Martha fetched the ingredients and set them down on the work area. "Now what?"

"Well, first I have to let the mixture cool. After that I'm going to form stiff balls and roll them in flour. And then—" Talia set her masher down and stared at Martha. "Oh darn, I just remembered. I need panko crumbs to do this."

Martha crossed her arms over her chest and looked at the mixture. "What's the big yank?" she said in a grumpy tone. "Why can't you swirl them through the batter you use for the fish?"

And just like that, the kinder, gentler Martha was gone, replaced by her crotchety old self.

"There's no reason," Talia said, keeping her tone even. "I liked the idea of the crispy panko coating, that's all. But you're right. I can use the batter this time around to test them, can't I?"

Martha shrugged. "Whatever floats your dinghy."

Talia gave a quiet sigh. She realized all at once how much she missed working with Bea Lambert. Bea was a rare treasure—kind, funny, quirky to the tenth power. She'd been like a second mother to Talia. If it hadn't been for her gentle prodding, Talia would never have taken over the eatery and morphed it into a deep-fried heaven.

"—too much flour on that one," Martha was scolding. She was aiming a thick finger at the lump of potato mixture in Talia's plastic-gloved hand. "Shake some of it off."

She was right, which irked Talia even more.

Over the next ten minutes Talia managed to coat and deep-fry six cheesy potato rounds. "Try one," she said to Martha, and nabbed one for herself.

Martha chomped on her potato round for what seemed an eternity. Talia ate hers carefully, testing the flavor and texture on her tongue. "Mmmm, nice and crispy," she said. "But I still think the panko coating would be better."

Her mouth full, Martha nodded and then swallowed. "You know what would be good inside these? Bacon."

Talia took another bite. She preferred making them meatless, but Martha did have a point. Lots of people loved bacon.

Martha ate two more and then pronounced herself as "stuffed as a holiday goose." Talia gave her the remaining two to take home, and by that time it was nearly seven.

"Time to roll," Martha said, whipping her smoky-smelling scarf off the door hook.

Talia resisted the urge to wrinkle her nose at the scarf as Martha shrugged on her peacoat. She was slipping on her own jacket when the eatery phone rang. Martha rolled her eyes when Talia answered it.

"Talia Marby?" a voice said.

"Yes, may I help you?"

With a snort of impatience, Martha set her green handbag on the front counter and headed for the bathroom.

"It's Andy Nash," the caller said. He sounded breathless. "I met you on Sunday, remember?"

Talia's heartbeat spiked. She remembered what Vivian had told her about him. "Yes, I remember. But I'm afraid the eatery is—"

"I'm not calling for takeout," he said urgently. "I've got a problem. I want to talk to you about it. Can you meet me at the diner in fifteen minutes? I know you close at seven."

No way, Talia thought. She did not intend to be Andy Nash's next stalkee.

"What does this concern?" Talia said, a hint of irritation in her voice.

Andy huffed loudly. "It's about that Ria woman who was killed. I don't want to say any more over the phone, but it's important."

"Andy, if you know something about Ria's death you need to go to the police."

"That's just it. I can't," he whimpered. "I—"

"And I'm afraid I can't help, Andy. Have a pleasant evening." Talia hung up the phone. It rang again almost immediately. She was tempted to ignore it. The problem was, her home number would be easy to find, and he might resort to calling her there. She lifted the receiver.

"Please please please," he begged. "I just need to talk to you for a few minutes, okay? We'll be in a public place with tons of people around. Nothing's going to happen."

In her head, Talia counted to five. "All right, but only for ten minutes or so. I'm very busy, and frankly I don't even have that much time to spare."

It was a slight exaggeration, but he didn't need to know that.

"Thank you." He blew out a noisy sigh. "I knew Peter Marby's daughter wouldn't let me down."

Martha emerged from the restroom. "Look what I found," she said, holding a plain brown shopping bag in the air.

Talia went over to her. "Someone forgot it, I guess. Where was it?" she asked Martha.

"In the corner near the bathroom. Shall we check it out?"

Talia smiled at her. "No, let's leave it here for now. I'm sure someone will show up to claim it tomorrow."

A cold breeze whipped across the cobblestone plaza, creeping under the sleeves of Talia's flared jacket. She hadn't yet dug her winter coat out of storage, but she planned to make the switch at the sight of the first snowflake.

Above the distant, rolling hills of the Berkshires, a white half-moon hung low in the charcoal sky. The shops on Main Street were mostly shut down at this hour. Lights twinkled in the darkened storefronts, many of which boasted charming Christmas displays.

Martha was quiet as they walked together to the town lot. Talia knew she was probably dying to find out who the mystery phone caller was. When they reached their cars, Martha slid inside her old monstrosity and revved the engine. Talia waved good-bye and hurried toward her own car.

She started her engine to warm up the Fiat, and then pulled out her cell. She sent a quick text to Ryan, letting him know where she was headed. That way, if anything happened . . .

Which it wouldn't. Something told Talia that Andy Nash was all talk. Annoying, for sure, but not dangerous, in spite of what Vivian had told her. Plus, for some reason he seemed to revere Talia's dad. He wouldn't do anything to hurt Peter Marby's daughter, right? She didn't know why he was so enamored of her dad, but maybe now he would enlighten her.

The Wrensdale Diner was barely a five-minute drive, located at the point where Main Street curved around toward the railroad track. Known for its "cloud high" roast beef sandwiches and bad-tempered waitstaff, it had been there for the better part of three decades. The available parking consisted of a series of diagonal lines painted on the street in front of the diner. Talia prayed she'd find a spot close by. Otherwise she'd have to park in the empty bank lot a half block away on the opposite side of the street.

Luck was on her side. She found a perfect spot close to the entrance. She locked the Fiat and dashed inside the busy diner. Andy was already seated in a booth for two about halfway down on the right. He waved to get her attention, and she slipped onto the bench seat across from him.

Andy's bespectacled face looked blotchy. Both his upper lip and his wide brow were dotted with tiny beads of perspiration. It was warm in there, but not that warm. Clearly he was extremely nervous.

"Thanks for coming, Talia. I knew you wouldn't let me down. Your dad always said—"

"Andy, how do you know my dad?" she asked him. "I don't recall him ever mentioning you."

Leaning closer, Andy gave her a lopsided smile. "Of course he didn't. Don't you see? It's all very confidential. No one's supposed to talk about the others in the group."

"What group?" Talia said wearily. She set her purse beside her on the padded bench.

Andy lowered his voice. "Back when your dad had that, you know, little *problem*? Well, I was part of the group. Youngest one of a dozen, in fact."

Talia's stomach twisted into a familiar knot. Suddenly, she got it.

When Talia was a teen, her dad had fallen victim to the gambling bug. It had been a bad time for her mom and for her. He'd lost a load of money that they couldn't afford to lose. It wasn't until her dad joined Gamblers Anonymous that he got help and eventually kicked the addiction.

"I see," Talia said quietly.

"Yeah, and your dad was like my mentor, you know? Anytime I was tempted to stray, he'd reel me back in. I love that guy. He's the best."

Talia agreed wholeheartedly, but she wasn't about to discuss her dad with someone she barely knew.

A middle-aged server with a thick ring of black liner around each eye came over and took their orders for coffee. She looked less than thrilled that they didn't order food. Talia felt bad. The diner was busy. She didn't like occupying a booth for a mere cup of coffee. She made a mental note to leave the woman a sizeable tip.

"You said you had something important to tell me," Talia prodded.

He spoke more quietly, lowering his voice. "Yeah, but I gotta explain something first, because I know people are prob'ly talking about it." He shifted on the padded vinyl bench. His face reddened. "I, um, did something a bunch of years ago that got me in a spot of trouble."

Ah, confession time.

"You see, there was this girl I liked who worked at the town hall. I asked her out a few times, but she turned me down. Anyway, I thought I could prove what a nice guy I was by sending her a dozen roses." He paused. When Talia said nothing, he continued. "She didn't take it very well. She told me to, well, I can't say the word she used. Basically she told me to get lost."

"So what did you do?" Talia said. She was curious to hear his version of the tale that Vivian had already related to her.

"I guess it was stupid when I look back," he said. "I wrote her a poem. A really romantic one." He flushed right up to his earlobes.

Talia forced a smile. "Go on, Andy."

"I left it under her windshield wiper while she was at work," he said. His face darkened. "She went nuclear and told the cops I was harassing her. Then her father threatened me with . . . well, bodily harm."

Something about his hangdog look made Talia feel bad for him. He seemed like one of those men who had a knack for never attracting the opposite sex. Still, he needed to understand that when a woman says no, she means it. "Women don't appreciate unwanted attention, Andy. It's very scary stuff these days."

He scowled. "Yeah, I know, but I never would've hurt her! I don't know why she didn't get that."

So many retorts whirled through Talia's head. *Are you really that clueless?* was one of the more polite ones. "So what did the police do?" she asked.

His pale blue eyes watered. "Took me in, questioned me. Scared the living spit out of me." He raised his eyeglasses and rubbed the heel of his hand over his right eyelid. "The girl ended up getting a restraining order, which was way overboard if you ask me."

Talia knew she was treading dangerous waters, but she couldn't stop herself. "Is that what you did to Ria?" she said softly. "Did you bother her, Andy? Harass her?"

Andy's hand dropped to the table with a thud. "What? I didn't do anything to Ria. I asked her out for a drink a few times, but she told me to . . . to take a hike, so I left her alone."

"But Andy," Talia said innocently, as if she might have gotten it wrong. "Didn't you ask her out again, and didn't she accept? I'm sure I overheard you say that she agreed to have a drink with you Sunday evening, after the fund-raiser."

Andy swallowed. "Okay, yeah. You heard right. She told me she'd have a drink with me one time, and one time only. Next thing I know, she texts me and says that our date is off.

That rich-looking dude must've have called her to say he was coming over. I saw him, barely half an hour later. He was hugging and kissing her right in front of everyone!"

"You saw that?" Talia said.

Andy's blue eyes hardened. "Yup. I had a clear view of her table from Santa's chair."

Talia sat back in her seat. Of course he did. He'd asked Scott to move the Christmas tree to give the kids a better view of Santa. What he really wanted was an unobstructed view of Ria's table. In Talia's mind, Andy Nash fit the profile of a stalker to a tee.

Another thought struck her, a far worse one. What if Andy was the killer? What if he'd snapped when Ria canceled their date and strangled her in a fit of rage? Maybe this entire meeting was a ruse to throw Talia off the track. But why would he single her out?

The server returned with their coffees and then scuttled away. Andy took a big gulp from his steaming mug. Talia plunked a packet of creamer into her coffee and stirred. She sensed it was time to pull back, to fake a little compassion for his romantic plight.

"You know," she said with a slight *tsk* in her voice, "that was really shabby of Ria to cancel your date at the last minute. Truly thoughtless in my book."

Andy's eyes brightened. "I know! That's what I said. I would never treat a lady that way. Never."

No, you'd just hound her until she caved from sheer mental exhaustion.

Talia nodded with understanding. "Women don't realize how tough it is for men sometimes. You know, having to risk rejection every time they ask someone out."

"Yeah, well, you're right about that." He seemed pacified,

at least for the moment. She only hoped she hadn't opened herself up to any unwanted attention.

"Anyway, that's partly why I asked you to meet me. Because of, you know, that incident way back then, the cops are now questioning me about Ria's death."

Interesting. So Talia wasn't the only person of interest hovering on their radar screen. "Andy, I think they're questioning everyone who even talked to Ria that day. They interviewed me for hours."

"Yeah, but you found the body. I didn't." He swallowed another mouthful of coffee, and then gave out a long sigh. "Look, it's pretty common knowledge that you solved a murder a few months ago."

Talia shook her head. "I didn't solve it. I was at the wrong place at the wrong time, that's all."

"But you were smart." His pale blue eyes beamed. "You figured it out."

Yeah, when it was almost too late, she thought wryly. She glanced at Andy and saw an odd look creep into his eyes.

"See, here's the thing," he said, leaning closer to her across the table. "I . . . um, saw something that day. The day Ria was killed."

Heart pounding, Talia took a slow sip from her mug. She waited. "Are you going to tell me what it was?"

Andy shot a look over his shoulder and then craned his head toward the front entrance. "That's just it. I can't really say right now. I gotta get more evidence so I can go to the police."

Now Talia was seriously exasperated. "You want my help, but you can't tell me what you saw? I'm sorry, Andy, but I—"

"Wait a minute. Listen to me for a sec, okay? Please?" His watery eyes widened in fear. "If I tell you what I saw and the wrong person finds out, my life won't be worth a three-dollar bill."

Talia spoke quietly. "Are you saying you know who the killer is?"

"I think so. Yeah, I'm pretty sure." He squeezed his eyes shut and swiped at his damp brow. "Maybe not one hundred percent, but . . ."

"Either way," Talia said gently, "the police have ways to protect you. Andy, if you saw something that might help them catch Ria's killer, you have to tell them."

He shook his head. "You don't get it, do you?" he said flatly. "We're not dealing with a normal person here. We're dealing with a vicious killer. That's why I need your help. You see things. You notice things. You can poke around quietly without anyone even realizing you're doing it."

Talia took another sip of her coffee. How could she make him understand that she couldn't help him? That he needed to go to the authorities with whatever his so-called information was?

"I'm not asking you to put yourself in danger." Andy curled his lower lip into a pout. "I'd never do that to Pete Marby's daughter. But keep this in mind. All those people you saw around Ria that day? One of them is acting. One of them is a cold-blooded killer."

Talia shivered in spite of her warm jacket. "I don't know what to say, other than that you need to go to the police." She blotted her lips with a napkin and fished a ten-dollar bill from her purse. "Andy, look, I have to go, okay? If I trip over anything significant, you'll be the first to know." *Not*, she thought silently, tucking the currency under her mug. "In the meantime, please think about what I said."

When she looked up, Andy was staring past her, his eyes

focused intently on the glass front window of the diner. Then, as abruptly as if someone had jolted him with a cattle prod, he pulled his gaze away, grabbed a five from his wallet, and tossed it on the table. "I have to go," he said, leaping out of the booth.

Andy hurried toward the back of the diner, nearly tripping over his own shoe as he shoved past a server carrying a carafe of coffee. "Hey, watch it, buster," the server sniped at him. "Can't you see I'm holding hot coffee?"

Talia swung her head around, toward the front of the diner. What had Andy been gawking at right before he fled? She peered beyond the glass front, where the words *Wrensdale Diner* had been inscribed in a large, curving line. Through the red lettering, she spied a car the size of a cruise ship, headlights off, idling in a front parking space.

Their server appeared at her elbow with a steaming carafe. "More coffee?" she said sweetly, noticing the excessive tip on the table.

"No thanks," Talia said. "I have to run."

She heaved her purse onto her shoulder and glanced toward the back of the diner. Had Andy fled into the men's room? Then she remembered. The diner had a rear door that led to a small, unpaved lot where the employees parked.

Andy was gone.

And Talia couldn't wait to get out of there.

She was headed for the door when she noticed a trio of men who'd just sauntered in together. She only saw the backs of their heads, but from their boisterous voices she suspected they all had a buzz on. Wearing ball caps, all three were facing into the larger dining room where an overhead television was broadcasting a basketball game. One of them called another one "Captain" and slapped him hard on the shoulder.

Talia scurried out the front door. After the stuffiness of the diner, the cold night air felt incredibly refreshing. She took a deep breath, and then another. But it wasn't the crisp night air she found herself inhaling. It was the stale scent of a smoky, unwashed scarf.

A scarf worn by one Martha Hoelscher.

Was that who'd scared Andy into fleeing like a fugitive?

8

"Martha, what are you doing here?" Talia said, although it came out like more of a squeak.

The handles of her green plastic handbag clasped in one hand, Martha stood there like a statue and stared at Talia. "What do you mean, what am I doing here? It's a diner, isn't it? I came to get supper."

"Oh." Talia glanced at Martha's car. The ambient lighting from the diner and from passing headlights lent a sickly sheen to its faded paint. All at once, something about the old car bothered her. What was it? Aside from its age and its size, it was pretty much the same as any other ancient clunker. She smiled at Martha. "You said you were stuffed as a holiday goose a little while ago."

"So? I was stuffed then. I'm not now. I may be old and on my way out, but I still have to eat," she said grumpily.

Talia couldn't resist a chuckle. "You're far from old,

Martha. Anyway, have a nice dinner. I hope you enjoy your meal."

Eyes on her shoes, Martha shuffled toward the entrance to the diner. "Don't worry, I plan to. Tuesday is chicken croquettes night."

Talia waved good-bye and headed home to her bungalow. The day she understood what made Martha tick would probably be the same day a U.S. spaceship landed on Mars.

Ten minutes after stepping inside her bungalow, Talia was curled up on her sofa with Bo. Reeking of kitty salmon, the little calico was busy cleaning her whiskers with one paw.

Talia was about to call her dad to pick his brain about Andy Nash when she remembered he was on a skiing trip in Colorado. He'd probably answer his cell, but she didn't want to bug him. He deserved a few days off without having to worry about her. She was just setting down the phone when it rang in her hand. The readout said, *PPrescott*. With a groan, she steeled herself. "What can I do for you, Detective Prescott?"

Prescott's message was short and quick. "I'm afraid I have a few more questions for you, Ms. Marby. Can you come down to the station tomorrow morning?"

"But I've told you everything I know," Talia protested a bit meekly.

"Some new evidence has come in," Prescott said tersely. "Eight o'clock?"

Talia sighed. "See you then, Detective."

"Great," Talia muttered to the cat. "Something else to worry about all night."

Talia must have been more exhausted than she realized. She drifted off watching a sitcom she'd seen a hundred times, awakening only when her alarm jarred her out of a sound sleep.

In an effort to look professional, Talia put on camel slacks and a navy blazer. She pinned her nana's poinsettia brooch to the jacket's lapel. When Nana was living, the brooch had been her favorite holiday accessory. Wearing it made Talia feel close to her.

All at once, Talia felt her eyes sting with unshed tears. On days like this, when her mind was weighted with worry, she missed Nana so much. Nana always knew what to say to make her feel better. The thought that her nana's lovely blue scarf had been used to murder someone made Talia all that much sadder. Even if the police returned it to her after the murder was solved, she knew she'd never be able to wear it again.

Talia blotted her eyes and swiped a hint of peach-colored shadow over the lids. It wasn't something she normally used during the day, but she didn't want Detective Prescott to think she'd been crying.

The detective was already in the "interview" room when Talia arrived at the Wrensdale police station. Prescott stood and ushered Talia into a chair. "Thank you for coming," she said, a hint of mystery shining in her nutmeg-colored eyes. "You understand this interview is being recorded?"

"I do," Talia said, taking a seat on the rock-hard chair. "I'm surprised Sergeant O'Donnell isn't here."

"Who said he isn't?" Prescott straightened the short stack of documents that rested on the table in front of her. She picked up the top one and appeared to study it.

Talia had to force herself not to roll her eyes. No doubt whatever the detective was reading had already been engraved into her memory. The woman was no fool, and Talia wouldn't make the mistake of taking her for one.

"Ms. Marby," Prescott said sternly, setting the paper down. "Do you recall opening the door to the supply closet the afternoon you found Ms. Butterforth's body?"

Okay, Talia did have to roll her eyes at that one. "Detective Prescott, if I'm not mistaken, I've told this same story at least six times. Of course I remember opening the door to the supply closet. How else would I have found . . . you know, Ria's body?" She swallowed. "Anyway, the answer is yes."

"Did you turn the doorknob?"

Talia wanted to scream. "Of course I turned the doorknob. How else would I have opened the door?"

Prescott shrugged. "Maybe the door was already ajar and you squinched it open with your fingers?"

"Squinched it?"

"My mother's word," Prescott explained. "And if my mother used a word, believe me, we didn't question it."

"Who's we?" Talia smiled at her. Had she spied a tiny glimpse into the detective's personality?

"Let's get on with the interview, shall we?" Prescott said.

Talia sucked in a breath and released it on a burst of air. "The door was not ajar. I used the doorknob."

Prescott nodded. "Thank you." She paused. "Can you guess whose fingerprints the lab found on that doorknob?"

"Let me guess," Talia said, clasping her hands on the table. "Mine?"

Prescott grinned, a toothy smile that radiated not an ounce of warmth. "Exactly. And do you know who else's prints were found on that same doorknob?"

A tiny moth of apprehension fluttered across Talia's rib

cage. She sensed Prescott was trying to trip her up, but she wasn't sure why. Or how. "No," she said quietly, "I can't. I'm afraid you'll have to tell me."

"Not necessarily," Prescott said. She looked at her paper again. "On to the next thing—the scarf."

Talia suppressed a groan. Hadn't they already gone over that four zillion times?

Prescott's eyes lasered in on Talia. "The lab found an interesting substance on the scarf, Ms. Marby. Can you guess what that was?"

Again with the guessing games. "No I can't." This time she was careful not to suggest that the detective tell her.

Prescott sat back in her chair. She looked like a cat who'd just swallowed a mouthful of fresh tuna. "Raspberry sauce."

Talia's heart did a lindy hop on her chest. Raspberry sauce? How did raspberry sauce get on the scarf? Her mind spun, trying to conjure up a rational response. Nothing flew out.

"You seem a bit dumbstruck, Ms. Marby. Is there a reason for that?"

Talia paused for a moment to gather her thoughts. Then she said, "First of all, Detective, you didn't ask me a question." Talia smiled sweetly at her. "Second, I can't see how that would implicate either me or anyone else. Raspberry sauce is sticky stuff. Anyone who bought a fried cake could have strolled past Ria's display and dribbled a bit of sauce on the scarf."

Prescott tapped a finger to her lips, as if that hadn't occurred to her. "Hmm, yes, that's true. Anyone could have stained the scarf."

The detective forced Talia to revisit the scene again. Talia marching across the gymnasium, seeing the scarf sticking out. Pushing aside the divider. Opening the door . . .

Talia knew what the police were doing—they were testing her. They wanted to see if she would contradict herself
by making her tell the same story over and over.

After another fifteen minutes of badgering, Prescott
announced, "I think we're done here. Thank you for your
cooperation." She rose, neatened her papers, and dipped her
head toward the door.

By that time, Talia's ire had been stoked. The entire "interview" had been a sham, and a huge waste of her time. Rising
from her own uncomfortable chair, Talia nodded at the detective and turned to leave.

"Oh, by the way," Prescott called after her. "There were
no other prints found on the doorknob."

Talia's mouth went dry. She turned and stared at Prescott.
"None?"

Prescott smiled. "Only yours."

Her hand shaking, Talia yanked open the door and stumbled into the hallway. Leaning against the wall, clipboard
in hand, was Sergeant Liam O'Donnell of the Massachusetts
State Police.

O'Donnell nodded at her. "Ms. Marby."

And then Talia knew. He'd been watching the entire performance through the two-way mirror.

9

"That's what cops do," Martha squawked, pointing a stainless steel whisk at Talia. "They try to confuse you. They try to trip you up so you'll spill your guts all over the place, even though you haven't done a single thing wrong."

In spite of the dark mood the police interrogation had put her in, Talia couldn't help smiling at Martha's observation. Her friend Bea had said nearly the exact same thing a few months ago, when the police were eyeing Bea for the murder of a fellow tenant in the arcade. Of course, the expressions Bea had brought with her from the UK gave the words a far more amusing twist. But the sentiment was pretty much the same.

"Sounds like you've had a few run-ins with the police," Talia teased. She scooped two tablespoons of chipotle sauce into the coleslaw mixture.

Martha's eyes beamed with mischief. "I've had my share," she said cryptically.

Lucas was peeling potatoes on the far side of the work area. "Were you, like, one of those protestors?" he said, sneaking a sly grin at her. "You look like you might have been around in the sixties," he added, and then blushed.

"You're right on target, Lucas."

"Really?" His blue eyes popped wide. "What did you protest? I mean, I know about Vietnam and all, but . . ."

"Well, the war was a biggie," Martha said, animated now. She cradled the bowl of Parmesan batter in the crook of her left arm. "But even before that I marched for civil rights. Later on I marched for equality for women. Even burned my bra when—"

Lucas dropped his peeler and covered his ears. A half-peeled potato rolled to the floor and landed next to Martha's black shoe. "Okay," he said. "Too much information. La la la la la. I can't hear you!"

Talia laughed at his antics. "Lucas is right, Martha. Some things are best left to the imagination. But you do seem to have a fascinating past."

Martha's fleeting smile exchanged places with a thoughtful frown. "Yeah. Fascinating," she said softly. She picked up the potato and flipped it into the sink.

Talia tossed the slaw with two large forks. Her mind couldn't stop hopping back to her interview with Detective Prescott. The whole thing still irked her. "Raspberry sauce," she muttered to herself. "How circumstantial can you get?"

"You know you're talking to yourself, right?" Martha said.

Talia shook her head. "Sorry. I was thinking about something that detective said to me."

Martha shot her a look. "Well, what was it?"

Talia sighed. "She said forensics found a spot of raspberry sauce on the scarf Ria was strangled with. Like that proves anything, right? How does that point to me as the killer? Anyone could have spilled it!"

Martha turned away. "Huh," was all she said.

"The whole thing was ridiculous," Talia said. She covered the bowl with plastic wrap and then squeezed past Martha to get to the commercial fridge.

"I'm getting a little tired of doing the bump with you," Martha griped. "This kitchen is just too small for three people and all these appliances."

Talia tucked the slaw in the fridge and pushed the door shut, a tad more forcefully than she'd intended. "Martha, I realize we're a bit cramped in here, but there's nothing we can do." She pasted on a cheery smile. "Let's just make the best of it, okay?"

Martha mumbled something Talia couldn't make out. Ignoring her, she went over to the brown shopping bag someone had left near the restroom the day before. So far, no one had called about it. For safekeeping, Talia had stored it under the table in the kitchen.

Talia pulled out the bag and peeked inside. Several mounds of white tissue rested atop one another. With all that tissue, she thought, the contents had to be fragile. She carefully removed one of the mounds from the bag. With a gentle touch, she peeled aside the sheets of tissue. When she saw what nested within, she gasped. A tiny angel crafted from layers of embossed foil lay inside the tissue. The angel's dress was gold, and her wings a lustrous blue. Her halo was crafted from shreds of gold tinsel, and her delicate face had been formed from minuscule scraps of cloth.

Martha peered over Talia's shoulder and gave a low whistle. "That looks pretty old," she said. "In that condition, I bet it's worth a few bills."

"It's absolutely gorgeous," Talia breathed. "I wonder who—" She stopped herself before she said any more. She had a sinking feeling she knew where they came from. She rewrapped the angel in the layers of tissue and gently returned it to the bag.

"Aren't you going to look at the others?" Martha nudged her arm.

"No. These are very special. I don't want to handle them. Someone must be missing them."

She didn't want to leave them under the kitchen table. Lucas was a sweetheart, but he was also a wee bit clumsy, to put it mildly. One crunch from his large sneaker and the ornaments would truly be history.

Talia removed the bag to the farthest corner of the kitchen. She'd have to decide what to do with the ornaments. For now she planned to bring them home and store them in a safe place.

The lunch hour grew extremely busy, which kept kitchen chatter to a minimum. Only one more potato bit the tiles—a new record low for Lucas. A little after one, he took a fast lunch break and fired up his iPad.

"Hey, Ms. Marby, look at this. We got a whole bunch of new Likes on our Facebook page. We're up to thirty-four. Listen to this. 'If you want to taste the best food in the Berkshires, don't miss out on the old fish and chips place in the Wrensdale Arcade. It's not just fish anymore. Their deep-fried meatballs and mini-dogs are awesome, and be sure to order a side of their deep-fried pickles.' "

Talia went over and peeked at his iPad. "Lucas, that's terrific. Do you know who posted it?"

"Yup. One of the guys at the Wrensdale fire station. But

he posted it on his personal page, not on ours. The good thing is, a bunch of his friends already shared it." He held up his right hand and Talia high-fived him.

"Wait a minute," Talia said. "He called it the old fish and chips place. He didn't mention the restaurant's name."

"Don't worry, Ms. Marby. People will figure it out."

"But—"

"First off," Martha interjected, "you gotta get that new sign up. Fry Me a Sliver is not the easiest name to remember. Plus, it's clunky. It doesn't flow off the tongue."

Talia dropped into one of the kitchen chairs. *Was* the name clunky? She'd been so thrilled the day it came to her. She'd been celebrating her takeover of Lambert's with Bea and Howie, her folks, and Ryan and his dad. When she asked if someone wanted the last slab of deep-fried apple-cinnamon bread, Ryan had come back with, "Sure, fry me a sliver."

She loved the name.

"Ms. Marby," Lucas said in a soft voice. "I gotta agree with Martha. The name *Fry Me a Sliver* is kind of a . . . you know, a tongue twister."

In her head, Talia tried repeating it three times, fast. She sighed. It wasn't the smoothest arrangement of words.

"But I've already ordered the sign," she said with a groan. "And it wasn't exactly cheap."

"Why don't you just call it Fry Me?" Martha suggested. "If they haven't inscribed the name yet, it might be doable."

Talia bit one side of her lip. "I need to give it some more thought."

"You don't have time for thought," Martha pointed out. "You only have time for action."

As annoying as Martha was, she was right. Talia was

beginning to wonder if she'd jumped into the whole restaurateur thing a bit too soon. Maybe she hadn't been ready. Maybe she'd needed more time to plan.

Maybe the whole enterprise was going to implode like a collapsed star.

10

Talia made it to the restaurant earlier than usual Thursday morning. She'd decided to clean the tables and chairs so that Martha wouldn't be stuck with the job. It was one of the things she hadn't really given much thought to—asking Martha to perform the same icky task as one of her regular duties. From this point on, Talia would share the work, both the fun stuff and the dreary chores.

Not that the tables and chairs were all that grimy. Keeping up with cleaning them every day helped, but for the most part, patrons weren't all that sloppy. Wiping down the captain's chairs in the dining room was probably the most labor-intensive job. All spindles and carved wood, they sucked up most of the cleaning time.

Talia was surprised to hear a tiny knock at the door just after nine o'clock. With Ria's murderer still running loose, she was hesitant to unlock it. The delivery people always used the rear door, so it couldn't be one of them. She dried her damp hands on a paper towel and trotted over to the door. "Who's there?" she called out.

A tiny voice responded, but Talia couldn't hear the name. Moving to the left, she peeked through one of the diamond-shaped window panes that looked out onto the plaza.

It was Kelsey Dakoulas.

"Hey there," Talia greeted her, opening the door.

"Hey yourself," Kelsey said. She wore a blue mohair sweater with sleeves that went over her thumbs, but her hands were bare. On her shoulder was a beige tote that looked like vintage macramé. She gave Talia a weak smile, but her puffy eyes belied any good cheer she might have felt. "Do you, um, have a few minutes to talk?"

"Of course. Come on in. I'll get us some coffee, okay?"

Kelsey rubbed the palms of her bare hands together. "I'd love that. It's freezing out there."

Talia pulled out one of the chairs she'd just scrubbed and asked Kelsey to make herself comfortable. Kelsey draped her tote over an empty chair, while Talia delivered a small tray to the table. She set a steaming mug of coffee in front of Kelsey.

Kelsey added three sugars to her coffee and stirred it with her spoon. Her large brown eyes brimmed with tears.

Talia sat down across from her. "Kelsey, what's wrong?" she said softly.

Kelsey grabbed a napkin from the tray and blotted her eyes. "I've been wanting to talk to you for a couple days now, but with everything that's been happening . . ." She broke off with a choked sob.

"Take your time," Talia said.

Kelsey sniffled loudly and swiped a strand of long brunette hair away from her face. "The police interviewed me twice," she said. "My mom is so upset. All this worry and anxiety isn't good for her condition."

Talia's heart wrenched. "I'm so sorry. If there's anything I can do . . ." It came out like an empty sentiment, but she really did want to help.

Kelsey reached into the macramé tote and dug out an envelope. The blue card peeking out from inside had a familiar look. "I know you told the police that I went back to the gym that day after I'd already left."

Talia winced. "I did," she admitted. "But I wasn't trying to throw you to the wolves. I was only relating what I saw." She clasped the handle of her mug. "For what it's worth, I don't believe you had anything to do with Ria's death."

Kelsey smiled, but her brown eyes welled up again. "Thank you, I guess." She pulled the blue card from the envelope. "This is why I went back that afternoon. By the time they announced the raffle winners, I had already left. But then Mr. Nash texted me to tell me I'd won a prize, so I went back for it."

Talia's attention was piqued. "Andy Nash texted you? Do you remember what time?"

Kelsey shrugged. "I don't know. Sometime before three, I think. Anyway, I was in Queenie's Variety picking up a few groceries for Mom when I got the text. I paid for my stuff and then went back to the gym to collect my prize." She smiled, somewhat ruefully. "Turns out I won the free fish and chips dinner for two."

"Hey, that's great." Talia grinned.

"Yeah. Problem is, I'm a vegetarian. I don't eat meat *or* fish. No offense, but I wouldn't even have gone back for the prize if I'd known what it was."

"No offense taken. Even some meat lovers don't eat fish." Talia gave her what she hoped was a disarming smile. "Mr. Nash didn't tell you what your prize was when he texted you?"

Kelsey shook her head. "No. Just that I'd won something and I could pick it up at the community center anytime before five. He told me to stop by his office. I managed to find a parking space in front of the building, so I didn't even go into the parking lot. When I got to Mr. Nash's office, though, his door was closed. The envelope was taped to his office door with my name on it."

"So you never saw Mr. Nash?"

"No, but I heard him talking and assumed he was on the phone. I just snagged the envelope off the door and left."

A piece of the puzzle was still missing. "Kelsey, run me through this, okay? You grabbed the envelope, but you didn't leave right away, did you? I saw you leaving the gym through the front entrance."

Kelsey flushed. "I was desperate to use the bathroom. I didn't think I could wait till I got home." She slid the envelope toward Talia. "Anyway, I can't really use this. Maybe you can give it to someone else?"

"You keep it, Kelsey," Talia insisted. "It doesn't expire, and you can always give it to someone as a gift."

Kelsey's brown eyes widened. "Gosh, you're right. I never even thought of that. My boyfriend loves fish and chips, and so does his dad." She grinned. "Thank you."

Talia's mind went to all the culinary tasks awaiting her in the kitchen. Lucas would take care of the potatoes, but she still had the slaw to think about, and a fresh batch of meatballs to prepare.

But this was more important. Kelsey was at the gym only moments before Talia found Ria's body. And while she was sure the police had already subjected Kelsey to a grueling "interview," it was always possible Kelsey saw something crucial without realizing its significance.

Talia fetched the carafe from the kitchen and refilled each of their mugs. "I wish I could offer you a breakfast treat," she told Kelsey, "but I don't really have anything that would fit the bill."

"That's okay. I had a glazed doughnut from Queenie's. It's my once-a-day guilty pleasure."

Talia returned the carafe to the kitchen and then sat down with Kelsey. "Kelsey," she said, "I know you didn't hurt Ria. But I did overhear you arguing with her that morning. Something about a cat?"

Kelsey reddened, and her face went taut. "I thought Ria was my friend," she said, her tone laced with anger. She reached for another sugar packet and emptied it into her mug. "Turned out she was nothing but a traitor." Kelsey spat the last word. "When I found out what she did, I knew then she'd never cared about anyone but herself. She was just like her mother." She sniffled loudly, and then dropped her face into her hands. "I'm sorry. I know it's not right to talk about her that way, especially after what someone, you know, did to her."

Talia waited, and then said, "It's okay to be angry at someone who hurt you, Kelsey. It wasn't your fault that she died." She reached over and squeezed Kelsey's shoulder. "I went through something similar with an ex-boyfriend. I know how it feels."

Kelsey dropped her hands and looked at Talia. "Was your boyfriend mean to you?"

Talia thought back to the four-plus years she'd spent with Chet. At one time she'd thought they were almost engaged.

She shook her head at her own naïveté. "No, he wasn't mean. He could actually be very sweet at times. But he was rigid and controlling, and wanted to make all the decisions, even down to how we decorated our bathroom. He strung me along for years, until I finally left." Talia gave a tepid laugh. "Later I found out he'd been seeing someone else. I'm glad I left him when I did."

"That's awful," Kelsey murmured.

"Tell me about the cat," Talia urged.

"Okay, here goes." She pulled in a breath. "So I'm a part-time volunteer at the animal shelter, right? Mostly I help with adoption counseling on Saturday afternoons."

Talia smiled. "That must be so rewarding."

"It is." She sighed heavily. "For a long time I've been hoping someone might surrender a Siamese cat to the shelter. My mom adores Siamese, and last year we lost our sweet Angelica to kidney failure. The cat was super old—eighteen—but she meant everything to us."

"I'm sorry to hear that," Talia said. "I recently adopted a calico. I'm already so attached to her! I know I'd be devastated if I lost her."

Kelsey blotted the corners of her eyes with her fingers. "Two Saturdays ago I was at the shelter. I found out someone had brought in a four-year-old Siamese female they couldn't keep anymore. Oh my God, I was so excited. I'd have taken a male, but I wanted a female. It was going to stretch my budget to buy all new supplies for her, but I had a paycheck from Once or Twice I still hadn't cashed. Plus, I had some birthday money saved, which would cover the adoption cost."

"Sounds like a great surprise for your mom," Talia said.

"Yeah, it would've been, if I hadn't opened my big dopey

mouth. I told Ria all about my plan to surprise Mom with the Siamese." Kelsey twisted her lips in disgust. "Next thing I know, Ria goes to the shelter behind my back and puts an application in for the cat. Two days later—voila! The cat is living with Ria and her mom."

"Oh, Kelsey, that really was low. I'm sorry she did that to you."

"She did it purposely," Kelsey said bleakly. "I was mad at her about something else she did to me. When I told her I deserved an apology, she laughed in my face. She *laughed*! And then she stole my cat. She was a very spiteful woman."

Talia was beginning to wonder if she'd leaped to a wrong conclusion. Could Kelsey's simmering anger toward Ria have led her to commit murder? Was Kelsey even strong enough to strangle her with a knitted scarf?

She remembered what Sergeant O'Donnell had said to her. *Did you know, Ms. Marby, that it only takes about three pounds of pressure to strangle someone?*

Even so, Talia couldn't picture Kelsey doing that to Ria.

Although . . . what had that gossipy Vivian said? That Kelsey had been arrested in another state for attacking someone with a chair? Talia wondered if there was any truth to the story. As much as she liked Kelsey, she needed to poke around in her head a little more.

"Kelsey," she said, "I'm still confused about something. If you and Ria weren't getting along, why did you agree to work for her?"

Kelsey groaned. "Because I needed the money, that's why. I wanted to put it toward my future tuition, and Ria was paying me pretty decently. If I don't get better at saving, I'll never be able to get my vet tech degree!"

"What about a student loan?" Talia suggested.

"I started to apply for one, but then Mom got sick and I didn't follow up on the paperwork. Which, by the way, is voluminous." She rolled her eyes. "Plus, I'd rather save as much as I can first."

"I get that," Talia said. She'd had a small student loan herself, and did a happy dance the day she sent off the final payment.

Kelsey looked at her watch and sighed. "Look, I know I'm keeping you from stuff," she said. "Plus, Mom has a doctor appointment at noon, so I'd better scoot home. Helping her get ready is kind of a chore."

Talia's heart went out to her. For such a young woman, Kelsey had a lot of responsibilities. Having a sick mom to care for couldn't be easy. And she'd been juggling two jobs, along with doing volunteer work.

"Are you going to look for another job?" Talia asked her.

Kelsey shrugged. "Maybe after the holidays. For now I'm still waitressing at the Wiltshire Inn. It's a really nice place, and the tips are good." She stood and snatched up her macramé tote.

Talia had so many more questions for her. There was so much more she wanted to know, especially about Ria. She felt sure that the key to finding Ria's killer was in learning more about Ria herself.

"Kelsey, before you go, can I ask you something?" Talia said.

"Sure," Kelsey said. Shoot."

"Did Ria ever mention a dragon to you?"

Kelsey furrowed her brow. "A dragon? No, I don't think so." She stared at the wall, as if trying to remember something. "Funny you say that, though. A little over a week ago, a man came into the shop with a box of trinkets. He said they'd belonged to his deceased mother. He wondered if Ria was interested in buying them." She looked back at Talia. "One of the trinkets was a green dragon pin made of painted pewter—kind of cartoonish, you know? It was really big, an unusual piece. I thought it might appeal to the right buyer." She shook her head slowly. "But Ria took one look at it and her face changed. She got really pale. She told the guy she hated dragons, and to get it out of her sight."

"How strange," Talia said. "Did she say why she hated dragons?"

"No, and the poor man was so flustered at her reaction that he left without selling her anything." Kelsey slid a lock of brunette hair behind one ear. She smiled. "Hey, I'd better go," she said. "I'm glad we finally got together. It's a relief to talk about all of this with someone." She paused with her hand on the door handle.

"I agree," Talia said. "Can we talk again soon?" She tried not to sound too anxious.

Kelsey's eyes lit up for a brief moment. "You know, I just got to thinking about something. I know Ria's only been dead a few days, but I wondered . . ." She groaned. "Would it be tacky if I asked Ria's mom if I can adopt the cat? I'm pretty sure she never really wanted it. Ria only gave her the poor creature to get under my skin."

The quarrel Ria'd had with her mother at the fund-raiser suddenly popped into Talia's head. *Who said I wanted a cat anyway?* Ria's mom had snapped at her.

"I think it's worth a try, Kelsey. If she really doesn't want the cat, you might even be doing her a favor."

Kelsey sagged in relief. "Thanks. I'll call her tonight."

A lightbulb in Talia's head sparked to life. "Kelsey, wait.

I have a better idea. If you're game and you don't mind some company, why don't the two of us pay her a condolence call this evening? I'll pick up a glazed lemon pound cake at Peggy's Bakery and ask them to put it in a pretty container."

"Oh, Talia, that would be super! I was dreading making the call. If you go with me, I'll feel so much better." She grabbed Talia in a jerky hug.

Talia smiled and returned the hug. They agreed that she would pick up Kelsey at seven thirty in front of the arcade. Kelsey was familiar with the condo in which Ria had lived with her mom. It was an easy ride from downtown.

Lucas arrived at ten forty, right on Martha's heels. In spite of Martha's crabby nature, Talia loved that both her employees always showed up early. She took it as a sign that they valued their jobs, and also that they enjoyed working together.

By eleven, Talia had prepared two large batches of meatballs and enough tangy slaw to feed half the town. The eatery had run short of slaw the day before, forcing Talia to whip up a fresh batch. With the Wrensdale fire station ordering takeout on a near daily basis, it wouldn't do to run out of any of the eatery's staples.

It wasn't until Lucas poured himself his usual mug of coffee that Talia noticed the bandage on his wrist.

"Don't tell me," she said, gazing at him with mock sternness. He flushed almost to the tips of his pale blond locks. "Yeah. I was practicing on the cobblestone real early this morning. It was, like, twenty degrees out. My hands were frozen. I got about halfway across the plaza when I took a header. Mom was really pi— I mean, she was really ticked off."

Martha peered at the bandage. "One of these days, kid, you're gonna break your a—"

"Martha." Talia looked at her.

Martha glowered back. "I was going to say his *anterior* muscle, which on Lucas has a lot less padding than it does on me."

Talia held Martha's gaze for a moment and then turned back to Lucas with concern. "Lucas, what if it's broken? Maybe you should go to the emergency room." In truth, she was worried about him. In her opinion, he took way too many risks with that skateboard of his.

"Nah. It's not a problem. In her old life, my mom was an LPN. She said it's only a sprain."

Talia wasn't convinced. "Does it hurt?" she asked, rubbing her own arm in sympathy.

"Not if I pop a few aspirin," he said. A huge grin lit his face. "Don't worry, okay? It's all cool. Plus, I got an idea I'm gonna try out. But don't ask me to reveal it. I'm keeping it under wraps until I've perfected it. I'll give you one clue, though: *wheels.*"

"Wheels," Talia repeated. She shrugged. "Well, I guess we'll have to wait to see what that means."

They shifted back into work mode, with everyone tackling their usual assigned tasks. Martha looked flummoxed when Talia told her she'd already wiped down the tables and chairs in the dining area. "You can start working on the batters, okay?" Talia told her. "And if you could unpack the new box of haddock, that would be great."

Martha parked one hand on her hip and eyed Talia with suspicion. "You setting me up for a pink slip?"

Talia threw up her hands. "Martha, of course not! I thought you'd be pleased with a more fair division of labor."

Martha worked her mouth for a moment, and then shrugged. "Okay. If you say so."

A few minutes before noon, Jay Ballard at the fire station called in an order. "Talia, we're two guys short today," he said, sounding desperate. "Flu's going around. I'm begging you, can you please send someone over here with the food? We'll tip the driver real good. That's a promise."

"Jay, I wish I could," she said, meaning it. "It's just that we—" She looked at Lucas, who was waving his arms like a windmill at her. "Hold on a minute."

"Ms. Marby, I don't mind delivering it," Lucas said. "The fire station's, like, two blocks from here, right past the town parking lot. With my long legs I can walk it in five minutes!"

Talia sighed. She knew if she caved, the firemen would push for regular delivery. Still, they'd become such good customers that she hated to say no. She covered the receiver. "What about your wrist?" she whispered to Lucas.

"It doesn't hurt, Ms. Marby. I swear." He raised his good hand.

Talia sighed and went back to the phone. "We'll do it, Jay, but only this one time, okay? I don't have enough employees right now for delivery."

"Aw, you're awesome," the young fireman gushed.

Twenty minutes later, Lucas jogged out the door carrying two large brown bags. He returned with a grin splitting his face and a fistful of currency in his hand. "Look at the tip they gave me!" he beamed. "It's almost fifteen bucks!"

Martha dredged two haddock fillets through a pan of flour. "How they can afford to do that?" she grumbled. "Don't get me wrong, kid. I'm not begrudging you," she added quickly.

"Think about it, Martha," Talia said. "If they each put in a few bucks, it adds up."

Maybe Martha had been right earlier. Offering a limited delivery service might be something Talia should consider. While she paid her two employees what she felt was a decent hourly wage, she knew Lucas could use the tips for tuition money, or at least for books.

The lunch rush kept them all scrambling until after one. It was nearly one thirty when a familiar face sauntered in. Forcing herself to smile, Talia snatched a menu off the counter and greeted Detective Patti Prescott in the dining area. "Lovely to see you again," she said, praying she wouldn't be struck dead for lying. "Would you like a seat near the window?"

The detective's eyes flashed, and the tiniest of smiles touched her lips. "Thanks, but I've already eaten. I only came in to give you some news."

Talia's heart jumped. "You caught the killer?" she said hopefully.

Prescott studied her for a long moment. Talia was beginning to feel like a bug pinned to a corkboard. "No, I'm afraid not," she said in a grim tone. "The ME released Ms. Butterforth's body this morning. Her mother's arranged for a memorial service to be held tomorrow at ten a.m. at the Dozier and Bay Funeral Home. I thought you'd want to know."

"Tomorrow? That's so soon!"

"Mrs. Butterforth wanted to hold the service as soon as possible. Apparently a friend of the victim's helped her with the arrangements."

A friend. That had to be Will Claiborne. He was probably

the only person with enough funds and the wherewithal to put the plans for the service in motion so quickly.

"I appreciate your letting me know, Detective," Talia said. "I would certainly like to attend, but the timing is tricky."

Then a thought struck Talia. Maybe her old friend Bea would be willing to fill in for her Friday morning. For the past several weeks, Bea had been devoting herself to helping her husband, Howie, recover from knee surgery complications. But it would only be for a few hours. Plus, Bea knew the ropes and would be a big help to Martha and Lucas in the kitchen.

"By the way, Ms. Marby, have you seen Andy Nash lately?"

The question hit Talia like a boomerang to the back of the neck. She swallowed, feeling the detective's eyes on her. Should she reveal what Andy had told her at the diner Tuesday evening? Part of her wanted desperately to share it with the detective, but a bigger part feared for Andy's safety. If anything happened to him because Talia blabbed, she'd feel guilty for the rest of her days.

"Um, why do you ask?" Talia said as a blush crept up her neck.

Prescott gave her a cagey look. "I ask because I want to know," she said. "We haven't been able to get in touch with him for a few days. His car is at the dealership where he works, but he hasn't shown up since Tuesday. His dad's worried about him."

Her stomach lodged in her throat, Talia motioned Prescott to a quiet corner. In a low voice, she told the detective about her meeting with Andy at the diner. "I'm sorry I didn't tell you yesterday," she said, steeling herself for the backlash.

"But part of me didn't believe him, and another part worried that he might actually be in danger. If anything happened to him because I snitched on him, I'd never forgive myself." She released a long sigh and said, "If it helps, which it probably doesn't, I begged him to go to the police with whatever info he had. But he was too scared. He told me his life wouldn't be worth a three-dollar bill if I told anyone."

Prescott nodded slowly, as if turning it all over in her brain. To Talia's surprise she said, "I understand where you're coming from, although it is unfortunate. We could have protected him—*if* he was in any real danger, that is."

That was an interesting comment, Talia thought. Did the police believe Andy pulled a vanishing act because he killed Ria?

"Strange that you put it that way, Detective." Talia frowned. "The whole time Andy was talking to me, a little voice in my head kept warning me that the whole thing might be an act. That he might be conning me, you know?"

"You're very observant, Talia," Prescott said softly. "And intuitive. I would it appreciate, however, if you would share what you know with the authorities instead of keeping it to yourself."

Talia breathed a sigh of sheer relief. "Agreed, Detective. I want Ria's killer caught as much as the police do."

Then another thought struck Talia, one that chilled her to the marrow. Maybe the detective was the one playing games. Maybe Prescott was trying to trick her into thinking the police were homing in on Andy as the killer. That way, if Talia was the real killer, she might lower her guard and let something slip.

Prescott's gaze drifted over Talia's shoulder, and all at

once her nutmeg-colored eyes lit up. Pretending to scoop a crumb off an adjacent table, Talia turned and aimed a sideways look into the kitchen. Martha had just removed two deep-fried meatballs from the fryer and was swirling a generous helping of marinara over them. "Sure I can't tempt you, Detective?"

This time Prescott actually smiled. A real smile, not the faux, sharklike smirk Talia had seen up until now. "No thank you, not today. But one of these days when I'm off duty, I'll definitely take you up on that. By the way, you may as well call me Patti."

Again, Talia wondered if the detective was trying to throw her off balance with a half-baked offer of friendship. Was that how the police got their suspects to confess? Or was she being too cynical? It might simply be that Prescott knew Talia wasn't Ria's killer and wanted to recruit her help.

"Okay, Patti who's not Patricia," Talia said with a friendly smile. "From this day forward you are Patti."

Prescott's lips curved into another genuine smile.

"So what *is* your real name?" Talia pushed. Now she really wanted to know.

"Sorry," the detective said, "but right now I don't think you have the patience to listen to the whole story. Let's just say it's a lot better than what kids called me in school."

"What did they call you?"

Prescott's eyes twinkled cryptically. "Think about it, Talia. What are my initials?" She waved, and in the next second she was out the door.

Talia smiled to herself. Patti Prescott. PP.

She returned the menu she was holding to the counter and then called Bea Lambert. Bea was thrilled to hear from her. "Ah, luvvy, I've missed you so," Bea said in that darling accent of hers. "Of course I'll help you out. I'd be scrubbing floors in the bloomin' pokey if you hadn't nabbed that killer!"

Talia laughed and told her she was exaggerating. Bea agreed to be at the eatery by nine Friday morning. That would give Talia plenty of time to get to the memorial service by ten.

Talia dashed home after the eatery closed, fed Bo, and changed into black slacks and a lilac sweater. Around her neck she tucked one of her favorite scarves—the purple one threaded with thin strands of silver. Given the circumstances, she didn't want to look festive, but she also didn't want to project an air of gloom.

The lemon pound cake, nestled in gold foil in a lovely moss-colored tin, was already in the back of the Fiat. Talia pulled up in front of the Wrensdale Arcade at seven twenty-five. As promised, Kelsey was waiting for her.

"Thanks so much for coming with me, Talia," Kelsey said gratefully as she hopped onto the passenger seat. "I don't think I could've done this alone."

"No problem, Kelsey. I think it's actually a good idea that both of us go anyway."

Talia put on her left blinker and eased into the traffic on

Main Street. Holiday lights blinked in several of the store-fronts, despite the shops having closed for the night. A gaggle of women streamed out of Popover Palace, a kitschy café that had opened about a year earlier. The Palace occupied the space that once housed the old Della's Restaurant, a local icon founded during the late fifties. Della's had been known less for its plain American fare than for its vertical neon sign, which for decades had beamed high over the entrance. Considered a landmark now, the sign still hung above the restaurant, although it no longer flashed the word DELLA'S in bright neon orange.

"Do you think she'll give me the cat?" Kelsey asked in a worried tone.

"She might," Talia said evenly. "But let's not bring it up right away, okay? We wouldn't want her to think that's the only reason we're calling on her."

"Okay," Kelsey said softly. Then she gave out a tiny giggle. "Calling on her. It sounds so old-fashioned when you say it like that."

Talia smiled. "It's something my Nana would've said. I think a lot of her expressions rubbed off on me."

"Does she live in Wrensdale?" Kelsey asked.

Talia nodded, feeling that familiar lump fill her throat. "She did, but I'm afraid we lost her this past spring. It was a very hard time for my family and me."

"I'm so sorry." Kelsey shifted to tuck her coat more securely underneath her. "I lost my gram when I was nine, but I don't remember her all that well."

For the next few minutes neither of them spoke, except for Kelsey to give directions over a series of side streets. The older streets were all familiar to Talia, but there were a few newer offshoots she didn't recognize. When they reached an area that Talia recalled had once been a small apple orchard, she was surprised to see that a cluster of duplexes had sprung up in its place. A tiny piece of her heart twisted, remembering the fun she and her dad used to have picking apples there every September.

"Go down this street," Kelsey instructed, pointing a gloved finger at a sign that read ORCHARD LANE. "It's the third duplex on the left. Six-A."

Following Kelsey's directions, Talia drove slowly along the darkened street until she came to a set of mailboxes with the numbers *6-A* and *6-B* reflecting off the front. The driveway on the *A* side of the duplex was empty, although Talia didn't expect to see Ria's Camry. She assumed it was still in the custody of the police.

Not a single light shone through any of the windows.

Kelsey leaned forward and peered through the windshield. "Oh, no, it's totally dark inside!" She grabbed the sleeve of Talia's jacket. "What if she's not home?"

The other side of the duplex was dark as well, almost as if the entire place had been abandoned. Thick shrubs that looked like rhododendron skirted both the front and the sides of the house. Each unit had a set of shallow steps that led to a white front door.

Talia glanced farther down the street. Brilliantly lit Christmas trees shone in several of the windows. In the bay window of one of the homes, a cherry red sign blinked the message HAPPY HOLIDAYS. The street itself was mostly empty, save for a pickup truck parked along the curb about three houses down. In front of another darkened unit, an SUV rested partway on the lawn.

Talia eased the Fiat into the driveway and shifted into Park. The engine was still running when Kelsey leaped out of the car and trotted up to the front door.

Talia shut off her engine, pulled her key out of the ignition, and trailed Kelsey up the front steps. "Wait," she called to Kelsey. "Maybe she's sleeping or resting."

"No," Kelsey said glumly. "She drives an old Taurus and it's not here." Kelsey pressed the doorbell. From inside the house came the soft sound of a melodic, dual-toned chime. Kelsey pressed the bell again, several times.

"It's okay, Kelsey," Talia said, trying to soothe her. "We'll come back again. There's a memorial service for Ria in the morning. Maybe we can come by after that. It's a little late for a visit anyway." She looped her hand gently around Kelsey's upper arm.

"It's *not* okay," Kelsey said, her teeth clenched. "Princess is alone in there, and there's not a single light on. At least she could've put one on a timer!"

Kelsey scurried down the steps and marched over to where the bay window rose about five feet from the ground above the dense shrubbery. She squeezed her slender form between two of the shrubs until she was standing directly below the window. The curtains had been drawn closed, preventing even a glimpse inside. "Princess," she called out in a singsong voice. "Are you in there?" She reached up with one hand and tapped her fingers on the window.

Worried that someone might spot them trying to peek through the window, Talia cast a look around at the nearby homes. If an alert neighbor decided to report two peepers to the police, they'd have to do some fast talking to explain why they weren't trying to break in.

Kelsey rapped the window with her knuckles and called

the cat's name again. All at once, a small head appeared through the opening in the curtains. Talia flicked on the mini-flashlight dangling from her ladybug keychain. It radiated a faint beam, barely enough to create an inch-wide circle of light on the window. "See, she is in there!" Kelsey cried.

A gorgeous pair of feline eyes gazed curiously at them through the glass. Kelsey reached her hand up and touched the window. Princess rubbed her face against the pane, as if she could feel Kelsey's tender touch. "Oh, Princess, you're in there all alone in the dark, aren't you?"

Talia moved closer to get a better look. The cat didn't appear to be in any distress. No doubt she was bored, but there was no reason to believe she was in any danger. "Kelsey, I'm sure Princess is fine, even without a light on. Don't cats see better in the dark than humans do?"

In the dull beam afforded by Talia's mini-light, Kelsey's face appeared pale and fragile. "Yeah, they do. Cats can't see with the same level of detail as humans. But in the dark, their retinas allow them to see about five times better we do." She splayed her gloved hand against the windowpane.

A sudden low *swoosh* from behind the house sent Talia's heart bumping up against her tonsils. She'd swear someone had just opened a window at the back of the unit.

No, not a window. A slider.

"Kelsey," she whispered. "We have to go. I heard something in the back."

"But Princess—"

"Princess is fine. If it will make you feel better, I'll call Mrs. Butterforth a little later."

Another, harsher sound left no doubt that someone was behind the duplex. Whoever opened the slider had pushed it shut.

That time Kelsey heard it. She grabbed Talia's sleeve and yanked her into a crouch. They huddled between the shrubs, and Talia quickly shut off her light. A cold rhododendron leaf poked at her eyelid, and she pushed it aside with her hand. They remained stock still for at least a minute, listening for any signs of the interloper. If it *was* an interloper. It might also have been Ria's mother, trying to avoid opening her door to visitors.

But that didn't make sense. If she'd wanted to hide from them, why wouldn't she just remain in the darkened house until they gave up and went away? And where was her car?

Another, more jarring noise rent the frigid December air— the sound of a car door closing three or four houses away. Then the street brightened, illuminated by a pair of headlights cutting through the gloom. An engine growled, and a dark pickup truck roared past the duplex.

Talia felt Kelsey's fingers curl around her own, and she squeezed Kelsey's hand in silent support. As if by unspoken consent, they waited another minute. Kelsey's fingers finally loosened, and she breathed a noisy sigh and rose from her crouch. "God, that was a close one, wasn't it?" Her voice was shaky.

"Not to mention a very uncomfortable one." Talia's knees crunched as she stood, and she gave out a little groan. "Come on, we'd better go. This didn't exactly go as planned, did it?"

Kelsey shuddered and shook her head, then dashed toward the Fiat.

Talia scampered inside her car and flicked the heater on high. Kelsey was quiet as she pulled her seat belt over and snugged it into place. Their attempt to visit Ria's mom had been a bust, a failure. In the muted light afforded by the dashboard, Kelsey looked as if she was ready to burst into tears.

Talia thought about the pound cake, tender and moist, infused with lemon and topped with a sugary glaze. It sat in a decorative tin in the back of the car, aching to be sampled.

"Kelsey, would you like to come over to my house for a little while? I'll make us some tea, and we can test out that pound cake sitting back there."

"Oh, Talia, I'd love that," Kelsey said. "But aren't you going to save the cake for Mrs. Butterforth?"

"I'll buy another one tomorrow. I'm sure this one would stay fresh, but why give her a day-old cake, right?"

Talia also had something in mind that she wanted to try with the cake.

"Then it sounds good to me." Kelsey's grin shone in her voice. She dredged her phone out of her macramé tote. "I'll let my mom know where I'm headed in case she starts to get worried."

What a good daughter, Talia thought.

Fifteen minutes later, Kelsey was seated at Talia's kitchen table rubbing noses with the calico cat. "Oh, you are so lucky to have a cat like this," Kelsey beamed. With her finger, she scooped up a smidge of glaze from the slice of pound cake sitting in front of her and held it out to Bo. The kitty licked it off her finger and then rubbed her face on Kelsey's hand, her purr rivaling that of a jet engine revving up for takeoff.

Talia refilled each of their mugs with steaming, fresh-brewed mango tea spiced with ginger and cloves. The blend came from Time for Tea, the specialty tea shop in the Wrens-dale Arcade, and was one of Talia's favorites.

"I got her quite by happenstance," Talia explained. "An elderly woman in the neighborhood had died, and her son apparently dumped her outside and left her." Talia shook her head.

"That's horrible!" Kelsey cried. "He should go to jail for that."

"It was heartless, that's for sure," Talia agreed. She recalled how frightened Bo had been—hungry, but leery of trusting anyone. She returned the teapot to the trivet on the table. "I tried luring her with tuna for a few days, and eventually she realized I wasn't going to harm her. She was also very hungry. Once she decided I was a safe bet, she strolled through the front door, sniffed around for a bit, and then curled up on my grandfather's ratty old chair." Talia grinned at the memory. "I took that as a sign that she wanted to stay."

"That's so adorable," Kelsey said. "So this was your grand-parents' house?"

Talia related the story of having bunked there temporarily until she could find a permanent place to live. At the time, the bungalow had been for sale and was attracting some interested buyers. Heartbroken at the thought of turning over her nana's beloved home to strangers, Talia was ecstatic when her mom and twin aunts came to the rescue. They sold her the house and took back a zero-interest mortgage, making it a deal she couldn't refuse.

Kelsey stroked Bo's head absently. Her face darkened. "I want that cat, Talia. I want Princess for my mom. Ria's mother doesn't care about her—I just know it! All she cares about is her stupid boyfriends."

"Boyfriends?" Talia said, lifting her mug even as her interest rose. "Does she have more than one?"

"Let's put it this way. Any male who crooks a finger at her is her boyfriend." Kelsey curled her lip in disgust. "But the one she's with now is this guy Ralphie. He works with her at Wrensdale Dry Cleaners. Weird-looking guy. Has hair growing out of his ears and a belly shaped like a doughnut." Kelsey gave a little shiver.

Ralphie. Now why did that name sound familiar?

Of course! He was Vivian's cousin. The one who supposedly told Vivian that Kelsey had been arrested for assault. If only she could figure out a way to ask Kelsey about it without revealing where she'd heard it.

"Kelsey, tell me more about Ria," she pressed quietly. "I knew her once as a lonely little girl. But after she and her mom moved out of town, I never saw her again until I walked into the shop that day. Even then, I didn't know who she was. The thing that shocked me was how angry she seemed. She nearly took your head off!"

Kelsey paled. She rested her elbows on the table and dropped her head into her hands. Bo must have sensed her change in demeanor. The cat jumped off her lap and relocated onto Talia's.

"We used to be good friends," Kelsey said, her voice barely above a whisper. "I looked up to her. She was like the big sister I never had, you know?" She paused for a long moment, her dark brown eyes growing moist.

"But something changed," Talia said.

Kelsey pushed a lock of her dark hair behind one ear. "One night after we left the Wiltshire Inn, she asked if I wanted to come over to her house and hang out. Her mom was out with some guy that night, as usual. Of course I said yes. I liked the idea of Ria and me becoming better friends."

Talia held up the teapot, and Kelsey nodded. She refilled both their mugs and added a dot of cream to her own.

"Anyway," Kelsey went on, "we sat in the living room and Ria opened a bottle of her mom's burgundy wine. Cheap stuff, but we didn't care. We started chugging, way too fast, and got very silly. It felt good, having a friend like Ria that I could be myself with. She was so much more sophisticated than I'll ever be."

"Don't sell yourself short, Kelsey," Talia said.

Kelsey blushed. "Anyway, after we'd gone through the first bottle, Ria got this crazy idea. She said that we should each tell the other a secret about herself—something no one else knew."

Talia felt her heartbeat kick up a notch. Trying not to look anxious, she took a slow sip of her tea.

"We swore—we *swore*—never to tell another soul," Kelsey said, her voice rattling. "So I went first." She shook her head, and her hair fell forward. "If I tell you, you have to promise me you won't breathe a word, okay?"

Inwardly, Talia winced. She hated to promise. What if Kelsey's secret was relevant to Ria's murder? "Kelsey, I'll promise, but only if you're sure it has nothing to do with Ria's death."

"It doesn't," Kelsey said. "Okay, here goes. About two and a half years ago, I was visiting my aunt Nancy in Maine. She's like my favorite aunt, and I used to spend a few weeks with her every summer. Anyway, we were out in her back yard soaking up some rays when I heard this awful, agonized cry. I turned around and saw my aunt's neighbor beating a cat with a heavy stick." She sucked in a strangled breath.

"Talia, it was so horrible. The cat was trying to get away but she'd grab it before it could run and then she'd just keep hitting it. If you could have heard the poor thing squealing . . ."

Sickened by the story, Talia placed a hand over Kelsey's arm. "That's terrible, Kelsey. Did you call the police?"

Kelsey shook her head. "By the time they got there, it would've been too late. Plus, I was like a . . . a crazy person, you know? I just reacted. I ran over and shrieked at her to leave the cat alone. She turned and gave me this evil grin and told me to get out of her, you know, bleeping face. She said the cat wrecked one of her plants and she was going to teach it a lesson it wouldn't forget."

Talia felt her stomach twist into a knot. Instinctively, she placed a protective hand over the tri-colored angel curled in her lap. She pushed aside her half-eaten cake. "Then what did you do?" she prompted quietly.

"Like I said, I just reacted. There was a kid-sized lounge chair close by. You know, the kind made with interwoven vinyl strips? I snatched it up and bashed her over the head with the seat. I wasn't trying to hurt her—I only wanted her to leave the cat alone. I guess it threw her off balance because she tumbled to the ground. I was so enraged I"—she swallowed—"I kicked her in the butt with my bare foot." She choked out a sob, and tears began trailing down her cheeks.

Talia pushed the pink-flowered napkin holder closer to Kelsey. Kelsey snagged three at once and blotted her eyes, then took a noisy sip of her tea.

"After that she turned on me like a cobra, spewing filth you wouldn't believe. I guess the edge of the chair scraped her cheek because blood started running down her face. Next thing I know the cops were there, along with an animal control officer." She gave out a bitter laugh. "Turned out the witch's husband had already called the police, and Aunt Nancy had called Animal Control to take the cat away."

Talia squeezed Kelsey's arm. "I'm so sorry you had to go through that."

Kelsey rubbed her face. "Everything happened real fast after that. The cops took us both into the station, and the Animal Control lady rescued the cat. The cat was so frightened it was cowering."

Talia's stomach clenched. Just hearing the story made her blood steam. She couldn't imagine having to watch it go down in person.

"Next thing I know the bimbo files an assault charge against me, so we both ended up in front of a judge the next morning. It was a one-horse town, and the courthouse was in the back of the library. The judge took us in her chambers." Kelsey clenched her fists in her lap. "You should've seen that awful woman, Talia. All sugary sweet, wearing a bow in her hair and a dowdy, pin-striped skirt. In this syrupy voice she told the judge she only hit the cat once, very lightly, to get it away from her plant. Said she was totally shocked when I attacked her, and showed the judge the scratch on her cheek where I supposedly mauled her." Kelsey made air quotes with her fingers.

Bo squirmed out of Talia's lap and padded in the direction of her litter box, almost as if she couldn't bear to listen any longer.

"The judge asked me what I had to say for myself. I very calmly told her what really happened. Luckily, the AC officer backed me up. She'd seen how terrified the cat was when she put her into the carrier."

"It was a good thing your aunt had the sense to call her," Talia said.

"Yeah, I know." Kelsey's gaze clouded. "The judge still looked torn, and I was terrified she'd sentence me to a few months in jail. Then the best thing happened. My aunt asked the judge if she could show her something. Turned out she'd used her phone to video the whole thing."

"Oh, that was so smart of her," Talia said. As much as she found some people's addiction to their cell phones irritating, there were times when the devices came in darned handy. "So what did the judge do?"

"She was very professional," Kelsey said, a glint in her eye. "She asked the woman—whose name was Dotty, by the way—if that was her in the video. The fool could hardly deny it. My aunt got some excellent close-up footage." Kelsey grinned, displaying perfect white teeth. "Anyway, the witch turned bright red and started apologizing to the judge. The charges against me were dropped, but *she* had to pay a hefty fine for animal cruelty. The judge also barred her from ever owning a cat."

Talia was thankful to hear that the judge had wielded her gavel wisely, but the cold glee in Kelsey's eyes was a tad frightening. "So . . . what happened to the cat?"

"Believe it or not, the judge adopted her. She was so incensed by what she saw on my aunt's video that she took the cat home herself. It was an almost perfect resolution."

"Almost?" Talia said quizzically.

Kelsey's jaw tightened. "Dotty is still walking free."

The words themselves made sense, but the hostile undertone in Kelsey's voice sent chills up Talia's arms.

All at once, Kelsey flushed pink, as if she feared she'd

revealed a part of herself that she wasn't altogether proud of. "I'm sorry that story got so long-winded," she said with a nervous laugh.

"You don't need to apologize." It struck Talia that in trying to learn more about Ria, she was finding out plenty about Kelsey.

Kelsey twisted her hands. "I was only trying to explain why I got so angry with Ria. She promised not to breathe a word of it to anyone, but apparently *anyone* didn't include her clueless mother."

"You think her mother blabbed it?"

"I know she did. A couple friends of my mom's mentioned it to her. Poor Mom defended me, but I know she felt weird about it. Anyway, I confronted Ria and she admitted she hadn't exactly kept it a secret. In her eyes it was just a silly story that didn't amount to a hill of coffee beans. She didn't understand why it bothered me so much."

"I do," Talia said. "She violated your trust, and your privacy."

Kelsey nodded. "Exactly. I gave her a real hard time about it. She repaid me by stealing Princess!"

It wasn't exactly a "theft," Talia thought, but Kelsey obviously saw it that way.

"Put it behind you, Kelsey," Talia suggested. "People have short memories. Once they latch on to the next bit of gossip, they won't even remember you. Besides, you did the right thing, rescuing that cat. Think where the kitty might be today if you hadn't intervened."

"Thank you. That makes me feel better." Kelsey frowned. "Problem is, I've been seeing my boyfriend for, like, five months now? His name's Josh and he's just the sweetest guy. He's smart, and works really hard at his job. I think he might even be, you know, *the one*?" Her cheeks morphed into two ripe apples.

Talia vaguely recalled Kelsey mentioning a boyfriend. Wasn't she planning to offer him and his dad the fish and chips gift certificate?

"Anyway, his folks are super conservative. I mean, they never even utter a curse word. If they find out about what happened in Maine—even though the charges were dropped—they'll never accept me into the family!"

"Kelsey, the only one who has to accept you is Josh."

"I know. I get that." She lifted her shoulders in a world-weary shrug. "I just don't want to start off on the wrong foot with them, you know? They're super sweet people and I want them to like me."

Talia thought back to the day she first met her ex-boyfriend's mother. She and Chet had been dating for about six months, and he felt it was time for her to meet "the maternal half." Cynthia Matthews Sholes met them at an upscale bistro in the Back Bay section of Boston, not far from the townhouse on Commonwealth Avenue she shared with hubby number three. Thin as a pencil with silvery blond hair, the milky skin on her face smooth as rubber, she tottered in on a pair of royal blue Manolos that had her teetering like a tall building in a stiff wind. Talia saw Chet cringe, and she realized instantly that his mom had a drinking problem. Throughout the meal Chet barely spoke, leaving Talia to weave small talk through Cynthia's nonstop stream of chatter. By the time they'd finished eating, Talia felt terribly sad for the woman. Despite her wealth, Cynthia's privileged life clearly held little joy. After that they rarely saw her, for which Talia had been secretly grateful.

Kelsey rose from her chair. "Thanks for inviting me over,

Talia. This was a treat for me." She lifted the handle of her macramé tote off the back of her chair, and one end slipped. A brick-sized rectangle of some brown confection wrapped in cellophane tumbled onto the floor. Kelsey made a face. "Oh, God, I forgot I had that thing. The chef at the Wiltshire Inn gave out mini-fruitcakes to all the waitstaff yesterday. Ugh. I *hate* fruitcake." She picked it up and stuffed it back inside her bag.

Talia laughed. "Most people do, I think, but I've actually tasted some pretty good ones." A thought crossed her mind. "Kelsey, I was going to try deep-frying a few chunks of the pound cake after you left. If you're game and you don't mind donating to the cause, would you like to stay a bit longer to help me deep fry some of your fruitcake? In fact, we can try it with both cakes and see which one we like better."

Kelsey grinned. "That would be fun. But I already know which one I'll like better." She dug the fruitcake out of her tote again. "Can I help?"

"You sure can." Talia smiled and moved her wooden cutting board from the counter to the kitchen table. "Why don't you cut some chunks of cake from both loaves while I make the batter. Make each one about an inch and a half long." She gave Kelsey a sharp knife and set her to work.

Talia pulled her small deep fryer from one of the lower cabinets, plugged it in, and filled it with fresh canola oil. While it heated, she whipped together a sweet batter of eggs, milk, sugar, and flour, adding a hefty dose of baking powder and a touch of vanilla. Ever since her takeover of the fish and chips shop, she'd been trying to come up with the perfect recipe for a basic sweet batter, one that could be modified to suit whatever delectable tidbits she happened to be frying.

Hmmm.

She opened her fridge and pulled out a carton of orange juice. Without measuring, she poured a tiny splat of the juice into the batter and whisked it in.

Talia glanced over at Kelsey, who was cutting chunks of fruitcake with surgical precision. "That's probably enough," she said kindly, noting the mountain of cake chunks piled on the cutting board. "We can start with those."

Kelsey moved the cutting board to the counter next to the batter bowl. "What next?"

Talia scrubbed her hands at the sink and dried them on a paper towel. "Let's start with two of each," she said, swirling a piece of lemon cake and then a piece of the fruitcake into the batter. She set them in the wire basket and lowered them into the fryer. The mouthwatering scent of hot oil and sweet batter filled every nook of the kitchen.

Kelsey closed her eyes and drew in a lungful of air. "That smells awesome," she said.

When the two fried cakes were the perfect shade of gold, Talia lifted the basket and drained them, then set them on a clean paper towel. From one of her nana's ancient Tupperware containers, she removed a shaker of confectioner's sugar and sprinkled it over the cakes.

Kelsey looked quizzically at her. "Why do you keep it in there?"

"To discourage the wrong kind of visitors," Talia said meaningfully. "You know . . ." She made a crawling motion with her fingers on the counter.

Kelsey grinned. "Ants."

Talia transferred the fried cakes to one of her pink-flowered dessert plates and gave Kelsey a fork. "Okay, time for the official test."

Looking appropriately serious, Kelsey bit into the first

one—the lemon cake. "Oh. My. Lord," she said. "This is to *die* for." She halted mid-chew and grimaced. "Sorry. I didn't mean to say that," she mumbled.

Talia smiled at her and lowered two more cake chunks into the fryer. "Don't fret over it. It's only an expression."

After a deep breath, Kelsey moved on to the fruitcake. "Here goes." After two bites she stared at Talia. "Wow. That's not half bad. It's almost like the batter lightened the cake instead of making it heavier."

Talia prepared the next two fried cakes and slid them onto a plate. She sampled the fruitcake first. The first flavor that tickled her taste buds was that of the dried cherries. Simultaneously sweet and tart, they complemented the hint of orange in the batter. "Kelsey, this is definitely one of the better fruitcakes I've had."

"The chef called it a British fruitcake. He told us that in some recipes they soak the fruits in rum, but he uses brandy."

After the second bite of the fruity concoction, Talia was hooked. The blend of brandy-laced fruits and nuts encased in golden fried batter was sheer perfection.

By the time they were through, Talia felt stuffed. It occurred to her that the cakes had served as her supper. She'd had nothing to eat since midafternoon when she fried a slice of haddock for herself and topped it with a scoop of tangy coleslaw.

"I have to go," Kelsey said, looking almost wistful. She scrubbed her fingers with a napkin. "Josh and I are planning to see a late movie."

Kelsey insisted that Talia keep what was left of the fruitcake, and Talia grabbed the keys to her Fiat so she could drive Kelsey to her car. Kelsey lifted Bo in her arms and planted a kiss on the little calico's whiskers.

Talia knew she was pushing her luck, but with Ria dead

and the killer still running free, she had to know. "Kelsey, there's one thing you still haven't told me. What was the secret Ria shared with you?"

Kelsey lowered Bo to the floor and let the cat slip out of her grasp. "She said that when she was a kid, she witnessed a murder. And that the killer never got caught."

12

Talia was surprised the next morning to receive a text from her mom. She was slipping on a pair of pantyhose—something she rarely wore—when the telltale ding of her cell phone alerted her. She dropped onto the bed and grabbed her phone, giggling when she saw the message.

> Surprise. the Js are coming sunday and staying for a weeek/ knew you would wnt 2 no.

"Yay!" Talia cried to Bo, who was gazing at her from her favorite perch on the night table. "Aunt Jennie and Aunt Josie will be here into two days!"

If the cat was startled by the news, she didn't let on. Instead she licked a paw and scrubbed it over her whiskers, no doubt in preparation for their visit.

Talia's twin aunts, Jennie and Josie Domenica, had moved

to Malibu twelve years earlier, after starting up their own greeting card company—Sunday Swizzle. Never married, they had always lived together, dubbing themselves "confirmed bachelorettes."

Josie, the creative half of the team, had distinguished herself in the greeting card world by embedding a well-disguised swizzle stick into every one of her designs. Often it was so cleverly hidden that it took several minutes and a magnifying glass to find it.

Aunt Jennie, on the other hand, would be hard-pressed to draw a straight line with a ruler. Quiet and somewhat reclusive, she ran the business end of the company. Her nose for numbers and savvy marketing skills had catapulted Sunday Swizzle into one of the top-rated businesses in the state of California.

Talia cranked out a return message to her mom, who she knew despised texting.

Why R U texting?

The Js always do it I have 2 show them Im no slouch

Talia giggled again and hit the speed dial for her mom's cell. "When does their plane get in to Bradley? I can't wait to see them!"

Natalie Marby laughed. "I know. Me, too. I had no idea they were planning a visit. They won't land until around five o'clock, but don't worry about picking them up. They've already arranged for a car rental."

Buoyed by the news of her aunts' impending visit, Talia finished tugging her pantyhose up to her waist. Glory be to heaven, had the things always felt so uncomfortable? She couldn't fathom how she'd worn them all those years when she worked as a commercial property manager and later as a commercial broker.

Now for something to wear. One by one, she fished through the hangers in her closet, eventually landing on a charcoal gray pencil skirt. Her tunic-style black sweater with the belted waist would go nicely with it. For the memorial service she wanted to look appropriately somber. She chose a dove gray scarf made from the softest Indian cotton to complete the ensemble.

After sticking her feet into her plain black plumps, she kissed Bo, swiped a bit of gloss over her lips, and then grabbed the brown shopping bag that held her "work" clothes.

Bea Lambert, the queen of punctuality, was waiting at the door of Fry Me a Sliver at precisely nine o'clock. She was wearing a screaming red sweatshirt adorned with appliquéd snowmen, and her green eyes sparkled when she spied Talia striding across the cobblestone plaza toward the eatery.

"Oooh, it is so good to see you, Bea," Talia squealed, encasing her old friend in a big squashy hug.

Bea planted a noisy kiss on Talia's cheek. "I've missed you, too, luvvy, more than you know. And I can't believe you have to go through this again! Finding that poor girl the way you did." She gave a forceful shake of her dyed black curls. "Wouldn't surprise me if you ended up solving *this* bloomin' murder, too, like you did the last one. Heaven knows you can't trust the coppers to do it!"

Talia laughed. Poor Bea had had her fill of police when they wrongly accused her of murdering Phil Turnbull a few months earlier. She slipped her arm around Bea's shoulder. "Come on, you. Let's go inside and get the coffeepot cranking."

Inside the eatery, Bea made a beeline for the "loo," as she

called it. Talia stuck her brown bag beneath the counter and
put the coffee on. Two minutes later, Bea motored into the
kitchen and poured herself a cup. In spite of having been born
and raised in the UK, Bea loathed tea, and had always chosen
coffee in its place, even at "teatime."

"Ah, I've missed these mornings with you, luvvy," Bea
said, her eyes growing moist.

Talia missed Bea, as well, more than she wanted to admit.
"I've missed you too, Bea. I swear, sometimes when I unlock
the door in the morning I still expect to see you standing there
at the work table, shredding cabbages and carrots for the
coleslaw."

Bea gave her a wistful smile. Talia gulped back the half
cup she'd poured for herself, rinsed the mug, and stuck it in
the dishwasher. She toyed with the idea of warning Bea
about Martha's moods. What was that expression? Fore-
warned is forearmed?

No, Bea didn't need any such warning. She was a kind
soul who loved everyone. By the time the lunch hour rolled
around, Bea and Martha would probably be fast friends.

Dozier and Bay was the name of Wrensdale's sole funeral
home. Over the years, jokes about the "doze" in Dozier had
made the rounds. The final doze. Doze in peace.

Talia was running early, which earned her a prime parking
space near the portico that graced the entrance to the two-
story white building. She parked her Fiat next to a cream-
colored Lexus that looked as if it had just been driven out of
the showroom. In a far corner of the lot was a dark gray sedan
that looked suspiciously like an unmarked cop car. Talia
would swear she spied a solitary figure sitting in the driver's

seat, but from her vantage point she couldn't make out any features.

A gleaming black hearse was parked directly in front of the portico. Talia's stomach clenched at the sight. Barely eight months ago she'd entered this same building for Nana's wake. Fueled that day solely by three cups of coffee, she'd been gripped by nausea the moment she entered the room where Nana's casket was on display. She remembered having to run to the restroom with a bad case of dry heaves.

Talia stepped inside the foyer, her black pumps noiseless on the plush carpeting. A thin, elderly gent with lush white hair and a pair of matching eyebrows greeted her soberly. Dressed in formal black with the exception of his crisp white shirt, he touched her elbow gently. "Are you here for Miss Butterforth?" he murmured.

Talia nodded and he extended a hand to his left, instructing her to follow the mauve runner to the Rose Garden Room at the end of the hallway. She followed his directions, pausing when she reached the entrance to the viewing room.

Several rows of padded chairs had been set up facing the casket. A few were already occupied by mourners. Talia wondered briefly if any of them were undercover state police officers.

She signed the guest book and then moved toward the mahogany coffin, which, to her relief, was closed. At one end, a massive arrangement of dozens of white roses perched on a table. A huge spray of pink snapdragons nestled in a sea of white mums was draped over the casket. In the center was a bright pink bow, the words BELOVED DAUGHTER printed on the ribbon. A plain wooden crucifix hung on the papered wall directly behind the casket.

Talia felt her throat fill, and she swallowed hard. Lifting

her hem slightly, she knelt before the coffin. She murmured a silent prayer for Ria's soul. When she was through, she crossed herself and added, *Please find her killer. She didn't deserve this.*

Along the far wall, beneath a serene painting of an English garden, was a tufted Victorian sofa the color of tea roses. A skinny woman with frizzy blond hair was seated in one corner, her scrawny fingers clasped around a wad of spent tissues. Talia recognized her from Sunday's fund-raiser—Ria's mom. The woman looked up at Talia with a shell-shocked expression, then dabbed at her puffy eyes. "Do I know you?" she said in a raspy voice.

"I'm Talia Marby, Mrs. Butterforth. I was a classmate of Ria's many years ago. I am so very sorry for your loss."

"I remember your name," she said with a slow nod. "You're the girl who took the rabbit from my Ria." Her eyes welled up and she mashed the tissue against them.

Talia stifled a groan. The rabbit again?

The woman sniffled. "You can call me Anita," she said, forcing a weak smile. "I never held a grudge about that, by the way. Ria shouldn't have took that dumb rabbit. It didn't belong to her in the first place."

Talia couldn't believe she was dissing her own child, but then she chided herself for her unkind thoughts. The poor woman had lost her daughter in a brutal way, and was probably in denial.

A man appeared suddenly at Talia's elbow, so close that his arm brushed hers. His citrusy aftershave failed miserably at masking the scent of unwashed clothes. Wearing a black ski jacket that curved snugly over his jiggling middle, he fixed Talia with a piercing look. "You doin' okay, Anita?"

With a polite smile, Talia stepped to one side to allow him a wide berth.

Anita reached for his hand and nodded. "Yeah, but you come sit here with me, okay, Ralphie? I don't like sitting here by my lonesome. Look at all these people coming in. I gotta talk to them, and I don't even know most of them!"

The man dropped onto the sofa with the grace of a fatted goose. "I'm here for you, honey. Don't worry." He patted her knee lightly.

"Mrs. Butterf—I mean, Anita," Talia said. "When it's convenient for you, would it be okay if I dropped by your home for a few minutes? Maybe this evening sometime?"

Anita looked at Ralphie and shrugged. "I guess so. You coming over, Ralphie?"

Ralphie averted his gaze. "Yeah, but not until later. Friday's bingo night, remember? I gotta take Ma over to the church hall. I'll be over after that, okay?"

Anita pushed her lower lip into a pout and looked up at Talia. "You might as well come over, then."

Oh, yay. She was first runner-up to Ralphie.

Anita rattled off the address, saving Talia the embarrassment of having to pretend she didn't know it. The last thing she wanted was for Anita to glean that she'd already been snooping around her duplex unit.

Talia glanced at her watch. It was five to ten. She headed toward the last row of chairs, hoping to spy someone she knew. Was Kelsey planning to attend? She'd forgotten to ask her.

"Good morning, Talia." The voice, soft and refined, came from behind and slightly to the left. Talia turned to see Will Claiborne. Impeccably dressed in a suit of black worsted wool, he looked at her with an expression so glum that it tore at her heart. His eyes were red and swollen, and his lower lip trembled faintly.

Instinctively, Talia reached up to hug him. "Good morning, Will. I'm so sorry you have to go through this."

He nodded, his emerald eyes filling with tears. "Thank you. Did you notice all the lovely flowers I ordered?" He glanced over at the explosion of white roses resting at the head of the coffin.

"Yes, and they're beautiful," Talia said. Much as she tried, she couldn't prevent her gaze from drifting to his tie tack. Carved from solid jade, it was a facsimile of the two-headed snake that graced his new ring. "The spray from Ria's mom is quite lovely, as well," she added, clearing her throat.

Will's lips twisted slightly. "Actually, and I don't mean to sound unkind or self-centered, but I purchased every floral arrangement in this room. Ria's mother seems to possess somewhat limited resources. I thought it only fair that I pick up the tab."

Talia suspected he'd picked up the tab for everything, including the elaborately carved mahogany coffin in which Ria now lay. She swallowed back the sob that threatened to burst from her. "I'd better get a seat," she said.

Will nodded gravely. "Pastor Rice should be along anytime," he said. "Perhaps we can chat later."

Talia nodded and hurried along the aisle between the wall and the rows of chairs. She was just sliding into a row about halfway back when she spotted Detective Prescott, seated in the last row. Looking appropriately solemn in a navy pantsuit, she appeared almost bored. Talia smiled and nodded at her, giving her a tiny wave as she lowered herself onto a padded chair. Prescott shot her a glance but pointedly ignored her.

Thanks for the snub, Talia thought to herself. The woman certainly did run hot and cold. Talia wouldn't be calling her "Patti" any time soon, she decided. What had she been thinking when she agreed to that?

The remaining seats began to fill. The white-haired gent who'd greeted her in the lobby came in. He leaned over Anita and spoke quietly. She nodded, and then she and Ralphie moved to the front row of chairs, murmuring to each other in hushed voices.

"Hey." A man brushed the chair next to Talia's and sat down.

Talia smiled up at Scott Pollard. "Hey yourself," Talia murmured. "It's good to see you, Scott." A clean, woodsy scent wafted from him, which Talia thought suited him well. Jacketless, he wore neatly pressed navy Dockers and a pin-striped shirt. His short blond hair had been styled with gel, and his face sported about a day's beard growth.

Scott fanned himself with his hand. "Is it warm in here, or is it me?" He glanced at his watch and then smiled at Talia. "I'm glad I didn't wear my jacket."

"It is pretty warm," Talia said softly, sneaking a look at his wristwatch. The face of the watch portrayed a snarling pirate, complete with the requisite evil grin. Talia stifled a smile. The man must really be into the whole pirate gig.

Pastor Rice came into the room. A spritz of gray hair sprouting from a balding pate, he clutched a prayer book in one hand and his reading glasses in the other. He spoke briefly to Anita Butterforth, after which he approached Will Claiborne. Will uttered a few words, and the pastor clasped Will's hands in both of his. Will took a seat next to Anita, and the pastor stood before the mourners.

"Dear friends and family of Oriana Fay Butterforth," he began in a well-modulated voice.

Oriana Fay. It was the first time Talia had heard Ria's full name. Inanely, she thought back to that awful day, almost thirty years ago, when she'd taken the stolen rabbit from Ria's small arms. The anguish in the girl's eyes still haunted her. If Talia could go back in time, she'd break into her saved allowance and buy Ria a rabbit of her own.

Talia pressed a finger to her eyes and choked back tears. When she looked up, she spied a last-minute mourner hustling into the room. Looking flushed and worried, Kelsey Dakoulas scooted onto the nearest chair. Talia waved, but Kelsey obviously hadn't noticed her.

The pastor spoke kindly of Ria. He praised her devotion to her mother, her love for animals, and her work in the community. Talia suspected that the man had never actually met Ria, but was doing his best to send her off to her Maker with glowing references.

When the pastor was through, he asked if anyone wished to say a few words. Hushed whispers sifted through the room, along with the shuffling noises of the mourners preparing to leave. Talia wondered why Will Claiborne didn't step up, but when she craned her head toward the front, she saw the reason. The poor man's face was buried in his hands, and he was weeping silently.

A solid arm pressed against hers. "Have you seen Andy Nash around lately?" Scott whispered in her ear.

Why was he asking? Talia wondered. Had Andy really gone missing? She shook her head and pointed at the exit, signaling that that they could chat later.

The pastor finally nodded to all, and then left the room. The mourners began filing out, except for one impeccably dressed woman who was determined to march in, oblivious of those around her who were trying to leave. Her brunette hair bound in an old-fashioned French twist, she wore a stylish black overcoat dress with a ruby red scarf tucked around her slender neck. Talia put her at fifty, maybe a tad older. *Faded beauty* were the words that came to mind.

Anxious to get a better look at the woman, Talia shuffled forward as quickly as she could without stepping on people's heels. She'd just reached the front row of chairs when she saw the woman stride over to Ria's coffin, her light hazel eyes burning with hatred. With one red-gloved hand, the woman snatched a bundle of white roses from the voluminous vase and threw them at the lid of the casket.

Will Claiborne leaped off his chair, his face the color of ripe tomatoes. He grabbed the woman's arm and pulled her away. "What are you doing here, Liliana?" Talia heard him hiss. "I told you to stay away."

"No one tells me what to do," she retorted. "I supposed you paid for all this," she said to Will, swinging her arm in a circle.

Will's face paled to a sickly gray. Releasing the woman's arm, he staggered slightly.

"Excuse me." Talia scooted around the slow-moving senior in front of her. She hurried over to Will and gripped his arm, then eased him back into his chair. "Are you okay, Will?"

He nodded dully, and the woman gave out a vicious laugh. "Well, isn't this predictable. You've already got a new strumpet lined up to take the place of the other one."

Talia gasped. Who *was* this woman? She started to respond when she felt two powerful arms move her deftly aside. With the grace of a big cat, Detective Patti Prescott circled around

Talia and looped her hand over the woman's upper arm. "Ma'am," she said quietly, "these people are grieving for a loved one. I'm going to have to ask you to show some respect."

"Who are you? Get your hands off me!" the woman shrieked, smacking her free hand at the detective's viselike grip.

The eyes of all who remained in the room swiveled toward the commotion.

Prescott discreetly showed the woman her badge. "Do that once more," she said softly, "and I'll take you in for assaulting an officer. Are we on the same page?"

The woman, Liliana, abruptly went silent. Then her whole body began trembling and she started to sob—waves of heartfelt agony that made Talia ache for her. Whoever the woman was, she'd obviously misinterpreted Talia's concern for Will. And she sure must have hated Ria to have pitched those roses at the coffin the way she did.

Prescott smiled at the cluster of people who'd stopped in their tracks to gawk. "Excuse us, folks," she said in a soothing tone. "We just need to get some air." She guided the woman gently toward the exit as if she were escorting the Queen of England to a waiting limo. Liliana's legs looked as if they might collapse beneath her, but Prescott kept a firm grip on her and ushered her through the doorway and into the lobby area.

Nicely done, thought Talia. Prescott had nipped the embarrassing scene in the bud with tact and quiet diplomacy. Talia couldn't imagine what might have happened if the detective hadn't been there.

Scott came up behind Talia. He placed one hand lightly on her back and the other on Will's shoulder. "Everyone all right here?" he said in a husky voice.

"I think so," she said, bending toward Will. "Are you all right, Will? Can I get you anything?"

Will pulled in a deep breath and shook his head. "I am so very sorry for all this," he said. "She threatened to make a scene at Ria's service. I had no idea she would actually go through with it."

"Who is she?" Talia asked.

Will looked at her with misery in his eyes. "That, I'm afraid, was my wife."

Walking to her car, Talia felt as if she'd been slammed in the back of the head with a rock. The last thing she'd ever have imagined was that Will Claiborne was married. *Estranged*, he'd called it, after he'd pulled himself together. Talia had always thought it was an odd way to refer to a marriage. In her mind, you were either married or you weren't.

Talia found her sympathies for him waning. She no longer felt as bad for Will as she had before, in spite of his insistence that his marriage had been dead for a long time. He'd apparently been trying to divorce Liliana for the better part of two years. She'd fought him every inch of the way, determined not to let him go. Every time he thought he was close, something always happened to delay the proceeding— a minor car crash, a surgical procedure, anything that would require a postponement. Liliana, he'd claimed, had an entire repertoire of stall tactics at her disposal, along with a high-priced lawyer.

Outside, Talia snugged the collar of her flared jacket closer around the folds of her scarf. It was time to dig out her winter coat, she thought wistfully. The mild fall weather that trickled into December had lulled her into a sense of inertia. Once

Mother Nature woke up and started to flex her muscles, they'd be in for some frigid weather, along with heaps of snow.

She didn't see Kelsey anywhere, but Scott Pollard caught up with her. "Hey, we never got a chance to talk, did we?" he said, behind her back.

Talia turned and smiled at him. "Hey, Scott," she said, noticing the twinkle in his brown eyes. She'd almost forgotten that he wanted to ask her something about Andy. "And no, we didn't. Unfortunately, things turned a bit chaotic at the end." The pale sun caught the highlights in his hair and danced there for a bit. She pulled her gaze away abruptly, not wanting to give him the idea she was interested in him.

"Yeah, tell me about it." He shook his head. "I gotta tell you, I really felt for that poor fellow. If that cop hadn't been there to intervene, his ex probably would've scratched his eyes out, or done something even worse."

His *almost*-ex, Talia thought, but didn't voice it. "I don't think she would have resorted to violence. To me she seemed overwhelmingly sad. I actually felt bad for her. She seemed, I don't know . . . desperate maybe?"

A chill suddenly rode up her arms. Could Liliana have been desperate enough to kill Ria? Was she someone the police should be looking at?

Scott shrugged, but his jaw hardened. "Maybe, but she came off like a nutcase. I mean, it was a memorial service, right? That's a terrible thing to do to someone's family."

Talia bit off a wry smile. If Liliana's histrionics had bothered Anita Butterforth, she certainly hadn't shown it. She'd sat right there with Ralphie the entire time, gawking as if she'd been watching an action movie. And when Prescott was leading Liliana through the doorway, Talia had distinctly heard Anita snicker.

Scott grinned as they came up alongside Talia's Fiat. "Well, you got a prime parking spot, didn't you?" He patted the roof. "Cute little car. How does it drive?"

"It drives fine, I guess. I don't know much about engines, but the ride is smooth, and it handles beautifully. Compared to the SUV that I used to drive, this car is a peach to park."

Scott rubbed his hand absently over the roof of the Fiat. "Hey, look," he said, his tone turning serious, "have you seen Andy Nash around lately? I haven't been able to get in touch with him since Sunday. I'm worried about him."

Interesting, Talia thought. Detective Prescott had asked her pretty much the same thing. Had something happened to Andy? Another, more disturbing thought popped into her head. Had the killer caught up to him and silenced him?

Remembering Andy's paranoia, Talia wasn't sure how much to reveal. "I think I saw him earlier in the week," she said, being deliberately vague.

Scott stood a bit straighter. "Really? Where?"

Again, Talia didn't want to hand out details, even though Scott seemed genuinely worried about Andy. "He was, um, leaving the diner, I think," she said. "Do you really think something happened to him?"

Scott bit his lip and gave her a worried look. "I don't know, but I'm afraid it might have. Wherever he is, I just hope he's all right."

"Me, too," Talia said distractedly, thinking back to that uncomfortable chat she'd had with Andy at the diner. Hadn't Detective Prescott said that Andy's dad was concerned about him, as well?

"We're pretty good buds," Scott said, "but he's a strange little dude, you know? I try to look out for him when I can. What scares me is that I think the cops might be looking for him, too."

Talia sensed that Scott knew something of Andy's past and was trying to prevent him from doing anything foolish. "He's lucky to have a good friend like you, Scott," Talia said.

Scott looked off into the distance, his eyes narrowing. "I didn't realize until the fund-raiser that he'd had a thing for Ria. Evidently she'd made a date with him and then canceled at the last minute. That's the type of thing that can really set him off, you know? Poor bas—I mean, the poor guy's had a lot of rejection in his life."

If Talia had been waiting for an opening, now was the perfect time. "Scott, is there any way . . . I mean, do you think he could have harmed Ria?"

"Andy?" He looked shocked at the question. "Nah, not a chance. At heart, he's a good guy. He talks the talk, but he doesn't walk the walk, if you catch what I'm saying."

"But if no one can find him, don't you think he could be hiding from the police?"

Scott chewed his lower lip and shook his head. "No way, Talia. I'm telling you, he's really a solid guy. People just need to stop being such jerks and give him a break." He sounded almost perturbed that he'd had to explain that to her.

Talia gave him a disarming smile and then glanced at her watch. It was close to eleven. She really had to fly.

"Hey, I'd better let you go," he said, as if reading her thoughts. "You've got fish to fry, right?"

Talia laughed. "I do, and I hope you'll check out our new menu one of these days. It's not all about fish anymore. We have some tasty new sides, and we're going to be experimenting with a lot of different deep-fried desserts."

"Tasty new sides, huh?" He drew out the word *tasty*. "Yeah, I heard that somewhere. I might stop in later if I have a chance. I've been straight out with a kitchen reno in Lenox, but I'm hoping to finish up today. Hey, if you ever need any home renovations, I'm you're man, okay?" He gave the roof of the Fiat a playful slap.

"I'll keep that in mind," she said, wary of promising anything.

By the time she slid inside the Fiat, she was shivering. The parking lot had emptied out, save for the dark-colored sedan in the far corner. She started her engine and flipped on the heat. When she looked to her left, she saw Will Claiborne climbing into the cream-colored Lexus. His face looked drawn, and achingly weary. He didn't wave, so apparently he hadn't noticed her sitting there. Instead of starting his engine, he stared through the windshield. Then he dropped his head onto the steering wheel and wept.

13

Talia made it back to the eatery at ten past eleven, just in time to see the very rings of Hades flying loose.

The moment she stepped through the door into the kitchen, Lucas looked at her with terror in his eyes. "Help me," he mouthed. The carrot he'd been holding hit the floor. He bent to retrieve it and promptly slipped on a slice of onion he'd apparently dropped earlier, nearly biting the tile floor himself.

Talia gripped his arm to keep him upright and then quickly shed her coat. She plopped it on the hook next to Martha's peacoat, which in turn had been draped over the foul-smelling scarf. At least the scarf was underneath the coat today, instead of over it.

Talia closed her eyes and took in a deep breath. When she opened them, Bea's arm was raised high, a wire whisk shaking in her fist. "You're using too much flour in the batter!" Bea was bellowing. "Give me that bowl right now before you ruin the whole batch!" She made a grab for it, but Martha pulled it away, her eyes alight with triumph. The batter sloshed in the bowl, skimming dangerously close to the edge.

"Hah! Too slow, old lady! Talia never complained about the way I make the batter, so get off my—"

"Martha," Talia warned, barely controlling the fury in her tone.

"I was going to say get off my *case*," Martha said with a pout. "Tell this one to leave me alone. She doesn't even work here. She's nothing but a temporary fill-in."

"A fill-in!" Bea spluttered, her black curls jutting from her head like springs. "I'll have you know I ran this place for over twenty years! How dare you call me—"

"Stop!" Talia ordered, making a time-out sign with her hands. "I *cannot* believe I'm hearing this. If I didn't know better, I'd think I wandered into an unruly kindergarten class. What is the matter with you two?"

Martha glowered at Bea, her thick arms curled around the batter bowl as if she were protecting it from marauders. She stuck her chin out. "She started it."

Bea huffed out a breath, her green eyes looking wild. "Don't you get cheeky with me, dragon lady." She waggled the whisk at her. "I've made thousands of bowls of batter in my day, and I know you're adding too much flour. You're not making batter, you're making *paste*!"

Martha stared her down. "I told you, *this* batter is for the meatballs, not for the fish. Maybe if you cut off a few of those crazy curls of yours, you could hear better!"

Bea lunged for the bowl, causing Martha to swivel away from her with a jerky motion. A tidal wave of batter slopped over the edge of the bowl and made a direct hit on Martha's sensible shoe.

Martha stopped dead and gave Bea a murderous look. "That does it. Now you're—"

Talia stepped between the pair. She grasped Bea by the shoulders and steered her through the opening between the wall and the speckled turquoise counter, into the dining area. "*You* take a break," she said. "Suzy has some of those holiday lip glosses you like. Why don't you mosey around in her shop for a while and cool down. While you're gone, I'll deal with Martha."

Bea's face fell. "Aw, luvvy, I'm so bleedin' sorry. I don't know what got into me. That woman—she just pushed all my buttons at once!"

"I know," Talia said quietly. *Believe me, I know.*

Her head hanging, Bea asked Talia to fetch her purse and then left through the front door.

Without a word, Talia went back into the kitchen. When she saw Martha swiping at the top of her loafer with a flimsy napkin, she tore off a fistful of paper towels from the roll over the sink. She dampened them under the faucet and went over to Martha.

"Stick out your shoe, Martha."

Looking too stunned to object, Martha clutched the counter for support and lifted the toe of her loafer. Talia scrubbed the shoe with the damp towels, then repeated the procedure until every speck of batter had been thoroughly removed. Finally, she wiped the floor of any spills and tossed the whole mess in the trash.

"Thank you," Martha muttered, and headed for the back door. She removed her peacoat from its hook and yanked at her scarf.

Talia gaped at her. "Martha, where are you going? We're opening in ten minutes."

"Aren't you firing me?" she said with a hangdog look.

"Of course not. Now put your coat back and finish up with the batter, please." Talia hoped she didn't sound too witchy, but sometimes Martha needed a firm tone. She intended to have a chat with her later, when the lunch crowd quieted down and they could snag a few minutes to talk privately. For now they needed to be ready to serve their customers. "Did you make the coleslaw?" she asked more gently.

Martha nodded. "And I made the tartar sauce. I didn't know if you might run late, and I didn't want us to get caught short."

"Thank you. That was smart thinking."

Talia realized she sounded patronizing, which she hadn't meant to do. Chuckling to herself, she couldn't help wondering if this was how Rachel spoke to the kids in her fourth-grade class.

She went to the sink and scrubbed her hands with soap. Lucas looked all aflutter, as if he didn't know what to do next. Talia smiled at him. "Lucas, have you finished cutting the potatoes?"

Panic flitted over his deep blue eyes. He swallowed. "Um, yeah, but I dropped a few so I have to peel a couple more."

Talia smiled at the poor kid. "That's okay. You can do that later, if we need them. In case we get any requests, are you interested in doing some local delivery again today?"

"Yes!" He crossed himself and thanked the Lord under his breath.

"Okay, we'll see what happens. Don't get your hopes up yet."

"Thank you, Ms. Marby. You're the best!"

Talia didn't feel like the best. Today she felt totally incompetent. What kind of restaurateur leaves for a few hours and returns to find that her eatery has erupted into chaos? With a quiet sigh, she glanced over at Martha, who was covering the batter bowl with plastic wrap. Not for the first time, she wondered how long the woman would last at the job.

The first lunch order came in at eleven thirty-one. Not only did the crew at the fire station want delivery again, but old Father Francese over at Saint Agatha's telephoned and requested the same.

"If you could, my child"—he coughed vociferously into the phone—"I've been laid up with a dreadful cold, and I never miss having my fish on Friday. Perhaps you might find it in your heart to send someone over with an order of fish and chips? And some of that tasty coleslaw, as well, with a heap of mushy peas? Bless you, child." He coughed again, even more loudly this time.

Talia couldn't help smiling. For someone suffering with such a bad cold, the priest had quite the appetite. He was also a bit of a con man, she thought, but in a kind way. The tiny rectory behind Saint Agatha's Church was only a short distance past the fire station. Technically, though, it was probably outside the area where Talia had thought about offering delivery.

She checked with Lucas, who said he'd be thrilled to deliver lunch to the ailing priest. With his youthful energy and long legs, he claimed, he could deliver both orders within the space of ten or twelve minutes and be back for another trip.

"I'm not going to charge Father Francese for his lunch today," she said to Lucas. "He really did sound awful. It's the least I can do."

Lucas grinned. "You're like, a real angel, Ms. Marby. If he offers me a tip, I'll tell him to give it to the soup kitchen instead. Either that or I'll stick it in the animal shelter donation can at Queenie's."

"That's very sweet of you, Lucas." She wondered if his folks realized what a kindhearted son they'd raised.

Around quarter to twelve, Bea strolled back in. The dining area had begun to fill, and she nodded at some of her old customers, who recognized and greeted her instantly. With a sheepish look, she went into the kitchen and handed Martha a bunch of tickets. "These are for Suzy's raffle," she said. "I bought them for you, Martha. If you win, you'll get a lovely basket filled with bath and body goodies. I don't know if you use that sort of thing, but, well, they do smell quite pretty."

Martha stuck them in the pocket of her brown slacks. "Thanks, Bea." She cleared her throat. "That was a nice thing to do, even if I'm not much for tarting myself up."

Bea chortled and gave her an awkward hug. "Well, I'm going to go along now, luvs. Howie has a therapy appointment for his knee at one thirty, and I wouldn't want him to be late."

"Martha, do you mind if I walk Bea to her car?" Talia said. "I want to pick up something from the bakery while I'm out. I won't be more than ten minutes."

"Go ahead." Martha waved a hand at her. "Lucas and I got it covered." She winked at her co-worker.

Over the distant hills, the sky had grown overcast. The trees were barren now, waiting for the first snowfall to coat their bare branches. Bea slipped her arm through Talia's. "Aw, luvvy, I do have to apologize for my bad behavior today. That wasn't like me, was it, going off on poor Martha like that?"

"Don't beat yourself up, Bea. And I'm so sorry I spoke harshly to you." She squeezed Bea's gloved hand with her own. "I don't think I've ever done that in my life."

"It's already forgotten, luv."

Bea's ancient brown Datsun was parked in the town lot, close to the sidewalk. Two spaces away was Martha's massive green clunker, looking even more dented than ever. Talia would swear that the deep scratch on the left front fender hadn't been there a week ago. Did the woman use her spare time to drive in demolition derbies? Talia pointed out Martha's car to Bea.

Bea stopped dead and gawked at it. "Ah, Talia, now I know why Martha was so flippin' angry with me. I poked fun at that horrid old car of hers!"

"You did?" Talia looked at her in surprise. "That is *so* not like you, Bea."

"But I didn't mean to, you see. I didn't even know it was hers! When she came in this morning and started complaining about how far she had to walk from the parking lot, I said, 'Well, at least you don't have to drive an old junker like the poor sod who owns the ugly green car I saw this morning.'" Bea shook her head. "How daft of me. No wonder she gave me the cold shoulder all morning."

Talia groaned. "She probably did take offense, but since you didn't know, it wasn't really your fault."

"Nonetheless, I don't like hurting people's feelings." Bea issued a noisy sigh.

"Bea," Talia said thoughtfully, "why did you call her dragon lady?"

"Oh, I was just spouting off," she said, unlocking the door of her Datsun. "Course now that I know she drives that old metal monster, it almost seems appropriate, doesn't it?" She shook her black curls. "Tell her I'm sorry, will you, luv?"

They hugged good-bye, and Talia hurried toward Peggy's Bakery. She purchased a dozen frosted holiday cookies and asked Peggy to tie a pretty bow around the box.

It wasn't until she'd gotten back to the eatery and changed into her "work" clothes that something odd occurred to her. She'd seen Martha's car this morning, too—right before she met Bea in front of the restaurant. Since Martha's shift at the eatery didn't start until ten, why had her car been in the lot so early? Not that it was any of Talia's business, but it was one more thing to ponder.

The remainder of the day stayed blessedly busy. Lucas left at four, delighted to have made five local deliveries. The guys at the firehouse had apparently blabbed, so the requests for delivery were increasing.

By seven, Talia felt mentally drained. The battle between Martha and Bea, short-lived as it was, had done a number on her. She hated confrontation, especially when it involved a dear friend like Bea.

She hurried home, fed Bo, and went off with her cookies to see Anita Butterforth.

14

Anita Butterforth took the bakery box from Talia's hands and waved her into the living room of her duplex unit. "Come on in. Take a load off." She took Talia's jacket and draped it over her arm. "You can sit there," she said, indicating a platform rocker that lilted slightly to one side.

"Thank you." Talia skimmed her gaze over the narrow living room, which gave a whole new meaning to the word *bland.* Beige walls, off-white furniture, tan wall-to-wall carpeting that had seen better days. She lowered herself onto the indicated chair. With its pattern of splashy red geraniums, it was the sole item in the room with a bit of color. The seat was so close to the floor that she felt like a grade-schooler.

Anita tossed Talia's jacket over the back of the sofa. "I was watching a Sandra Bullock movie," she said, dipping her nose at the flat screen television against the far wall. She grabbed the remote off a scarred wooden coffee table and muted the sound. "You ever seen that one where she goes undercover at a beauty pageant? It's a hoot and a half!"

Talia gave her polite smile. "Yes, I think I have. It was pretty funny." She rested her purse in her lap.

Anita ripped the bow off the white bakery box and lifted the lid. "Oh, don't these look delicious," she said, snagging a frosted, bell-shaped cookie. "It was awful nice of you to bring them. Want one?" She held out the box to Talia.

"No thanks," Talia said. "I want you to have them."

Anita shrugged and plunked the box on the coffee table that sat between them. "It's real nice of you to visit," she said, biting off a corner of the cookie. "Ria didn't have a lot of friends. Most of my friends are people I work with at the dry cleaners."

"Does your friend Ralphie work with you?" Talia knew the answer, but she was curious to see if Anita would refer to him as a boyfriend.

"Oh yeah. He's been there a long time." She ran a hand through her frizzy blond hair and brushed at something on her velour pants. "The boss is always ragging on him, but believe you me, they couldn't run that place without him." She pointed a yellowed fingernail at Talia to emphasize her point.

Meooooowww.

Talia peeked around the edge of the sofa. A darling little Siamese was meandering toward them from what appeared to be the kitchen. "Oh, look, you have a cat," she said, playing Dora the Dunce again. She held out her hand to the kitty. "What's your name, sweetheart?"

"Ria named her Princess," Anita said flatly, with a sideways look at the cat. She rolled her eyes. "For some reason, Ria thought I wanted a cat. This one's okay, but they're a lot

of work, you know? And I hate cleaning that freaking litter box."

Hmmm. Maybe there was hope that Kelsey could adopt
Princess after all.

"Hey, there, sweetheart," Talia cooed. "Come over here
and see me."

"Cripes, don't encourage her. She'll just get cat hair all
over you." Anita snapped her fingers at the cat. "Princess,
leave our company alone, and don't you dare go near those
cookies!"

"She's fine, Anita. I have a cat, too. Please don't worry
about it."

With a slow blink and a lift of her elegant chin, the cat
ignored her owner's admonition and promptly jumped into
Talia's lap. Talia grinned and stroked the cat's silky head.
"Look at you," she said, "with those gorgeous blue eyes. You're
a pretty girl, aren't you?" She set her purse aside so Princess
could have a comfier seat. The cat revved up her purr machine
and curled into a cozy circle on Talia's lap.

"You want a Pepsi or anything?" Anita fidgeted nervously. "Ria and me didn't get company too often, so there's
not much to drink in the fridge."

"No thanks. I'm fine," Talia said. "I really came only to
pay my condolences. This must be such a difficult time for
you." She squirmed a bit from the lie, but Anita didn't seem
to notice.

"Yeah, it is. I talked to more cops this week that I ever did
in my life." Her eyes flashed with anger. "You'd think they'd've
caught the killer by now, right? I mean, what do they get paid
for?" She bit off another chunk of her cookie.

"I understand your feelings," Talia said, stroking Princess
under the chin, "but I'm sure they'll find the killer soon. Did

they ask you who might have wanted to harm Ria? Like, whether she might have had an old boyfriend with a grudge? Something like that?"

Anita gave out a disgusted laugh. "Yeah, like a million times. Funny thing about Ria, though. Pretty as she was, she never dated a lot of guys. She was too fussy, you know? Kinda stuck-up about who she hung with. I kept telling her, 'Ria, you're never gonna snag a man with that attitude of yours,' but she never listened to me."

An overwhelming wave of sadness for Ria welled up in Talia's chest. She got the distinct impression that Anita's hunt for her own man had always taken precedence over her daughter's needs.

"Course the cops knew she'd been seeing Will Claiborne. Man, that guy sure did love my Ria," she said, her eyes welling up. It was the first time Talia had seen Anita show any real emotion over Ria's death.

"Anita," Talia said, "Forgive me, but something I overheard Ria say to you at the fund-raiser on Sunday stuck in my head. It sounded like she said, 'I saw the dragon. The dragon is back.'"

Anita snapped her gaze at Talia. "You heard that, huh?" She blew out a shaky breath. "Ria and that freaking dragon," she said softly. "I guess she never got over it."

"The thing is," Talia pressed in a quiet voice, "I couldn't help wondering if it might have had anything to do with, you know, the person who harmed her."

For a long moment Anita stared at the wall. Finally, after a long sigh she said, "No, it was nothing like that. The dragon was just a"—she snapped her fingers—"you know, a filament of Ria's imagination." She absently brushed a cookie crumb from her velour top. "It started when she was a kid. Drove me nuts for a long time, let me tell you. I mean, here I was raising a kid on my own and I constantly had to listen to that dragon crap."

For a moment, Talia was taken aback. The insensitivity in Anita's tone horrified her. Had the woman forgotten that her daughter's life had been snuffed out in a brutal manner?

"Ah, I know what you're thinking. I can tell by the look on your face."

Talia felt herself flushing. She hadn't meant for her reaction to be so visible, but she'd never been good at hiding her feelings. Almost as if she'd felt her dismay, Princess lifted her head and looked up at Talia.

On second thought, Talia wondered if she was being too tough on Anita. Maybe recalling Ria's childhood shortcomings was the only way she could deal with her death. Everyone handled grief in a different way.

Anita stared at her through narrowed eyes. "It's a weird story, if you wanna hear it."

Talia wanted desperately to hear it. Something in Ria's tone that day had set her senses on high alert. If the dragon, whatever it was, had anything to do with the killer, maybe she could make sense of it in a way that Anita had never been able to.

"I think it might help you to talk about it, Anita," Talia said quietly.

Anita looked away, her fingers twitching as if she needed a cigarette. "Back when Ria was young, six or seven, we were living in Agawam. Ria's father was long gone, so it was just me and her. Anyways, this one night—it was real hot out—I was out of cigarettes, so I drove to the convenience store down the street. I left Ria in the car, in the parking lot behind the store. I guess I was in there longer than I thought." She reddened. "I ran into an old flame of mine—you know how it is—and we got talking about old times."

I know I'd never leave a six-year-old alone in the car at night, Talia wanted to say. She forced a smile. "Sure, I've done that," she fibbed.

"Anyways, me and Donny talked for a while, and he asked if he could come over to my place and have a beer with me. Even offered to bring a six-pack, which was fine with me. When I got back to the car, Ria was acting weird. She was huddled real low in the front seat, hugging herself like she was scared. I asked her what was wrong, and she said, 'I saw a lady get hurt, and a dragon did it.' Well, I knew that didn't make any sense, but that was Ria, you know? Always spinning silly tales to get attention."

That poor little girl. The thought that Ria had to dream up stories to get her mother's attention broke Talia's heart. Even if Anita was exaggerating, it was immensely sad to think of the lonely childhood Ria must have had.

Anita pursed her lips. "I told her to *stop* telling lies and tell me what really happened. Kid always had a wild imagination, you know? It got on every last one of my nerves."

Talia stroked the cat's head, ire rising in her chest. "So what did she say?"

"Well, then her voice got a little smaller, the way it always did when she was lying." Anita's eyes blazed. "She insisted, though, that she saw a dragon hurt a lady. I asked her where the dragon was, and she said it was gone. When I asked her where the lady was, she told me the dragon took her away. At that point I was like, wicked ticked, you know? I smacked her on the leg and told her to sit up straight. I told her Donny was coming over, and she'd better behave herself while he was there and not bother us. Plus, I wanted to get home and grab a quick shower before he got there, and she was being a royal pain in my patoot.

"Anyways, once we got home I warned her to keep her mouth shut and watch TV. My . . . I mean, Donny, my friend, ended up spending the night," she said, "so I let Ria sleep on the sofa." Her face colored.

Let her sleep on the sofa? More like forced her to, Talia wanted to blurt out. She would've bet her Fiat it hadn't been the first time little Ria had been relegated to sleeping alone in the living room.

Anita's face suddenly changed—a twinge of guilt maybe?—and the lines around her eyes deepened. "I heard her crying in the night, poor little kid," she went on, a bit more softly. "But I couldn't go out to see what was wrong because I would've woken up Donny, and he had to go to work real early the next morning."

Talia felt her entire body stiffen. What a pathetic excuse for a mother Anita had been.

Princess obviously felt Talia's distress. She jumped off Talia's lap, opting instead to leap onto the sofa and curl up against her jacket.

Anita didn't seem to notice. "Couple days later, a report came on the TV about a woman who went missing. She was eighteen or nineteen, I think, a local girl. Went out with her boyfriend that Friday night and never came home." She blew out a breath. "When they flashed the girl's picture on the TV, Ria started to go nuts. Kept insisting the dragon took the girl, and that I had to find the dragon." Anita snatched another cookie—a Santa face—from the bakery box. The kitty's ears perked and she padded over to investigate the sugary treat. Anita shoved her aside with her forearm. "Get away, cat. Leave my cookie alone."

Princess sat upright in a regal stance and regarded Anita with her cool blue gaze.

"Did you think she might have seen something?" Talia asked, hoping to distract Anita from the cat. "Did you go to the police?"

Anita made a face. "Course not! What was I going to tell them? That my crazy little girl said a dragon took that woman?"

Crazy little girl. The words struck like arrows to the heart. The more Anita went on with the story, the better Talia understood the simmering anger that had influenced Ria's actions.

It was clear that Ria had always played second fiddle in her mother's life. Second to whatever man happened to catch Anita's fancy, or maybe it was the other way around. Talia suspected Anita hadn't been very discerning in her choice of suitors.

Nonetheless, Talia knew that if she had any hope of making sense of the dragon, she would have to squelch her distaste for Anita and encourage her to spill the whole story. She folded her hands in her lap and gazed with feigned sympathy at the woman. "Did you try talking to her?" she said gently. "Wasn't it possible that Ria might have seen something that night that could've helped the police?"

"Course I tried," Anita said defensively. "But all she did was draw pictures of the dragon, over and over again. The pictures were cartoonish, childish. Didn't look much like a dragon at all. Not to me anyway. Aren't dragons supposed to have wings?"

"I . . . I'm not sure," Talia said. She thought back to all the images of dragons she'd seen, but she couldn't recall if she'd ever noticed any wings. "Did she draw the pictures with crayons?"

"No, she didn't have any crayons, not after she pulled a hissy one day and broke them all. I refused to buy her any more after that." Anita snorted. "Besides, the kid was no artist. Bad enough she went through a whole pad of my paper making pencil sketches of that stupid imaginary dragon. When she asked for another pad, I told her to can it with the dragon. I found out later she was saving all her pictures. She stuffed them in an empty oatmeal box and hid it in the back of the coat closet. There was something else she'd saved in there, too, but I can't remember what it was." She bit off half of Santa's face and chomped on it.

All at once, something struck Talia. She closed her eyes and tried to picture the engraving on Will Claiborne's jade ring—a two-headed snake coiled around the stem of a tulip. Could Ria have thought that was a dragon? But that didn't make sense, did it? Will's ring was new. It wasn't likely Ria would have seen his family crest anywhere else.

"Did the missing woman ever turn up?" Talia asked, wanting to push Anita along a bit faster.

Anita grew quiet. "Yeah, she sure did. A few months later, close to Thanksgiving, a couple of hunters found her in the woods. Poor girl had been dead all that time . . ." Her gaze lost its focus, her words drifting to a bare whisper.

The dragon killed her. The thought came automatically, as if Talia had known it all along. "Did the police figure out who did it?" Her voice came out wobbly.

Anita uncrossed her legs, and then crossed them again the other way. "Yeah, it ended up being a no-brainer. The cops had been looking at her boyfriend all along—a guy named Kyle something or other—but he swore he hadn't seen her that night. A buddy of his backed up his story, so he figured he was golden." She guffawed. "Well, that alibi got blown out of the water when they found evidence of him, you know . . . having relations with the girl. He changed his tune after that. He admitted he *had* been with her, but he claimed they'd fought afterward and he dropped her off a couple of blocks from her folks' house." She paused and looked at Talia. "You sure you don't want something to drink?"

"Actually, a glass of water would be nice," Talia said. "I'm feeling a little dry."

Anita hopped off the sofa and disappeared into the kitchen. Talia quickly jumped off her chair and scooped up Princess. "Come sit with me," she whispered. "I'm going to find you a home where people will appreciate you, okay?" She kissed the cat's forehead and reclaimed her seat in the rickety rocker.

Anita returned with a plastic cup filled with water. She scowled when she saw Princess in Talia's lap again. "I hope tap water's okay. The bottled stuff's too expensive."

"It's fine," Talia said, and took a long sip. "So what happened to that Kyle fellow? Did he get convicted?"

"Yup. Still doing time, as far as I know. Judge gave him life without parole."

"Did Ria ever mention the dragon again?"

"No," Anita huffed, "and she was still guarding those sketches like they were made of freaking gold. One day when she was at school, I went into the closet where she'd stashed them. I was going to throw them in the trash, get rid of them once and for all. But they were gone. Either she'd tossed them out herself or moved them to a better hiding place. She was clever that way." Her gaze softened, and a wistful look crossed her face.

Talia was willing to bet Ria had never thrown out the sketches. Was it possible she might have kept them all these years? Maybe squirreled them away in another secret hiding place?

"Funny thing is," Anita said with a rueful smile, "I don't think she threw them away. I think she took them with her when we moved to Wrensdale. Remember the house we were living in when Ria stole the rabbit? The two-story on Hampton Avenue?"

"I remember," Talia said, her mind wanting to shut out that awful day.

"Well, this one day I kept calling and calling her and she wasn't answering me. I was furious. Tired from work and in *no* mood. Anyways, I caught her sneaking out of her closet with this guilty look on her face. What's the kid up to? I wondered. She wouldn't say anything, so I sent her to bed early with no television. The next day I searched the closet but I couldn't find anything. Whatever she hid there, she hid it good." Anita's eyes filled with tears. "I shouldn't've gotten so mad at her the way I did." She snuffled and pressed her tissue to her eyes again.

In spite of Anita's rough ways, Talia's couldn't help feeling bad for her. "You miss her, don't you?"

She sniffled. "Of course I do! I wish I could tell her how sorry I am for some of things I did when she was growing up. All those times I ignored her, or left her alone. If I did that today, the cops would haul me away in cuffs, wouldn't they?" She sucked in a noisy sob.

Probably, Talia thought, but didn't voice it. "I'm sure Ria knew you loved her," she said, her voice sounding flat even to her own ears. "So when was it that you and Ria moved to Wrensdale?"

Anita thought for a moment. "Actually, it wasn't too long after that Kyle guy got convicted for the girl's murder. Donny and me had started seeing each other again. When he got the chance to take a construction job in Wrensdale, him and me and Ria all moved into an apartment there." She frowned. "It didn't last long. He found someone else and moved out a few months later, leaving me stuck with the lease. Creep. Ria and me finally moved to a cheaper apartment in Pittsfield. It wasn't as nice, but I least I could make the rent." She shook her head sadly.

Talia sighed. Anita's life certainly hadn't been a bed of daisies. Maybe her search for a man had been more about finding a provider for her and her daughter than snagging a companion for herself. She decided to cut her a little slack and stop being so judgmental.

But she couldn't get the dragon out of her head.

"Anita, I know this might sound strange, but did the dragon look anything like a snake? Maybe a two-headed snake?"

Anita frowned. "No, I don't think so. Tell you the truth, it didn't look much like a dragon, either. I guess I'm not sure what it looked like. Like I said, Ria was no artist. What are you getting at?"

Talia hesitated. If she described Will's family crest, would Anita keep it to herself, or would she go blabbing Talia's suspicions to Will?

She decided not to say anything, at least not yet. She had trouble believing Will was even capable of harming Ria. His wife, Liliana, was another matter . . .

"Hey, I gotta ask you something," Anita said suddenly. "Would you mind if I showed you Ria's room?"

"Not at all," Talia said. "I would love to see it."

She set Princess gently on the cushion of the rocker and

followed Anita up a carpeted staircase. Ria's room was on the left side of a narrow hallway, opposite the full bath.

"I kept everything just like she left it," Anita said, pushing the door open. She pulled a crumpled tissue from the pocket of her velour pants and squashed it against her eyes.

Talia was stunned at the contrast between Ria's bedroom and the rest of the drab unit. The walls had been papered in a Victorian print of tiny pink roses. The double bed frame was cast iron, painted white in a distressed style, with a heart-shaped scroll at the head. The spread itself was white chenille, the lacy pillow shams a shade of pink that complemented the wallpaper beautifully. A tall, distressed white bureau graced the opposite wall. Atop the bureau was a vintage vase filled with dried pink hydrangeas.

"Oh my, what a lovely room," Talia breathed. "So feminine and tasteful."

Anita spied Princess peeking at them through the doorway, and immediately closed the door. "That cat's been itching to come in here," she said testily, "but I've been keeping her out. I don't want cat hair all over Ria's bed." Her tone immediately softened. "Ria was a good decorator, wasn't she?"

She was a fabulous decorator, Talia thought. No wonder she opened a vintage clothing store. Clearly it was her passion. "Yes, and it's immaculate, too. Ria was obviously a neatnik."

Anita's expression darkened. "Not as much as you think," she said, and gave a slight shudder. "That's what I wanted to show you. See that nightie on the pillowcase?"

Talia glanced at the frilly pink nightdress that had been folded carefully atop one of the plump pink pillows. "Yes, it's pretty."

"Well, Ria didn't leave it like that. I *know* she didn't. She always used to toss it on the bed when she got dressed in the morning and leave it there in a heap."

Talia swiveled and looked at Anita. "Are you saying . . . you think someone else was in here?"

"I'm saying I *know* someone else was in here. Whoever it was must've broken in last night when I was out to dinner with Ralphie. When I got home, that nightie was folded just like that." She rubbed the arms of her velour top. "And I know Ria didn't leave it that way."

Talia felt a shiver race through her. If Anita was right, then someone must have been in here, looking for something. "Was anything taken? Are you missing anything?"

Anita slowly shook her head. "Not that I could tell. Far as I could see, the rest of the house was untouched." She went over to Ria's closet and opened the door. A slew of dresses, blouses, and slacks were lined up neatly across the metal rack. "See how everything is hanging so tidy?" Anita said. "Well, I know for a fact Ria didn't leave it this way. She used to jam things in where they didn't fit. Sometimes it looked like a clown closet." She gave out a bittersweet laugh.

A bad feeling was beginning to crawl over Talia. She wondered if the intruder had been the person she and Kelsey had heard closing the slider in the back the night before.

One thing she knew for sure. Whoever broke into Anita's duplex hadn't been there just to straighten up. "Anita, you reported this to the police, right?"

"Yeah, for all the good it did," she said gruffly. "Two uniformed cops came over, looked around for barely ten minutes, took some half-baked notes, and then left. They acted like I was nuts for reporting a room that was too neat." She closed the closet door quietly.

"How do you think the intruder got in?" Talia asked her.

Anita rubbed the back of her neck. "Well, Mr. Bay at the funeral home warned me about keeping my doors locked. Problem is, the lock on the sliding door out back doesn't catch right anymore. A five-year-old could've jimmied it open. The two cops looked at it but didn't see anything out of place." Her jaw tightened. "I could tell they didn't believe a word of what I was saying."

"I believe you," Talia said. "If you don't mind, Anita, I'm going to mention this to Detective Prescott."

Anita shrugged. "Be my guest. I guess I should have thought to call either her or that O'Donnell guy at the state police, but I figured the cops who showed up would know enough to report it."

Talia agreed. They should have known enough to do that. "Anita, I'm not sure you should be staying here alone until, you know . . . the police figure out who did this." She heard the tremor in her own voice, and realized she was frightened for Anita.

"Don't worry." Anita flushed slightly. "Ralphie's coming over after he takes his mother home from bingo. He doesn't like me staying alone, either."

Well, score one for Ralphie, Talia thought. Maybe he had more sense than she gave him credit for.

When Talia was leaving, she gave Anita an impulsive hug. Maybe the woman hadn't been the best mother, but not having walked in her shoes, she didn't have any right to judge.

Anita seemed pleased by the gesture, if a tad embarrassed. "Hey, thanks for the cookies," she said, her eyes filling again.

"You're welcome." Talia paused, wondering whether or not she should mention Princess. She decided she had nothing to lose. "Anita, if Princess is too much for you to cope with right now, I know a family that would love to have her. You wouldn't have to worry about her, and they'd give her a great home. All you have to do is let me know, okay?" She didn't mention Kelsey's name, since she wasn't sure how Anita felt about her.

Anita's eyes widened as if she favored the idea, but then she heaved out a sigh. "Yeah, problem is, she was Ria's cat, you know? I'd feel awful guilty if I gave her away."

"That's okay. You can think about it anyway. I know Ria would want Princess to have the best home possible."

There. She'd planted the seed. Maybe after Anita thought it over, she would do the right thing.

15

As soon as Talia settled herself in her car, she locked her doors, pulled out her phone, and punched in the number for Detective Prescott. Her call went straight to voice mail, so she left a message for the detective to call her as soon as possible. "It's fairly urgent," she told her, "and it's about Ria's murder."

The more she thought about Anita's intruder, the more it made the hair on her arms prickle. Straightening Ria's closet, folding her nightie on the pillow? In Talia's view, it had all the earmarks of a stalker. And when she thought of a stalker, her thoughts went immediately to Andy Nash.

That was another thing. Didn't the detective confirm that Andy's other job was working for a car dealership? If he'd wanted to switch his car for another vehicle—like maybe a truck?—he was working in the ideal business.

The short ride back to her bungalow seemed darker than

ever, the moon half hidden by clusters of clouds. The calendar was creeping toward the shortest day of the year, and snow was predicted for early the following week. If she were a skier, like her dad, she'd welcome the onset of winter in the Berkshires. Depending on conditions, her dad would be spending most of his weekends either at Jiminy Peak or Bousquet Mountain, conquering the slopes with the skill of the athlete he'd been in his youth.

Talia, unfortunately, didn't have a single athletic gene spiraling through her DNA. For her, yoga was about the extent of her exercise program, and she practiced that only sporadically. Ever since she'd returned to Wrensdale in September, she'd been spending so much time in the fish and chips shop that she didn't have time for much else. One of these mornings she was going to awaken to find that she'd sprouted gills overnight.

She pulled into her driveway, struck by how stark her bungalow looked compared to the other homes on the street. Vicki and Grace, the couple who lived a few houses away, had strung tiny blue lights around each of their windows. Their gorgeous tree, the tip of which kissed the ceiling of their living room, sparkled red and blue and silver through the bay window. Across the street, even old Mrs. Polerski had hung a massive evergreen wreath on her front door. Its bright red bow was nearly as big as she was.

"Nana would be so mad at me," Talia groaned to herself. "I haven't put up a single decoration yet!" Since the eatery was closed on Monday, she vowed to devote part of that day to putting a colorful wreath on the door and buying a few decorations for the house. She wasn't sure she'd have time to do the whole Christmas tree thing, but at least she could add some cheery holiday touches to the bungalow.

Bo welcomed her with a face full of furry kisses and a not-too-subtle demand for dinner. "Don't worry, I can see that you're starving," Talia said, cradling the cat in her arms. She kissed Bo's whiskered cheek and then set her down. "How about savory salmon tonight?" she said, idly flipping through the row of kitty food cans in her cabinet. She took Bo's wide-eyed silence as a yes, and spooned the contents of the can into her dish.

Her cell rang just as the last spoonful of stinky salmon wafted into her face. She plopped the can in the sink and grabbed the phone off her table. "Detective Prescott?"

"At your service." The detective's tone was cautious. "You have news about Ms. Butterforth's murder?" No greeting, no pleasantries. *Slam bam tell me, ma'am.*

Talia cut directly to the purpose of her call, explaining that Anita had experienced a break-in of sorts, and that someone had apparently riffled through Ria's belongings.

"You're saying that she found things out of place?" the detective said doubtfully, "but that nothing was taken?"

"Sort of," Talia said with an irritated sigh. It was hard to explain an intruder breaking in and making things *neater* instead of messier.

For a moment, only dead silence filtered through the phone. "I'll look into it," Prescott finally said. "And I'll make sure Derek knows about the pair who took the call. I suspect it was Garner and Grabowski. Those two couldn't find a pimple on their noses if they were staring straight into a mirror. And you didn't hear that from me, by the way."

Talia chuckled. Maybe the detective had a sense of humor after all. "Any word on Andy Nash?" she said, pushing her luck right to the edge of the cliff.

"Not yet," Prescott said in a clipped tone. "And even if I

knew something, I don't think you'd have the patience to listen while I explained it to you. But thank you for the information, Talia. I'll be in touch if necessary."

"But what if—" Talia started to blurt out before she was cut off like a pushy telemarketer. She wished she could have slammed down the phone, the way people did before they had cell phones. And that was the second time Prescott had implied that Talia didn't have any patience. What was up with that?

She slept fitfully that night. Visions of Ria's folded pink nightie kept floating through her brain. Deep in her bones, she felt certain it was the killer who'd folded that nightgown.

16

It was Saturday, and Martha was in a mood.

"I don't suppose you gave any more thought to rearranging this kitchen," she griped.

Talia watched her stir enough Parmesan cheese into her batter bowl to glue a cruise ship together. "That's too much cheese, Martha," she offered quietly. "Add another egg and a little more flour and milk."

She was determined not to fight with the woman today, in spite of the fact that Martha had shown up for work armed with a pair of verbal boxing gloves. Had something happened to send her into a snit?

Martha slammed the bowl onto the worktable. She whipped open the fridge door, nearly pulling it off its hinges, and pulled out another egg and a carton of milk. She poured the milk into the bowl, sloshing it onto the table. With the utmost tact, Talia pulled a paper towel from the roll and wiped up the spill.

"I can clean up my own mess," Martha said.

Talia couldn't resist an eye roll. "Is something wrong, Martha?" she asked. "Do you want to talk about it?"

"What I *want*," Martha said, "is enough room to get my job done. Working in this kitchen is like working in a tunnel."

Talia stared at her. It took every ounce of restraint she had not to throw a retort at her. She took three deep breaths. "I'm going next door for a few minutes. I'll be right back." She grabbed her purse and scurried out the front door.

In Sage & Seaweed, Suzy Sato was kneeling in front of a shelf lined with pastel-colored bubble baths. "Is that Talia I hear?" She turned and smiled up at her friend.

Talia laughed. "Okay, that's the second time you nailed me. What do you have, eyes in the back of your head?"

Suzy blushed. "Help me up?" she said, sticking out an arm.

Talia grabbed her arm and lifted her gently upward. Suzy brushed off the knees of her bright red maternity leggings. "Come with me."

Baffled, Talia followed her over to a display case on the opposite side of the boutique. Cut glass bottles in a variety of shapes lined the shelves, each bearing a shell-shaped label identifying the scent within.

"This is a brand-new line," Suzy explained. "I didn't want to say anything before, but there is a certain . . . *aroma* that follows you."

Oh dear God, was Suzy about to tell her she had body odor? But how could that be? She showered every day. She washed her clothes.

"Don't look so frightened," Suzy said, her sky blue eyes beaming. "I'm only pointing out that there's a slight *eau de deep fry* that tends to cling to your clothing."

Talia swallowed. "There is?"

"Don't worry, it's not a bad smell. It's actually a very delectable scent! But you don't want to carry it all the time, do you?"

"No, I . . . I guess not."

Suzy lifted one of the bottles from the shelf. Shaped like an old-fashioned teapot, it was filled with a pale green liquid. "This delicate scent," she explained, "is made from green tea with a slight overtone of citrus. It's perfect for disguising any lingering traces of deep-fried food that might cling to you." She removed the stopper and waved it under Talia's nose.

Talia took a deep breath. "Oh, wow, that's really nice. Barely there, but lovely."

"Exactly!" Suzy's laugh flitted through the shop. "It doesn't overpower. It simply complements. And covers." She winked at Talia.

Talia peeked at the price tag. It wasn't cheap, but it certainly wouldn't bust her budget. And since she hadn't done much shopping lately at all, she decided to treat herself. "I'll splurge on it," she said. "And I want to pick up some of your raffle tickets, too."

Suzy rang up the transaction while Talia filled out the raffle stubs. "Well, look at that," Suzy said slyly, her Southern roots slipping into her silky tone. When Talia looked up, Suzy was craning her neck and peering through the front window of the shop. "Is that who I think it is?"

Talia turned and followed her gaze. She gasped. "That's Liliana Claiborne!"

Suzy looked shocked. "You know her?"

"No, but I met her at Ria Butterforth's memorial service. Well, *kind of* met her. She sort of crashed the scene and had to be escorted out."

"That poor Mr. Claiborne." Suzy shook her head full of springy red curls. "She cheated on him for years, you know, with a boy toy she picked up one evening at a charity event. The boy toy was the bartender, and from what I've seen, Liliana Claiborne is no stranger to the bottle."

"Oh my. I didn't realize that. I didn't even know you knew our landlord."

"Kenji and I met him, briefly, when I first opened the shop. He's devilishly handsome, isn't he? And as sweet as pecan pie."

Talia grinned. "I found him to be very pleasant," she agreed. "And that's all I'm going to say. How do you know that about his wife?"

Suzy huffed and pulled out a salmon-colored gift bag from beneath the counter. "She came with him to the shop's opening. Glory, what a scene she made! I'd been serving miniature glasses of champagne on a tray, and she kept slugging them back like they were nothing more than lemonade! Will spoke to her quietly, several times, but Liliana just kept getting louder and more abrasive. People started to stare, and . . . well, honestly, I didn't know what to do. I stopped serving champagne for a little while, and Will finally made his apologies to me and they left." She jammed two sheets of silver tissue into the bag.

"That must have been embarrassing for everyone," Talia said. "How did you know about the, um, boy toy?"

"Well," Suzy went on, "as I was milling about serving canapés to the guests that day, I overheard two women talking about her." She flushed. "Yes, I eavesdropped, and I can't say I'm proud of it. But when I realized who they were dishing about, I kind of stood behind them so I could catch the whole thing. Let me tell you, I got an earful. Liliana, it seems, has always had a roving eye for the studly types." She pushed the bag across the counter toward Talia.

But if that were true, Talia mused, why was Liliana so intent on keeping Will? Why didn't she just let him out of the marriage?

"Oh, I know I shouldn't be gossiping like this," Suzy said, a hint of apology in her tone. "I've been the subject of a lot of hateful gossip myself, and believe me, it's not fun. I guess I'm just still miffed at her for spoiling my grand opening that way. Not that she *really* spoiled it, but . . . oh, you know what I mean."

Her thoughts whirling, Talia grabbed the bag that held her new scent, hugged Suzy good-bye, and headed outside onto the plaza. She'd snagged her purse but not her jacket when she left Fry Me a Sliver, and the December chill now gnawed at her like sharp icicle teeth.

She glanced over at Once or Twice. Liliana Claiborne, clad in a full-length black wool coat with a furry collar, was attempting to unlock the door. Either she had the wrong key, or the key just wasn't working. When Talia saw Liliana kick the door with the toe of her red leather boot, she dashed over.

"Can I help?" Talia said kindly, coming up behind her. "You look like you're having trouble with your key."

Liliana, her brunette hair flying loose about her face, turned and stared at her through eyes that looked bloodshot and unfocused. "You're that woman," she said. "The one from the funeral." She said it matter-of-factly, without a hint of malice.

"Yes, I'm Talia Marby. And you're Liliana, right?"

Liliana's breath was stale. Her blood-red lipstick had been applied with a too-generous hand. She nodded absently, and then went back to jiggling the key in the lock. When it refused to open, she cursed and slapped her hand on the door.

Concerned for her, Talia stepped a bit closer. She wasn't even sure if Liliana had any right to enter Ria's shop, but the torment in the woman's eyes was so intense that she had to do something to help. "Here, let me try." Talia reached for the key, and Liliana immediately snatched her own hand away. The key jiggled, but wouldn't turn. Talia suspected it was the key from the shop's prior incarnation and wasn't going to fit no matter how long they stood there and fussed with it.

"I don't think it's going to budge, Liliana. Is there something you need? Maybe I can help."

Liliana began to shake. Tears slid down her sculpted cheeks, leaving tracks in her makeup. "You can't help," she said softly. "No one can help."

Talia's heart twisted. The poor woman looked absolutely lost, as if she didn't have a friend in the world to care about her.

"Liliana, you look like you could use a cup of hot coffee to warm you up. Why don't you come with me?" She slipped her arm through Liliana's and tugged her gently toward the plaza. Liliana didn't resist. She clomped along next to Talia, stumbling a few times on the uneven cobblestone.

Martha shot them an odd look when they entered the dining room.

"Why don't you sit over here," Talia said, propelling her over to a table at the back of the dining area, near the restroom. She wanted to keep her out of Martha's line of vision so Liliana could have some privacy. "How do you take your coffee?"

Liliana brushed her hands over the table, as if testing it for cleanliness. "With whiskey," she said in a low voice. She looked up at Talia with a sad smile. "Black, please, and as strong as you can make it."

Talia smiled. "Our French roast is pretty powerful. I'll be right back."

Ignoring Martha's gawking, Talia poured a mugful of coffee for Liliana. She wished she could have offered her something to eat, but it was too early for lunch and she didn't have anything really suitable for breakfast.

Talia set the mug and a napkin on the table, and then slid into the chair facing Liliana. Liliana wrapped her hands around the mug and closed her eyes for a moment. Then she took a long, careful sip. "That's actually very good," she said, setting her mug down. "I expected it to be typical fast-food coffee."

Talia didn't know if she should be insulted by the "fast-food" comment, but she decided it was probably just Liliana's way of speaking. She struck Talia as a woman who'd been spoiled much of her life by having the best of everything.

Liliana lifted her elegant chin and took a deep breath. "I don't smell anything frying," she said, almost wistfully.

Talia smiled at her. "Actually, it's a tad too early. We don't open until eleven thirty. I'm sorry I don't have any breakfast food to offer you."

A smile touched Liliana's lips, and all at once Talia saw the stunning beauty she had to have been in her youth. In her mind, she pictured how Liliana and Will must have looked when they were first married—what a handsome couple they must have made. Talia couldn't help wondering what had caused the first crack in the relationship.

In a honeyed voice Liliana said, "When I was a little girl, we had a cook who was from Edinburg. Oh, she used to make the most fabulous breakfasts for me! Have you ever heard of a Scotch egg?"

Surprised by the fast one-eighty Liliana's mood had taken, Talia felt some of her own tension drain. She liked this gentler version of Will Claiborne's wife. It was so much more pleasant than the angry one. "I've heard of a Scotch egg," Talia said in response, "but I've never had one. Isn't it a hard-boiled egg wrapped in sausage?" She thought back to those wonderful mornings as a kid when Nana used to serve her favorite breakfast—French toast made from thick slices of hearty Italian bread, with a dab of ricotta cheese whisked into the egg mixture. And even when Talia was young, Nana would permit her to have a half-filled cup of coffee, so long as she added a hefty dollop of milk. Talia was sure it was the reason that coffee had always been her comfort drink of choice.

"That's right," Liliana said, "and then the whole thing was deep-fried." Her smooth brow furrowed for a brief moment as she skipped along memory lane. "Of course these days most people bake them instead of deep-frying them, but the original way is the best." She took a delicate sip from her mug. Her face lit up as if she were a child again. "Our Maidie knew how to season the pork sausage to perfection. Oh, her Scotch eggs were just marvelous! Although on some days, when I'd overslept and was running late for school, she would simply deep fry the egg by itself." She gave out a slight laugh. "All that lovely grease. Terrible for the arteries, but back then I didn't care."

Talia studied Liliana for a moment. The woman looked as if she could use a decent meal. She was stick-thin, and her coloring was deathly pale. "Liliana, have you eaten any-thing this morning?"

Liliana's smiled faded. She pushed a strand of brunette hair away from her face. "I don't normally eat in the morning. I'm not usually . . . up for it." Her pale hazel eyes brightened. "Oddly enough, coming in here has made me a bit hungry."

Martha appeared suddenly next to the table, coffeepot in hand. "Would you like a refill, ma'am?"

"Thank you. That would be delightful," Liliana said.

Martha poured a steaming refill into Liliana's mug. "If you're interested," she said in a quiet voice, "I know how to deep-fry an egg."

Talia sat back, flummoxed. Martha was full of surprises today, wasn't she? She'd shown up for work on a broom, and all of a sudden she was skimming across the sky on a cloud of fluff. And she'd clearly been eavesdropping on their conversation. She must have heard every word Liliana had spoken.

Liliana splayed a manicured hand against her chest. "Oh, my," she breathed. "No one has made a deep-fried egg for me in a *very* long time."

That was all Martha needed. She cocked a finger at Liliana and promised to return in a few. Talia smiled at Liliana. "Excuse me, I'll be right back."

Talia rose and trailed Martha into the kitchen. She didn't trust herself to say anything, so instead she opened the fridge. She pulled out the remains of the fruitcake Kelsey had given her the night before and sliced off a chunk about a half-inch thick.

Martha, meanwhile, had cracked open an egg and was guiding it expertly into a small fry pan of boiling vegetable oil. Talia watched with interest as the egg sizzled. She'd never before seen an egg prepared this way. With practiced moves, Martha used a wooden spoon to roll the egg gently around in the pan. When it was perfectly browned, she lifted it onto a paper towel with a slotted spoon, and then transferred it onto a plate.

Talia microwaved the fruitcake for half a minute and then placed it carefully next to the egg. "Thank you, Martha. I'll take it from here."

When she returned to the dining room, she saw that Liliana had slid off her coat and draped it over the back of the chair. Talia set the plate down in front of her, along with a few more napkins and some plastic ware. The egg did smell delicious, she thought grudgingly. She almost wished Martha had whipped up one for her, too.

Liliana's eyes widened when she saw the plate, and tears poised on her lashes. "Oh my, I can hardly believe what I'm seeing. It looks exactly like the ones Maidie used to fry up for me. And I simply adore fruitcake." She placed a napkin carefully across her lap and sliced into the egg with her plastic knife. The gooey yolk drifted lazily over the crispy whites, making Talia's mouth water. How the heck did Martha learn to do this?

While Liliana dove into her breakfast, Talia nabbed a cup of coffee for herself. She still had so much to do, but she wanted to question Liliana before she let her escape.

"You people are so thoughtful," Liliana said, lowering her gaze. She pushed aside her empty plate. Talia was pleased to see she'd eaten every speck, right down to the last crumb of fruitcake. "I'm sorry I was so horrible to you yesterday. I . . . I wasn't myself."

"I understand," Talia said softly.

"Will wanted to marry that woman, you know." Her voice was bitter. "He loved her the way he once loved me. He even had a pendant made for her with that horrid two-headed snake on it."

The snake again. That awful family crest. Talia shivered. "Did he ever have one made for you?"

"No, apparently I wasn't *worthy*, for which I am grateful to the good Lord." She rolled her hazel eyes at the ceiling.

"Why were you trying to get into Ria's shop?"

Liliana shrugged. "I just wanted to see it, maybe trash a few things. It was childish of me, I know, but when I woke up this morning I had a vicious headache. I guess I made a bad choice." Looking somewhat embarrassed, she tossed her crumpled napkin onto her empty plate. "Strangely, I feel a thousand times better. I suspect the delectable breakfast you fed me has something to do with it."

Talia silently agreed. Food had a way of soothing the body, as well as the mind. Martha's single act of deep-frying an egg for Liliana had worked like a miracle drug. She would have to remember to thank Martha, even if she was a grump.

Not wanting to get distracted, Talia turned back to the conversation. "Are you and Will going to go through with the divorce?" she asked quietly.

Liliana gave her a flat smile. "He told you about that, did he? Yes, I think we are. I can't fight him any longer. I've made so many thoughtless mistakes, and now it's too late to make up for them."

Talia wondered if she would elaborate. Feigning nonchalance, she took a sip from her own mug, hoping to elicit a bit more info from Liliana.

"You may as well know. I . . . cheated on Will. When we were first married, he traveled a lot on business, trying to make a name for himself buying up commercial property. I couldn't bear it when he was gone. I felt so horribly alone." She choked back a sob, although Talia wasn't sure it was genuine. She suspected Liliana had a touch of the dramatic in her.

"I can understand that," Talia said. *Not the cheating part, though*.

"I followed in my mother's footsteps," Liliana went on, her tone filled with regret. "When I was sixteen, she left Daddy and me for some gigolo she met at the tennis club. I'm afraid I did pretty much the same thing to Will, except for the leaving part."

Talia shifted in her chair. "How long have you and Will been together? I mean, you know . . ."

"We were married twenty-two years ago," she said, her eyes glazing over. "Will desperately wanted a child, and at first I went along with it. Then one day when I was shopping, I saw a woman struggling to soothe a screaming infant. The baby's face was covered in drool, and a ripe smell was coming from its diaper." She made a face. "God forgive me, but I just couldn't see myself doing that. I faced a hard truth that day—I wasn't cut out to be a mother. Without telling Will, I did something unforgivable. I went to my doctor, and he . . . made sure I could never get pregnant."

Talia didn't know what to say. The baby part she got. Motherhood wasn't for everyone. But going behind Will's back to ensure she'd never get pregnant? There was no way Talia could empathize with that.

"I had to tell him eventually," Liliana said. "Our *efforts*"— she made air quotes—"to get pregnant weren't working, and he wanted us to have tests. That was the beginning of the end," she said sadly. "In a way, I guess I deserved it."

The door crashed open, saving Talia from coming up with a response. Skateboard tucked under his arm, Lucas tripped inside, freezing when he saw that Talia wasn't alone. "Oh, um, sorry about that," he said, blushing to the tips of his ears.

"Good morning, Lucas," Talia said. She noticed that Liliana was grinning broadly at him.

Lucas mumbled a greeting and shot into the kitchen. Talia heard his skateboard clang against the back wall, where he always propped it.

The noise didn't seem to bother Liliana. "My, what a *handsome* young man," she purred.

Talia felt herself tense. Lucas was nineteen! She couldn't seriously be interested in him, could she?

Oh, chill, she told herself. Liliana was only paying him a compliment. Besides, Lucas *was* handsome, even if he was still a teenager who tripped over his own shoelaces every five minutes.

Liliana slipped her arms into her wool coat and rose. "I'm sorry if I bent your ear too long," she said. "You've been very patient with me." From her deep, slanted pocket she removed a Coach wallet that was a gorgeous shade of teal. "What do I owe you for your generosity?"

"Nothing," Talia said. "It was our pleasure, and I enjoyed our chat. I hope you'll visit again when you can sample our fish and chips, or some of our other deep-fried treats." She walked Liliana to the door and stepped out onto the plaza with her. "Liliana, this might sound like a strange question, but did Will ever refer to the two-headed snake on his ring as a dragon?"

Liliana's smooth brow furrowed for a moment. "A dragon? No, I don't think so, but he did call it something else. Amphis . . . amphee . . . something like that. Frankly, I never cared enough to remember it. Even one snake is too many for me."

"I'm with you there," Talia said. She made a mental note about the "amphis" or "amphee" name, hoping she could retain it long enough to Google it. She bade Liliana good-bye, watching as the woman strode over the cobblestone toward Main Street. Liliana seemed much steadier now, probably because she'd gotten some solid food into her.

Talia was waving a final good-bye when she saw Liliana turn and enter Sage & Seaweed.

Oh, boy. Suzy was in for a surprise.

17

The lunch orders were coming in almost faster than Talia could answer the phone.

"We are, like, slammed, Ms. Marby," Lucas said grimly. "I mean, it's great having the business, but—"

"I know, Lucas." Talia slung a slab of golden fried haddock into a takeout box, next to a container of mushy peas. "We're going to have to forgo delivery until we can figure out a better system. Today is out of the question." She added a slew of sizzling hot fries, closed the box, and shoved it into a brown bag, attaching a slip with the customer's name to the top.

His large hands covered in disposable gloves, Lucas lowered two handfuls of hand-cut potatoes into the deep fryer. Talia squeezed past him, wincing as Lucas sucked in his breath to let her pass. Her arm bumped his, and one of the fry baskets jiggled. Sparks of hot oil flew up and landed on Lucas's already bruised wrist.

"Lucas, I'm so sorry," Talia cried. "Are you all right?"

Grimacing, Lucas rubbed discreetly at a spot on his wrist. "Yeah, don't worry. It's okay, I barely felt it," he said.

Talia gently took his hand and examined it. A dime-sized red welt was forming on the inside of his wrist. "You are not okay. Take off your glove and run some cold water over it while I get some salve and a Band-Aid."

"Really, Ms. Marby. It's only—"

Talia felt her hands shaking. "Please do as I say, Lucas." She dug out the first aid kit from underneath the sink.

Lucas did as instructed, and then patted his wrist dry with a clean paper towel. Talia applied some anesthetizing ointment and then covered the burn with the largest Band-Aid she could find in the kit.

"You're, like, really pale, Ms. Marby." Lucas said nervously. "Honestly, it's only a tiny burn. You're not going to pass out, are you?"

Behind her, Talia heard a snort. She poured herself a glass of water and gulped it down, then pressed the side of the glass to her forehead. "I'm not going to pass out, Lucas, but why don't you go home. Martha and I can take over. Once the lunch crush is over, it won't be bad."

"No way," he protested. "You need me here, and my wrist doesn't even hurt."

Talia looked at him and suppressed a smile. Lucas had never stood up to her before. "All right. But if it starts to throb, I want you to tell me right away, okay?"

He crossed his heart with his forefinger. "I promise."

Martha eyed her balefully. "Still think we have enough room in here?"

Squelching a retort, Talia glanced out at the dining area. Nearly all the tables were occupied. Business was booming!

"You and I will talk later," she said quietly to Martha.

They made it through the crunch without any further accidents. As kitchen burns went, Lucas's was fairly minor, but it made Talia sick to think how much worse it could've been. A few times, she'd caught him touching the tender area with his fingertips and wincing—a sure sign that it hurt more than he was saying. Around one thirty, she insisted that he go home.

After he left, she took a mini-break with a mug of coffee and a small hunk of deep-fried haddock. Martha bustled around the dining area clearing the tables. Normally she would plop herself at the table with Talia and take a few minutes to have lunch. Her grim mood today had apparently squashed her appetite.

Talia sighed. If Martha quit, it would be yet another problem to deal with. She had to admit that with the added menu items, their kitchen had grown somewhat chaotic. Not to mention that the extra fryer she'd had to install reduced some of the precious food prep area.

She hadn't thought it all through very well, had she? What kind of a restaurateur was she? Was she one of the ones doomed to fail? Would she be another sad statistic in the column of those who just couldn't cut it?

By two thirty or so, things had drifted into a lull. Grateful for the quiet time, Talia began wiping down tables and chairs to prepare for the supper crowd. She was just returning her spray bottle to the shelf underneath the counter when the entrance door swung open. In stepped Scott Pollard, looking as fine as ever in a long-sleeved gray polo shirt and crisp, form-fitting jeans that looked hand-tailored just for him. Talia would swear the man ironed his jeans! He sauntered up to the blue-speckled counter and leaned his muscular arms over it. "Hey," he said with a wide grin.

"Hey, yourself, Scott!" Talia returned his grin. "It's great to see you again."

"So, what does the chef recommend today?" He leaned his chin on the palm of his hand and searched her face with glittering brown eyes.

His intense stare making her squirm a little, Talia pulled an order pad from the pocket of her blue apron. She pasted on a perky smile. "The chef recommends our classic fish and chips meal, complete with tangy slaw, mushy peas, and our home-made tartar sauce."

He slapped the counter lightly. "Sounds like a plan. Hey, you got a minute to talk while your pretty gal over there whips up my order?" He winked at Martha.

Martha smiled sweetly at him. "Coming right up, sir."

Grateful that Scott's exaggerated flattery hadn't set Martha off, she led him over to the table near the restroom—the same one Liliana Claiborne had occupied only a few hours earlier.

Scott rested his arms on the table, concern etched on his features. "I take it you still haven't seen Andy Nash, right?" he said in a low voice.

"No, I haven't." She debated whether or not to tell him that Detective Prescott had inquired about him, too. Instead, she turned the tables on him. "Why?" she said. "Have the police been asking you about him?"

After a long sigh, Scott nodded. "Yeah, and the longer he stays away, the guiltier he looks. Man, I wish I knew where he was. I'd make him march right into the police station and tell them he's innocent!" He ran his fingers through his short blond hair.

Talia wondered if Scott knew how naïve he sounded. The authorities didn't cross your name off their suspect list simply because you proclaimed your innocence. The state police certainly weren't chumps, nor was Detective Prescott.

Scott scratched underneath his left forearm. "Is it hot in here, or is it me?" he said.

Talia laughed. "The restaurant's always toasty because of the kitchen. In the summer we really have to crank the AC." She realized that she'd never seen Scott wear a jacket. He must be one of those people who hated being too warm.

He chuckled. "I can't stand summer. Love it when the weather turns cold." He pushed up his left sleeve and scratched his arm again. "Course it doesn't help that every winter I get a case of eczema on this one arm, especially the elbow. Never get it on the other one. I think it's because I use my right hand when I'm working, while my left is usually resting on something."

Talia almost giggled out loud when she spied the tat that stretched along his left forearm. The image was of a swash-buckling pirate, complete with a plumed purple hat and an evil-looking 'stache.

Scott noticed her staring and grinned. "You like it? It's Captain Hook, from *Peter Pan*."

"Oh gosh, I should have recognized him," Talia said. "The . . . artist did a good job."

"When I was a kid, I played the role of the good captain in a school play. I swear, it was about the most fun I ever had. After that it kind of stuck with me, you know? Mostly because the other kids never let me forget it. So when I was sixteen, I got this tat done, much to my father's dismay. I thought he'd kill me when he saw it!" Scott laughed and tugged his sleeve down. "Ah, the things we do when we're young, right?" He sat back and folded his arms over his chest, his brown-eyed gaze deepening. "So, um, what do you say? Wanna be my Peter Pan?"

Talia shifted uncomfortably on her chair. Feeling a blush creep into her cheeks, she waved a hand at him. "Scott, you're such a teaser," she said. "Let me check on your fish and chips, okay?" She nearly tripped over her own foot leaping off the chair.

In the kitchen, Martha was just sliding his crispy fried haddock into a lined cone. She finished preparing the meal, and Talia plunked it all onto a tray, along with a glass of ice water. When she delivered it to his table, she saw that he was talking on his cell, the lines around his eyes creased with annoyance. "I told you," he said tightly, "I'm having lunch. I'll call you when I'm free." He disconnected and grinned up at Talia.

Using the excuse that she wanted to let him enjoy his meal in peace, Talia dashed back into the kitchen. Martha, staying unusually silent, was busy preparing herself a small snack of fries and coleslaw. Talia had told her the day she hired her that she could eat whatever she wanted, so long as it didn't interfere with her job.

"Hey, that was terrific," Scott said, strolling up to the counter. He picked up the short stack of menus that rested there and straightened them. "Best meal I've had in a long time." He paid the bill, and with a wink handed Martha a fiver.

"Sir, that's not—" Martha started to say, but Scott shook his head.

"You take it," he said in a kindhearted tone. "You're a wonderful cook."

Talia resisted an eye-roll. Was he genuine, or was he laying it on a little too thick? Well, what did it matter? Martha got a nice tip out of the deal.

Scott slid his business card across the counter. "Talia, I'm serious. If you ever need any renovations done, please give me a call, okay? I'm booked up through the end of the year, but I can always make room for you, depending on how big the job is."

"Thanks, Scott. I appreciate that."

He waved a cheery good-bye and left. With a sigh of relief, Talia tucked his card in her purse.

"He's got the hots for you, you know," Martha quipped, carrying her plate over to the table in the corner of the kitchen. She dropped onto one of the chairs with a thud.

"Don't be silly." Talia turned away so Martha wouldn't see her cheeks burning. "After you finish eating, I think we need to talk."

"We can talk right now." Martha shoveled a forkful of slaw into her mouth.

Talia took a deep breath and sat down opposite her employee. She folded her hands over the table, feeling oddly like a schoolteacher about to give a stern lecture to a student. "Martha," she said in a deliberate tone. "What happened today with Lucas made me realize how short on space we really are in here. You're absolutely right about that. The problem is, there's nothing I can do about it. I can't wave a magic wand and make the kitchen bigger, can I?"

Martha shrugged. "Nope." She popped a crispy fry into her mouth.

"So we're all going to have to learn to work around it. We'll do the best we can, okay?"

Martha wiped her fingers on a napkin. "Do you know what I did in my old job?"

"I know you worked for a national insurance company," Talia said, her patience waning.

"I was a leasing expert and a space planner," Martha said. "The company had offices in all fifty states, plus one in Puerto Rico. Every time they downsized—or upsized when times were good—it was my job to find and design the right office space for them. The company had formulas for how much office or cube space each employee could have. No one liked it, but they had to live with it. If they were allowed an office that was six by eight, then by George, that's what they got. My job was to squeeze it all in and make everyone happy in the allotted office space."

"It sounds very challenging," Talia said, already losing interest. "But I don't see—"

"No, you don't, and that's because you're only half listening."

Talia looked at her, openmouthed. "I . . . I—"

"Do you know why I got fired?"

Talia shook her head.

"One of the offices in the northwest region was cutting their employees from nine to six. Real nice for those folks who got axed, huh?" Her voice had an edge to it.

"I'm sure it was terrible for them," Talia said. She'd witnessed similar job cuts when she worked as a property manager in Boston. It was so sad, watching longtime employees clean out their desks while someone stood over them to be sure they didn't trash anything.

"It *was* terrible," Martha said levelly, "and it was all because the head honcho of that office was the bright-eyed offspring of the witch on wheels who supervised the entire region. Rumor had it that in order to increase her son's salary to the level she felt he deserved, she had to sacrifice those other jobs. Well, let me tell you—it was more than rumor. I got it from a very good source."

"But that's so unfair!" Talia threw her arms up.

"Darn right it was. Especially since the guy didn't know a casualty policy from his a—"

"Martha."

"From his ankle," Martha said, fire in her eyes. "Anyway, when he discovered that his new office was going to be the company-allotted fourteen-by-ten jail cell, he threw an all-out tantrum. E-mailed me forty times a day cussing me out. Demanded I submit a new floor plan for the office. Day after day, I ignored him. Finally the jerk calls me up on the phone one day and rips me a new one."

Talia leaned forward. "I hope you stood your ground, Martha."

"Oh, I stood it all right. I told him right where he could shove his complaints, and believe me, I didn't mince words."

Talia smiled. "I'm sure you didn't," she said, and then her smile faded. "That's why you got fired, isn't it?"

Martha nodded, and a rare blush colored her cheeks. "You figured that out, huh? Good. Now that I've gotten all that off my chest, I have something to give you." She hoisted herself off her chair and went over to her peacoat. From the right-hand pocket she pulled out a folded sheet of paper.

Oh, no, it's her resignation.

Talia watched silently as Martha unfolded the paper and smoothed it out. It was large enough to be the Declaration of Independence, so it had to be one heck of a resignation letter.

Martha sat again and spread the paper out before her. It took Talia a minute to realize what she was looking at—it was a sketch of the eatery's kitchen, except that everything was out of place. "I've been spending my evenings playing around with this," Martha said, "and I've come up with a floor plan I think will work."

"You . . . did this at home?" Talia said, stunned.

"Yep. Cut into my reading time, too," she griped. "Now look here." She plunked a finger on the sketch. "The biggest elephant in the room is the fridge. It's right opposite the main work counter. Every time someone opens it, which is about six hundred times a day, it shortens the gap to about a foot. That's why we're always doing the samba to get around each other in here. And let me tell you"—she jabbed a finger at her own chest—"this chick don't dance."

Suppressing a chuckle, Talia studied the sketch. Martha had obviously put a lot of thought into redesigning the kitchen—on paper, at least. She'd apparently taken measurements of everything when Talia wasn't looking, because the dimensions were printed neatly on every single item. "So you'd put the fridge over there, next to the storage closet?"

"Darn right I would," Martha said. "It's the only logical place for it. And this table"—she slapped the table top—"needs to go. It never fit into this space anyway. A round table would work better, and it would leave room for us to add three narrow lockers for our coats and personal doodads. *And* our skateboards, should we have one," she added with a wink. "Those coat hooks on the door are an eyesore. They definitely need to go. Like they say in the NFL, you've run out of real estate."

Talia didn't know what to say. Martha had obviously given the layout of the kitchen a lot of thought. Still, something about the sketch was off, something she couldn't quite put her finger on.

"Now here's the part you won't like," Martha said, as if she'd read Talia's mind. "In order to make this work, you're gonna need to cut into the rear of the dining area by about a foot and a half. The good thing is, you can do it without losing any vital dining space. That table, the one where Scott was just sitting? Right now it seats four, but if you replaced it with a smaller one where one or two people could sit, you'd have plenty of room for the buildout. Ever notice sometimes when a lone customer comes in, how they look around for a corner table so they won't feel self-conscious eating alone?"

Talia mulled it over. She realized Martha was right. When she worked in downtown Boston, she'd eaten lunch alone in restaurants hundreds of times. She'd always felt more comfortable sitting at a small corner table than somewhere in the center of the room.

Wow, Martha had really thought this through. Talia was impressed. Her gaze skimmed the sketch for a few more minutes. Martha had even allowed space for a second work-table where the nonfish foods could be prepped.

"One last thing," Martha said. "I know you're fond of those captain's chairs in the dining area. They remind you of an old English fish and chips shop, *blah blah blah*. But not only are they a pain to clean every day—they take up too much space."

"But Bea loved those chairs!" Talia protested, somewhat miffed at Martha's comment.

"I know," Martha said, "and I understand your loyalty to her. But she turned this place over to you because she loves you and trusts you to do the right thing." Her voice grew quiet. "I get that you want to follow in Bea's footsteps. But that doesn't mean you can't squish your feet around in them and make them a little bigger, does it?"

Talia smiled. Sometimes Martha had a way of cutting right to the core.

Martha flipped over the sketch of the kitchen. "I wrote down a few links for you to check out when you have a chance. You can get some funky-looking restaurant chairs that are sleek and easy to care for, plus they're a lot smaller.

They'd be a nice contrast to the wooden tables, and they'd go with your new theme. I bet you could sell those captain's chairs, easy."

"Martha, I don't know what to say," Talia said. "All of this"—she tapped the sketch and then folded it neatly—"tells me that you really like this job and want to stay." She pushed back the lump blossoming in her throat.

"Of course I want to stay." Martha looked incensed. "Why would you think I didn't?"

Instead of responding, Talia said, "Martha, why did you leave New Hampshire? Why didn't you just look for a different job there?"

"I did look. *Believe* me, I looked. None of the jobs I could've had would have paid anywhere near what I'd been getting."

"Okay, I get that, but . . . that doesn't explain why you left the state," Talia said quietly. "I'm sure what you're earning here doesn't even come close to the money you were making. Do you have family around here?"

Martha's face fell, and she broke eye contact with Talia. "No, my only family was there," she said, in a voice Talia could barely hear. "I had a foster child, a sweet, bright, beautiful girl named Dakota. She's fifteen now. After I lost my job, I couldn't support her anymore. Not the way I had before anyway."

Talia felt her jaw slowly drop. Martha, with a foster child? The woman who claimed she stayed as far away from kids as possible?

"She didn't want to leave, but I told the social worker I wouldn't be able to take care of her anymore. Not on unemployment. The state helps out with foster care, of course, but it's nowhere near enough to raise a kid. And my prospects for a decent job weren't looking too good. I'm old, you know—"

"Stop it with that old stuff, Martha," Talia said. "You might not be as limber as you used to be, but you're very smart, and you have more energy than most thirty-year-olds."

"Thanks, I guess." Her shoulders sagged. The forlorn look in her eyes was heart-wrenching. "Anyway, I don't think Dakota will ever forgive me. But I only wanted what was best for her. If there was a way I could've made it work, I would have, but . . ." She broke off, as if her mind was coasting backward to her old, happier life. She swiped a hand quickly over her right eye. "She's with a good family now, with some foster sibs. That's all that matters."

Talia's heart jerked in her chest. So many little things fell into place. Martha drawing animal faces with mustard and marinara for the little ones she'd thought were "too quiet." And wearing that silly green frog hat at the fund-raiser.

The truth was, Martha loved kids.

"Is that why you bought that nutty green hat Sunday? To amuse the kids?"

Martha frowned, and her face went into the red zone. "Uh . . . no, not exactly. You know that Ria woman, the one who was murdered?" She grimaced slightly.

"Yesss . . ." Talia said slowly.

"Well, I, um, didn't want her to recognize me."

Talia wasn't sure if she wanted to hear this, but she rolled her hand in a *tell me everything* motion.

"That morning, I think I told you, I had to park about a block away because I couldn't fit into any of those dinky spaces behind the community center. Anyway, I *kind of sort of* brushed the back end of another car when I was parallel parking on the street behind the lot."

Talia tried unsuccessfully to picture that scene in her head. It must have been like parallel parking a Coast Guard cutter. "Oh, no, don't tell me. Ria saw you, right?"

"Yeah, but I didn't realize it at first. I was getting ready to leave the driver a note when I saw her go slowly past me in a red car. I didn't know who she was, but she glared at me and made a nasty face, like she was memorizing my mug for a lineup. I figured she'd go straight to the cops and report me, so I whipped out of that space and took off. I had to park another block away."

"So you never left the driver the note?" Talia asked her.

"No," she said glumly, "but I keep looking out for that car. I really do want to pay for the damage. I just don't want to report it to my insurance company—I've got too many points on my record now. If my premiums get any higher, I'll have to live in the freakin' car.

"Anyway, when I saw that same woman come in to the gym—I couldn't miss that red hair—and plunk her stuff on the table next to ours, I almost popped an artery. I was terrified she'd recognize me, so I did the only thing I could think of—I bought a disguise."

Talia smiled and shook her head. "Martha, you never cease to amaze me. Your creativity knows no bounds."

"My sneakiness, you mean." Martha snorted.

"And I appreciate all the work you did on this floor plan. But even if I agreed with everything, I'm not sure if I can afford the renovations right now. Plus, we'd have to close for at least a week."

Martha shrugged. "Look, I hear you, sister. I never said it would be easy. Course there might be someone local who can help. Someone who specializes in that sort of thing." She winked at Talia. "Bet he'd give you a fair price, too."

Talia felt a rush of heat go directly to her cheeks. She was obviously talking about Scott Pollard. "Well, that's out of the question. I'm pretty sure he only does home renovations."

"Maybe." Martha eased herself out of her chair. "But you won't know until you ask, will you?"

They quickly cleaned up the table. There was one more thing bugging Talia, something she had to ask. "Martha, did you always drive that car, the one you have now?"

Martha chuckled. "No. Cars have never been my thing, but I did have a decent set of wheels—a Nissan. When I lost my job, I sold it for a cheaper car. It gave me a few more months' padding while I looked for another job. Plus, I wanted some extra cash to start a savings account. If I'd known the way that monstrosity sucks gas, I'd never have bought it. It was really a dumb thing to do."

Martha had obviously needed the cash to pay living expenses, Talia thought sadly. But why the savings account?

"When I look at your face, I can tell exactly what you're thinking," Martha said, a glint of humor in her eye. "It's getting so I can read you like a book. Look, I never saved much money. I didn't even participate in the 401(k). I gave most of my discretionary income, as they say, to causes I favored." She shook her head. "I guess it was shortsighted of me."

"So you started a savings account a bit late in life," Talia said. "There's nothing wrong with that."

"Yeah, but it's not for me," Martha explained. "I opened the savings account for Dakota, for when she goes to college. She doesn't know about it. I'm not going to give it to her till she turns eighteen." Martha closed her eyes and squeezed the bridge of her nose. In a voice so tiny it was almost a whisper, she added, "It was the least I could do for her. Selling the car was the only way I could do it."

With that, Talia lost it. She turned and sprinted into the restroom, sat on the commode, and cried until no more tears would come. All this time she'd been calling Martha a grump and a complainer, poking fun at that ridiculous car she drove. Turns out she was probably the most unselfish person Talia had ever met.

Get it together, Talia scolded herself. *Stop being such a crybaby.*

Five minutes later, she ran the cold water and splashed it over her eyes and cheeks, and then dried her face with paper towels. With her puffy eyes and red nose, she looked like a wreck, but there was no way to hide it—not without a jar of pancake makeup and a garden trowel. By now Martha probably figured she'd fallen into the drain.

She returned to the kitchen, avoiding Martha's line of vision. Martha, the batter queen, was already whipping up another batch of Parmesan batter for the meatballs. This past week, Talia noticed that the supper hour had been getting a little busier. In addition to needing more space, Talia was beginning to wonder if they would need to hire another employee. Lucas was only part time. He loved doing lunchtime deliveries, and it made sense to offer the service to her loyal customers.

As for the kitchen itself, should she contact Scott about getting an estimate for renovations? Would he even consider doing commercial work? She'd probably have to take out a small loan, but with business doing so well—fingers crossed—it might just be doable.

Well, she didn't have to make a decision today, did she?

It would be something to think about after the holidays were over. For now they were getting by, making do.

"Talia," Martha said in a quiet voice, "there's one more thing I have to tell you."

Uh-oh. Now Martha was scaring her. "Do I really want to hear it?"

"Probably not, but I have to tell you anyway. It was me who spilled the raspberry sauce on the scarf that strangled Ria."

"What?" Talia gasped.

Martha sighed. "While you were taking a break that day, we had a tiny lull in business. I was starving, so I made myself a snack and drenched it with raspberry sauce. Ria had left to go to the bathroom, I guess. I was dying to look at her stuff so I moseyed over there. The scarf was so pretty I fingered it. I didn't realize I had sauce on my thumb. I tried to wipe it off, but that only made it worse."

Talia shook her head and chuckled. "Forget about it, Martha. That raspberry sauce proves nothing. And I know you didn't kill Ria."

"I'll tell the cops if you want me to," Martha said meekly.

"No," Talia said. "Let's let sleeping sauces lie, okay?"

Martha looked relieved. "That sentence doesn't really make sense, but I'll accept it."

After Martha left, Talia stuck the floor plan in her purse so that she could peruse it later at home, maybe tweak it here and there. Ryan was cooking dinner at his condo for her this evening. She was so looking forward to spending a relaxing (romantic!) evening with him. Maybe she'd bring the drawing with her and get his opinion.

The *romantic* part was scaring her a little. So far, Ryan

hadn't pressured her, but she knew he yearned for a more intimate relationship. Well, she did, too, but she also needed to feel ready to take that step. She'd left Chet only four months earlier. Not that she was mourning their split, but in her mind they'd been on the cusp of marriage. Being alone was something she was still getting used to.

To her surprise, she was finding that she enjoyed evenings alone with her cat. She could read to her heart's content, eat Cheerios for supper, and indulge in whatever she wanted to watch on TV. With Chet they were always on the go—dining out with his friends or his co-workers, or going to sporting events she had no interest in. Relaxing evenings at home had been few and far between.

Now that she'd bought Nana's charming bungalow, Talia craved the chance to be on her own for a while. She'd already added a few personal touches to the house, but had a lot more in mind. Which reminded her, she still needed to pick up some Christmas decorations. Something for the front door, at least.

The one thing marring her contented mood was that Ria's killer was still out there. She wished the police had made more progress. The investigation seemed to be in limbo, at least the parts she was privy to. Andy Nash was still missing. Was he on the run from the police?

The dragon thing was driving Talia crazy. Most likely it had nothing to do with the murder, but she wished she knew for sure. What had Liliana called the two-headed snake? Amphis? Amphee?

She had to remember to Google it as soon as she got home. Either that or ask Ryan for help.

18

"I think I found what you're looking for," Ryan said, sliding his finger over his iPad.

They were nestled on Ryan's leather sofa, arms touching, Talia sipping a glass of buttery chardonnay. She'd brought him up to speed on the week's events, including her encounter with Liliana Claiborne.

Sitting here with Ryan in his condo, the faux oak blinds shutting out the shadows of the night and his bronze torchère lamp casting a soft glow over the room, she could almost believe that her life was perfect.

One glance at Ryan's iPad and she snapped back to reality. Nearly a week had gone by since Ria's death, and her killer was still free. She bolted upright and plopped her wineglass on the coffee table, which was actually an old restored steamer trunk. "You found the snake, I see." Her voice rose in pitch.

"A two-headed snake is easy to find—it's the dragon connection I'm looking for. This website—who knows how reliable it is?—makes reference to the fact that some people think the concept of a dragon originally came from serpents."

"I guess that makes sense," she said with a slight shudder. "They all look pretty scaly and slimy. Is there anything about an *amphis* or an *amphee*?"

Ryan's swiped his fingers over the tablet with quick, expert moves. "I think this is the word we're looking for. *Amphisbaena*—I have no idea how to pronounce it—is a two-headed serpent. According to this, there's a head on each end."

Talia shivered twice, once for each head. "But there's no such thing, right? I mean, there can't really be a two-headed snake?"

Ryan cleared his throat. "Um, sorry to burst your bubble, but I'm looking at one right now. And it's not only an image—it's a real photograph. The difference is that both heads are at the same end." He read for a few seconds, the dimple in his cheek deepening as he concentrated on the photo. "This article says that two-headed snakes are very rare, but they do occur in nature. It happens when the snake embryo in the egg doesn't fully divide and doesn't separate properly from its twin."

Talia took a fast peek and then turned away. "All I can say is ugh. Ugh times two." How could a snake have two heads? Wasn't one head bad enough? It was like a creature out of a nightmare.

Ryan continued flying through the images on his tablet. "There are some great depictions of two-headed dragons, but obviously they're the product of creative imaginations. Snakes and dragons are two different things. Snakes are real. Dragons are not."

Talia knew Ryan wasn't patronizing her. He was only emphasizing a point—there was no such thing as a dragon.

She sat back and thought for a moment. Anita had referred to the dragon as a *filament* of Ria's imagination. She'd probably meant *figment*, but either way, she was saying that the dragon wasn't real.

Of course it wasn't. Dragons didn't exist. But Anita had said something else. Something about—

"Wings." Talia sat up straighter. "Anita said that Ria's dragon didn't have wings. Are they supposed to?"

She peeked over Ryan's arm while he flipped through several more images. "Looks like most of them do. But remember, she was a little girl. She was drawing what she supposedly saw, and what she saw looked like a dragon."

It looked like a dragon. But what if it wasn't?

"Ryan, could Will Claiborne have thought of his family crest as a dragon, some sort of hybrid creature with two heads? He never used the word *dragon* when he showed me his ring, but now I'm beginning to wonder."

"Sure, anything's possible." Ryan shook his head. "But the real question, in my opinion, is why he would want to murder the woman he loved. Or claimed he loved."

Claimed he loved.

"That's the part that doesn't make sense." Talia groaned. "I've thought about it every which way, and I can't come up with any possible motive. He loved her, Ryan. Her death crushed him. That's why he can't be guilty, no matter how many snake heads are on his family crest!"

Ryan regarded her seriously. "So, Hercule, are you crossing him off your suspect list?"

She loved the way he pronounced "Hercule." Very Belgian.

"*Trés* amusing," she quipped. "But I can't exactly see myself sporting a waxed mustache and lecturing people about little gray cells, can you?" She grinned up at him, loving the way his eyes shone through his rimless glasses.

"Hmmm, not sure about the little gray cells part, but I'm willing to test the mustache theory." With a tender smile, he slid one arm over her shoulders and then leaned in and kissed her, drawing it out until every nerve in her body tingled. "Nope. I'll take you without the 'stache anytime. All the time," he added softly.

Talia's heart drummed in her chest. She felt sure that if she tried to stand, her knees would morph into two puddles of vanilla rice pudding.

Ryan touched her cheek. "Honey, I'm a little worried that you're getting so involved in finding Ria's killer. I keep thinking about what happened the last time."

Talia looked into his face and her heart melted. "I know, Ryan, and I get it." *And I love you for it.* "But what happened last time was a total fluke. Wrong place, wrong time, remember?" She said it lightly, hoping to deflect his concern. "And I'm not really trying to find her killer. Can I help it if people keep confiding in me about their troubles?" Her voice ended in a squeak, a sure sign that she was fibbing a little. "Okay, I guess I do want to find Ria's killer. Or at least steer the police in the right direction," she added quietly.

Ryan sighed. "It's just that you seem to be talking to all sorts of people who had reasons to hate Ria. Didn't you say Andy Nash was furious when she canceled their date? And now he's missing?"

"It is strange that he took a powder," Talia said. She bit her lip. "Either he's guilty and he's running from the police, or he saw something that day . . ." She let the thought drift off.

"And your landlord's wife seems a little unstable. She knew her husband wanted to marry Ria, so she definitely had a motive. You can't cross her off the list."

A list? Did she even have a list?

"And what about Kelsey? From the way you described your conversations with her, she had plenty of reasons to hate Ria."

Talia shook her head. She still couldn't see Kelsey as a killer. How could anyone who loved cats the way Kelsey did harm a human being?

"And, of course, there's Will." Talia blew out a sigh. "I can't get that ugly family crest out of my head. Now that I know there really is a two-headed snake, I'll probably have nightmares about it."

"You said Ria's mother has a boyfriend. Could he have killed Ria out of jealousy? Maybe because he wanted her mother all to himself?"

"No, and if you'd met Anita, you'd know why I say that. She made it pretty clear that the man in her life, whoever it was, always came first. I think Ria grew up as a very lonely child."

Ryan looked away, his frown deepening. Was he thinking of his own mother? Talia knew she had a PhD in economics and was steeped in the world of academia. Even in the family photos that lined the mantel over Ryan's fake fireplace, her face wore an air of bored resignation. Thank heaven for Ryan's dad, a kind and intelligent man who doted on his son.

"I know this sounds like an empty request," Ryan said, anxiety etched in his voice, "but will you promise me that you'll be extra careful?"

Talia leaned over and kissed him on the nose. "I promise, and I'm not just paying you lip service. I don't want anything to happen to me, either. You'll be happy to know I've been remembering to keep my cell charged, and I have you on speed dial, so to speak."

"Good." He took her hand and squeezed it gently. "And now, speaking of lip service, I have a great idea."

His eyes twinkling, he led her into the kitchen. A delectable aroma was seeping from the oven, something cheesy and creamy and down home delicious. The round white table was set with dark blue stoneware. Cloth napkins the color of burnished gold graced the left side of each plate, and a set of utensils had been carefully placed in the center. At the back of the table rested a white tile trivet that had a charming picture of an English castle.

Ryan pulled out a chair for her. "Every time you've eaten here, I've served either fast-food Chinese or pizza." He gave her a sober look. "Truth is—scary music, please—I'm a terrible cook." He pulled two wineglasses from a sleek-looking oak hutch at the back of the kitchen and set them on the table. Then he opened a fresh bottle of chardonnay and filled each of the glasses.

"Impossible," Talia said, inhaling deeply. "My nose tells me otherwise, and if it's working properly, you've made one of my favorite meals."

Ryan grinned. "Turns out it's one of my favorites, too. In fact, it's about the only thing I know how to make."

"Can I help?"

"Nope," he said. "You've worked hard enough cooking for the masses this week. It's my turn to serve you."

Ryan snagged two oven mitts off the side of the stainless steel fridge. He opened the oven and very carefully removed a vintage blue and gold casserole dish brimming with golden macaroni and cheese.

"My mom's recipe," he said, setting it down on the trivet.

"Ryan, that looks fantastic," Talia said.

"But wait, there's more!" Beaming, he whipped a prepared salad out of the fridge. "It has a hint of vinaigrette dressing, but I have plenty if you'd like more. I remembered that you didn't like dressing that overpowered."

Yet another thing she adored about Ryan. He listened to every word she said and filed it away for the future. With Chet, she could always tell that his eyes were glazing over after three or four sentences of "how was your day" chatter during dinner. After that, she might as well have talked to the utensils hanging on the rack next to the stove. She'd learned to keep her part of their conversations short and snappy.

"I was going to make some mini-burgers—my only other specialty—but I thought it would be too much."

"They would have been delicious, but I think you're right."

"Yeah, I'll save those for another night," he said. "But we can't have a meal without rolls, can we?" He reached into the oven again and removed a foil-wrapped mound. "Now I didn't bake these from scratch, but they're pretty good. Do you like Parker House rolls?"

"Yum. Who doesn't?" Gazing over the goodies on the table, she felt her taste buds dancing. More than that, she felt her heart swelling for this adorable man who'd gone through so much trouble to please her.

Ryan sat opposite Talia and held up his wineglass. "To you, sweetheart," he said huskily. "May we enjoy many, many more evenings together like this one."

Talia sensed he wanted to say more, but she was grateful he'd kept it light. They clinked their glasses together and dug into the food. "Ryan, this mac and cheese is unbelievable," she said after swallowing a cheesy mouthful.

"Oh, phew, thank God you like it!" He smiled at her. "Like I said, it's my mother's recipe. She calls it the busy woman's mac and cheese. Instead of preparing a cheese sauce, you just slice squares of cheddar and layer them between the cooked shells. Then you pour whole milk over it all and bake it. It's amazing how it makes its own cheese sauce while it's baking." His smile faded. "Mom was never much for making meals, or even for doing things together as a family. Academia was her main gig. Still is."

Ryan had hinted before that his mother had been somewhat distant. It made Talia appreciate her own mom and dad even more.

The mac and cheese was filling, but absolutely scrumptious. The squares of cheese on top had hardened to a golden crisp. Ideas began sparking in Talia's brain. Could she deep-fry squares of baked macaroni and cheese? Hadn't she seen that on a cooking show?

After dinner, Ryan plunked everything into the dishwasher. He offered her some ice cream, but Talia was too full to eat another bite. The evening so far had been wonderful— almost too good to be true. The lights low, they sat on the sofa for a while and watched television, although none of the shows tickled either of their fancies. She felt tension building inside her, roaring through her bloodstream like a waterfall. If Ryan asked her to, should she stay?

Ryan muted the television and tossed aside the remote. He pulled her close, and she sank into his arms. It felt so right, so perfect. It felt like the forever place she was always meant to be.

"I've been meaning to tell you," he said, plopping a kiss on her nose. "You smell really nice this evening. New perfume?"

Yay! He'd noticed her new scent—her "barely there" spritz of the green tea fragrance she'd bought from Suzy. "I'm glad you like it," she said, grateful that she'd splurged on it.

Finally, when Ryan was holding her so tightly her breath caught in her chest, he loosened his grip. "I think it's time I drove you home," he said hoarsely, kissing her forehead.

A surge of relief, mixed with disappointment, swelled through her. She'd almost forgotten that he'd picked her up and would have to deliver her back to her bungalow.

Ryan was helping her slip into her jacket when she said, "Oh, Ryan, I almost forgot. Can I show you something Martha did today?"

"Of course!"

Talia fished Martha's sketch out of her purse and showed it to Ryan, giving him a brief rundown of Martha's complaints about the setup of the kitchen. She wanted to tell him more about her conversation with Martha, but if she stayed there much longer, she knew she'd never leave.

Ryan spread out the paper and studied the sketch. Talia could almost see the wheels in his head turning, his analytical mind taking in every detail. "She's a savvy lady," Ryan pronounced. "She knows her stuff. And I agree that you'll need to build out into the dining area to accomplish this. But"—he held up a finger—"in the meantime, you could still move the fridge and do some rearranging to make your work space roomier. I like the locker idea, too."

Talia wrinkled her nose. "That's the part I wasn't wild about. Won't it look like a high school locker room?"

"It doesn't have to. They make some lockers now that aren't all gray metal and ugly. You could get some very attractive ones that will be so unobtrusive they'll blend right into the background. Just thinking, though, you might need an electrical upgrade. You've already added another fryer, right?"

"Right, and I'm thinking about replacing the fridge with a more modern one. Bea bought the one I have so long ago I can't even remember how old it is!"

"Good idea, Tal. You'll save on energy, too. I think this is very doable, depending on your budget." He swallowed and held her gaze. "I'll do whatever I can to help, okay?" he added softly. "Just let me know what you need and I'm there."

Talia felt her throat well up. She didn't know if he was offering help with the buildout itself or with the financing, but all at once she was overwhelmed.

By the time she was back in her bungalow, thoughts were tumbling in her head like the objects in a kaleidoscope. As brilliant and stunning as the colors were, they were equally confusing.

Feeling thirsty, she poured herself a half glass of apple juice and gulped it back. She poked through her cupboards, anxiety making her itch for something to nibble on. Her shelves were looking pretty bare these days. She hardly ever had time to shop anymore, except to keep Bo supplied with cat food.

She plunked down on the sofa. Normally when she was in thinking mode, she'd grab one of her throw pillows and hug it to her chest. These days she had Bo, who made a much sweeter hugging pillow. She smiled when the little calico leaped onto her lap. Scratching Bo under the chin, she said, "What do you say, Bo? Should I renovate the kitchen at Fry Me? Should I take the plunge?"

She was avoiding the real question tripping through her head. *Should I have spent the night at Ryan's?*

Bo rubbed her head against Talia's arm and gave her a tiny lick. Right then, she made a decision.

Talia dug both her cell phone and Scott Pollard's business card out of her purse. She sent him a quick text, asking if they could get together sometime during the week to discuss possible renovations.

She was surprised when her phone buzzed about three minutes later. She'd figured he wouldn't respond until Monday, the next business day, but he'd already texted her back.

Totally jammed all week. U free tomorrow morning?

Tomorrow was Sunday. An idea was germinating in her brain, something that had been triggered by her conversation with Anita. Sunday morning was when she had planned to put it into action. She texted back.

Can u make 11:30 at the restaurant?

Scott's response was immediate.

Put on the coffee and I'll be there.

Talia was impressed. Quick service, and except for the "U," he didn't use typical text-speak. She texted Scott back, agreeing to make coffee and telling him to knock at the door when he got there so she could let him in.

She thought about texting Ryan and asking if he wanted to join them. His input could be immensely valuable.

With a resigned sigh, she set her phone aside. That would really be taking advantage, she decided. Ryan spent every

Sunday with his dad, Arthur, at the Wrensdale Pines. She definitely didn't want to cut into their time together.

She was an independent woman now, and a business owner. If she couldn't handle it herself, then she wasn't cut out to own a restaurant.

19

The two-family house on Hampton Avenue hadn't changed much since Talia had last seen it. She'd been a kid then, but in her memory it had always looked the same.

She parked her Fiat in front of the house, beneath the ancient oak where she'd once plunked her bike on a mission to rescue a stolen rabbit. A weird sensation shimmied up her arms. She had no idea who lived here now, but she was about to ask the owner if she could search one of the closets in the second-story apartment. How crazy was that?

Over the years, this dreary-looking abode had woven its way into the occasional dream. The house taunted her, like an unfinished story. The aftermath of the dreams was always an inexplicable sadness, a feeling that she'd failed at a task she'd been sworn to carry out.

Talia swung her legs out of her car, feeling the December chill sidle underneath her flared jacket. Why was she still wearing it anyway? She had a winter coat, all dry-cleaned and hanging in protective plastic in the bungalow's coat closet. It was a gorgeous coat, stunning and stylish in rich navy wool, with a round collar and deeply slit side pockets. Chet had bought it for her last Christmas.

She sighed and locked her car. She'd answered her own question, hadn't she? Anything even vaguely reminiscent of Chet bugged her these days. She'd kicked him out of her head and her heart, and she didn't want any reminders. The Coat d'Azure on Main Street had some great fashions for realistic prices. She vowed to squeeze an hour from one of her days this coming week and buy a new coat.

Talia stepped carefully over the cracked walkway leading to the sad-looking clapboard house. The narrow front porch sagged a little, and screamed for a fresh coat of paint. Painted a dull gray with a peeling charcoal trim, it bore the same tired look it had over thirty years ago.

Praying someone would be home, she climbed the porch stairs and studied the two buzzers adjacent to the front door. The lower buzzer was labeled WANGER, and the upper one read KINSLEA.

Ria and her mom had lived upstairs, so she pressed the upper button. A muted drone sounded in the distance, so the bell must be working. After three minutes or so when no one had answered, she pressed the buzzer again.

Underneath her flared jacket she was wearing the wine-colored pantsuit she'd bought when she was still working in Boston. With her crisp white blouse and her favorite lady-bug scarf tucked around her neck, she looked neat and professional—just in case she'd be invited to remove her jacket.

When no one answered the buzzer after the third try, she

blew out a disappointed sigh. She was about to press the lower button when she heard a key turn in the lock. The door slowly opened. An elderly woman, her gray hair pasted to her head with bobby pins, gaped at her through a pair of thick eyeglasses. Dressed in a ratty blue robe and sporting fuzzy slippers, she looked as if she'd just tumbled out of bed. "What do you want?" she said in a scratchy voice.

Talia pasted on a cheery smile. She'd practiced what she planned to say, but now it all seemed to have floated right out of her head. "Good morning, ma'am. My name is Talia Marby. I live here in Wrensdale. I own the deep-fry restaurant on the Wrensdale Arcade."

The woman frowned. "Never heard of it," she said, starting to close the door.

"Wait . . . please," Talia said. "May I come in for a moment? I promise not to stay long."

Suspicion flared in the old woman's faded blue eyes. She looked past Talia out to the street, as if expecting to see a windowless van ready to whisk her off to a waiting spaceship. In fact, with all those pin curls, she looked almost ready for outer space. "You from one of those religious cults?" she bleated.

"No, not at all. I—"

"Then I'll say it again. What do you want?"

"Are you Mrs. Kinslea?"

The woman paused. "I might be."

This was not going to be easy. In truth, Talia didn't blame the woman for being overly cautious. These days all sorts of lowlifes were out there preying on the elderly.

Talia gave the woman a sheepish smile. "You see, about thirty years ago there was a family that lived here—a woman and her daughter. Their name was Butterforth."

"Means nothing to me," the woman said.

She obviously hadn't been paying much attention to the news, Talia thought, but that was probably a good thing. "I spoke to Mrs. Butterforth recently, and she thinks her daughter might have hidden something in the apartment. Something that was very valuable to the family. Not in a monetary sense," she added quickly, "but something that was deeply sentimental."

It was a huge exaggeration, but it was the only story Talia could come up with that wouldn't raise too many questions. As it was, the woman was staring at her as if she had loose bolts rattling around in her head.

The woman looked her up and down. "You want me to look for it?" she said, her horrified gaze cracking the wrinkles on her face.

"No, no. Not at all," Talia said. "This little girl, she used to hide things in her bedroom closet. Her mother thinks it might still be there. If I could just have a quick look around that particular closet, I'll be out of your hair in a flash."

With a world-weary sigh, the woman opened the door. "All right. Go on upstairs," she said, "and don't touch anything till I get there. I've got nine-one-one on speed dial, so if you're trying to pull a fast one I'll have the cops here in a jiffy. Go on," she added impatiently. "It'll take me a few minutes to get back up there with these creaky old knees of mine."

Talia did as instructed, her shadow preceding her as she climbed the stairs quietly in her low-heeled pumps. The sole source of illumination was the weak lightbulb attached to the ceiling over the foot of the staircase. When she reached the apartment, the door to which was partway open, she waited in the narrow hallway. A strong scent wafted from the kitchen, a blend of boiled cauliflower and arthritis cream.

She resisted the urge to cover her nose, smiling sweetly as Mrs. Kinslea finally made it to the top. The poor woman was wheezing as if she'd just climbed Mount Greylock.

"Follow me," she said. "I'll give you three minutes, tops, and then you better skedaddle."

Three minutes wasn't much, but if that's all she had, she'd work with it. She remembered Anita telling her that she'd caught Ria coming out of her bedroom closet one day, a secretive look on her face. Anita claimed she later searched the closet and found nothing, but Talia wouldn't be satisfied until she'd explored it herself.

"It was that room," Talia said, indicating the door to Ria's old bedroom.

With a nod, Mrs. Kinslea turned the knob and pushed open the door, sending a cloud of dust motes swirling through the room. Talia tried not to cough as she skimmed her gaze around the cluttered mess that greeted her. Ria's former bedroom was freezing cold and full of junk—everything from old chairs and tables to a battered Royal typewriter with most of its keys missing. In her mind's eye she saw the makeshift cage Ria had constructed for the rabbit. The little girl had cut up two big cardboard boxes and duct-taped them together, making a cozy little enclosure for her furry friend. The cage had sat right beneath the window, where the bunny could enjoy the summer breezes as well as an occasional swatch of sunlight.

"I don't use this room much," Mrs. Kinslea said. "Only for storage."

No kidding.

"I'll only be a few minutes," Talia promised, darting toward the closet. Inside, a row of heavy coats hung on the rack, above which was a wooden shelf packed with old-style hatboxes. Dozens of shoes were piled in a heap on the floor. The overpowering scent of mothballs made her eyes water, and she rubbed her lids with the back of her hand.

Talia pulled out her ladybug keychain and flicked on the tiny flashlight. How could she do a decent search in three minutes? The closet was a mess! She prayed the woman wouldn't actually time her while she was riffling through all this stuff.

"Are all these clothes yours?" Talia asked her, glancing over the array of pastel-colored hatboxes.

"You bet, missy. I was quite the fashion plate in my day, you know. Worked at the old England Brothers in Pittsfield for thirty-three years and got a discount on everything. After my Sammy died, I lugged these all these things with me from our place on Boylston Street in Pittsfield. Now *that* was a nice apartment," she said sourly, as if Talia had been the one who'd forced her to move.

Talia turned back to the task at hand. If everything in the closet belonged to Mrs. Kinslea, then Ria couldn't have hidden anything in one of the hatboxes or in any of the boots or shoes. Talia flicked her light all around the closet, praying she'd spy an attic door cut into the ceiling, or a secret slot cut into a side wall.

She heard Mrs. Kinslea's plodding footsteps recede into the distance. Was she leaving so she could call the police? Talia had to move quickly.

Of course, it would help if she were tall enough to search behind the shelf, but there was no way she could reach that far back. Did she dare ask Mrs. Kinslea if she could borrow a step stool?

Aware of the imaginary clock ticking in her head, she

decided against it. With a sigh of exasperation, she shone her penlight into every nook she could find.

She suddenly felt like an idiot. Did she seriously think she was going to find anything? She was on a fool's errand, without a clue where to begin. With a resigned sigh, she made one last sweep around the floor with her light. No, nothing in the corners, except—

Wait a minute. What was behind the coats? She shoved aside a bunch of the coats, her heartbeat going bonkers. Yes, it was a door! A trapdoor about four feet tall and maybe a yard wide, it was cut cleverly into the back of the closet so as to be nearly invisible. It had one of those flimsy latches consisting of nothing more than a curved hook fitted into a metal ring screwed into the wall.

Pulse pounding, Talia dropped to her knees. She set her mini-light on the floor and crawled over the mound of shoes. A spiked heel jabbed into her shin, but she kept going until she could reach the latch. When her fingers found the metal hook, she lifted it. She pushed on the door, but it wouldn't budge. Years of neglect and lack of use had no doubt made it stick in place.

Talia looked around frantically. Any second now, Mrs. Kinslea would be trotting back in to announce that her time was up. Her gaze landed on a black boot with a Cuban heel, circa 1965. She grabbed it by the toe and smacked the heel against the door, over and over until she heard something give. This time when she pushed on the door, it opened.

She snatched up her light again and shone it into a space so creepy it made shivers waltz up her arms. Cobwebs formed the primary décor, along with dust so thick it looked like a lamb's wool coat. A spider the size of an orange scuttled away from her mini-beam, and she let out an involuntary squeal.

From somewhere behind her she heard footsteps approaching, a bit more sprightly this time. She had to move fast. Blowing dust out of her face, she swept her beam all around. She didn't see much other than a filthy, empty attic space. After three sweeps, her beam caught something. Tucked against the wall to her left was a cylinder of some sort. About ten inches tall, it was coated with so much dust and grime she couldn't tell what it was. From the shape and size, though—

"Miss, are you done in there? What was all that pounding?" Mrs. Kinslea's screechy voice echoed through the closet. "I called my son, and he said I shouldn't have let a stranger in the house. You have to leave right now."

"Coming!" Talia called. Gingerly, she reached for the cylinder, her pulse skipping when she recognized what it was—an old oatmeal box. She grabbed it and blew off as much dust as she could, sneezing twice as she backed out of the space.

"My son says you have to go," Mrs. Kinslea squawked, "or he'll call the police."

"I'm coming, Mrs. Kinslea." She sneezed again and pulled the trapdoor shut, latching it closed.

Mrs. Kinslea gaped at the filthy oatmeal box. "How did you ever find that? I didn't even know anything was back there."

Still holding the box, Talia got to her feet and brushed off her pants. "There's a trapdoor at the back of the closet, but there was nothing behind it except a century's worth of dust. And this."

Mrs. Kinslea stared at the box and frowned. "Is it filled

with stolen goods or something?" Her gaze narrowed. "Are you a jewel thief?"

"No, I'm not," Talia assured her. "Do you have one of those plastic grocery bags I could use to put this in?"

Her curiosity apparently trumping her fear that Talia was a criminal sort, Mrs. Kinslea picked up her pace and returned in less than a minute with a plastic Price Chopper bag. Talia slid the oatmeal box inside and then pried off the cover. To her amazement, it lifted with ease. *Thank you, Quaker Oats, for making such a sturdy container.* She peered inside.

Mrs. Kinslea's faded eyes lit up through her thick glasses. "What's in there? Money?"

Talia pulled out the contents, which consisted of several sheets of yellowed paper curled into a tube. Something else was down there, too, something covered in cellophane. A cigarette wrapper? Trying to keep her fingers from trembling, Talia gently unfolded the papers. The top sheet portrayed a childish sketch of an animal of some kind, drawn with a green colored pencil. Her pulse raced. She was anxious to look at all the drawings, but this wasn't the place to do it.

Mrs. Kinslea's disappointment was evident in her scowl. "That's what you came here for? Some kid's scribblings?"

Talia pasted on her best smile. "Yes, well, as I said, they have great sentimental value to her mother."

She had to get out of there. If the woman's son really had called the police, she could get nailed. She could just imagine herself explaining this little intrusion to Detective Patti Prescott. *Not.*

She dug into her purse and pulled out a gift certificate for two free fish and chips dinners, thanking the angels that she'd thought to bring it with her. "I'm sorry I troubled you, Mrs. Kinslea. Please accept this in return for my barging in on you like this. It's good for two free dinners at my restaurant."

Mrs. Kinslea snatched it out of Talia's hand, her mouth twisting as she studied it. "Fish, huh? Well, I do like fish, so long as it's fresh. Maybe my son will take me over there for lunch one of these days."

"Our fish is very fresh," Talia said, "and I hope to see you both soon." She looped the grocery bag over her wrist and headed for the stairs. "It was nice meeting you, and I'm sorry for interrupting your morning!"

Talia fled down the shadowy staircase and out the front door. She sucked in a cleansing breath, hoping her new scent would cover any lingering odor of mothballs. She hopped into her car and slammed the door shut, resting the grocery bag on her front seat.

The quick glance she'd gotten of the one sketch told her she might have found something important. She desperately wanted to examine all the sketches, but Scott was meeting her at the eatery at eleven thirty. It was a few minutes before eleven. Plenty of time for her to get there, put on a pot of coffee, and go through at the box's contents before he arrived.

She started the car and was flicking on the heater when she spotted a dark green vehicle creeping into her side view mirror. Oh no, it looked like a pickup. Her stomach lurching, she locked her doors and shifted into Drive. She started to pull away when the pickup driver rolled down his passenger side window and waved frantically at her. "Talia, wait!"

She looked over. When she saw who it was, bile rose in her throat. Andy Nash was signaling to her to roll down her window.

"Andy, go away!" she said.

He leaped out of his truck, and for a moment Talia thought he was going to block her path with his body. Instead he came over and knocked on the roof of her Fiat. "Please, can I talk to you for a minute?"

She felt her entire body shaking. Andy was driving a dark pickup, the same kind of vehicle she and Kelsey had encountered a few nights ago in front of Anita's condo. Was he the one who'd broken in and folded Ria's nightdress over her pillow? The thought made her insides curdle.

"I swear, Andy, I'll call the police right now!" With a shaky hand she reached into her purse and dug around for her cell phone. Naturally it had journeyed to the molten core of the earth. It didn't help that her fingers couldn't stop trembling.

"Oh God, Talia, please don't call the cops. Just listen to me first, okay?" His glasses hanging crookedly from his ears, he gave her a wild look.

No, she wouldn't be tricked again into listening to another tale of woe from a man who might well have murdered Ria. The fact that he'd apparently followed her here like the stalker he was only added to her suspicions.

Finally, her fingers found her cell phone. She snatched it out of her purse and held it up so Andy could see she was calling the police.

His face red and stricken with terror, he raced around to the driver's side of his pickup and tore off. At the next corner he made a hard right, and then roared off through the residential neighborhood at nearly warp speed.

Her fingers freezing, Talia punched in Detective Prescott's number. She groaned when the detective's voice mail kicked in. Talia left her a detailed message, giving a recap of her encounter with Andy. She omitted the part about tricking an old woman into letting her search her closet—that would come later after Andy was behind bars. Unfortunately, in her haste to dig out her phone, she'd failed to notice the tag number on the pickup. Some detective she was.

It was ten past eleven when she got to the arcade. She made sure no one was following her before she parked in one of the diagonal parking slots on the street behind the plaza.

More than ever, she wanted to examine Ria's drawings. She was confident that before long the police would catch up with Andy. In the meantime, if anything in the oatmeal box pointed to his guilt, she wanted to figure out what it was.

She hurried across the cobblestone plaza, anxious to get inside. It was the kind of December day she'd always loved in the Berkshires, when the air teased with a promise of snow and Wrensdale's main drag boasted the same seasonal decorations it had for decades past. Today the arcade was quiet. Suzy's bath shop was closed. The tea shop didn't open until one on Sundays. Normally Talia would appreciate the lull and enjoy strolling over the cobblestone. Right now all she craved was the safety of her restaurant.

Once inside, she instantly locked the door. The first thing she did was set the Price Chopper bag on the floor near one of the corner tables. With all that dust on the oatmeal box, she didn't want to risk contaminating anything, nor did she want to attempt to wipe it. In case the police questioned where she'd gotten it, she wanted the dust from Mrs. Kinslea's attic to remain exactly as it was.

Rubbing the chill from her arms, she went over and turned up the thermostat. She shoved her purse under the counter. After that, she exchanged her pumps for her favorite polka-dot Keds and put on a pot of coffee. Martha's scarf, she noticed, was hanging on the back of the kitchen door again. She must have forgotten it when she left yesterday.

Talia pulled in a calming breath. In the scheme of things, it was minor irritation. Once they each had a locker, Martha's scarf would be stashed away—out of sight, out of mind, out of olfactory range. The thought made her smile. The idea of renovating the kitchen was beginning to appeal to her more and more.

The oatmeal box was calling to her, and she was itching to examine the contents. Scott was due in about ten minutes, assuming he was the punctual sort. Detective Prescott still hadn't returned her call, but she was confident the detective had already listened to her message. Talia remembered her saying that she listened to her voice mail nearly twenty-four/ seven. Had Prescott already put out an APB, or whatever it was called, on Andy Nash?

Talia poured herself a mug of steaming coffee. She plopped in a dollop of cream and grabbed a plastic trash bag from underneath the counter. She draped the trash bag over one of the tables near the door, making a tablecloth of sorts. After setting her mug down, she reached into the grocery bag and pried the cap off the oatmeal box. The drawings were curled loosely around one another, their edges yellowed with age. It would be a miracle if they didn't crumble when she examined them.

The cellophane item she'd spotted at the bottom of the box turned out to be an empty Lucky Strike cigarette pack. Strange thing for a kid to save, even a child as secretive as Ria. But Talia knew from personal experience that kids saved odd things. In fourth grade, she herself had rescued a Mr. Goodbar wrapper from a waste can after a boy she'd been crushing on had tossed it away. The memory made her cringe.

Eager to look at the drawings, Talia set them gently atop the trash bag. There were seven drawings in all, each one done in green pencil.

The first drawing was a set of random scribbles, so juvenile it didn't resemble much of anything. With a heavy hand, Ria had crossed out sections where she'd made mistakes. It was almost as if she'd been struggling to get it just right.

Talia's suspicions were confirmed when she went through the remaining sketches. With each successive drawing, Ria's artistic skills had improved. The pictures still didn't bear any resemblance to a dragon, but each one showed slightly more detail than the preceding one.

The last sketch set Talia's heart racing. Something about this particular drawing nibbled at the edge of her brain.

In bold green pencil, Ria had drawn an angular creature with vaguely reptilian features. It had a long, flat snout with jagged teeth, and clawed feet attached to short legs. A memory nagged at her, but she couldn't quite pin it down. The sketch resembled an animated beast she remembered from long ago. But what . . . *what?*

She thought about Will Claiborne's family crest—the two-headed snake curled around a tulip. Ugly as it was, it didn't look like any of the creatures Ria had drawn. The realization gave Talia a sense of relief, even though she was pretty sure Andy was the killer. But how was Andy connected to the dragon?

A hard knock at the door startled her. Her heart did a pole vault over her ribs. She folded the trash bag over the sketches and left them on the edge of the table.

Another knock sounded, louder this time. Praying it was

Scott and not Andy, she moved toward the door and called, "Who is it?"

"It's Scott!" said a cheery voice. "And I come bearing doughnuts."

Talia let out the painful breath she'd been holding. She unlocked the door, so relieved to see Scott standing there that she almost wept.

His brown eyes twinkling under his blond eyebrows, he stepped inside. Dressed in navy Dockers and a long-sleeved blue polo shirt over a crisp white shirt, he looked like an ad for a country gentleman. "Hey there," he said, "you're looking mighty pretty today." He went over to a table near the door and set down his brown doughnut bag. "Fresh from Queenie's. I got glazed, jelly, and cinnamon. Hope you like one of those."

"I like all of them." Talia smiled, relishing the scent of warm cinnamon that wafted through the dining area. "Thanks, Scott. You didn't have to do that. Aren't you cold? You're not even wearing a jacket!"

He laughed. "It's gotta get down to zero before I wear a jacket." He winked at her. "I'm hot-blooded, remember?"

"Let me get you some coffee," she said quickly, feeling her cheeks flush. Sometimes she didn't know how to take his comments. She couldn't tell if he was flirting or just being friendly.

A minute later she set a fresh mug of coffee on the table for Scott, along with sugar packets and creamers and a bunch of napkins. One of the sugar packs slid to the floor, and she bent to scoop it up.

"Here, grab a doughnut," Scott said, opening the bag. "You seem a little jittery. Are you okay?"

His tone was so kind, Talia found herself wanting to confide in him. For a moment, she debated whether or not to tell him about Andy Nash. By now, she hoped, the police had probably caught up with Andy. She might as well give Scott a heads-up. As Andy's friend, she reasoned, he would want to know.

First she needed a good sugar rush. She removed a cinnamon doughnut from the bag and set it in front of her on a napkin. She took a large bite and swallowed, savoring the cakey texture and burst of cinnamon on her tongue.

She looked soberly at Scott. "Scott, this morning I was visiting an elderly friend over near the park," she said, being intentionally vague. "As I was leaving, I realized that a pickup truck must have followed me there. It turned out to be Andy Nash, and he was absolutely frantic. He desperately tried to get me to let him inside my car. He was pounding on my roof!"

Except for a slight twitch under his right eye, Scott's face remained passive. "Talia, that's terrible," he said quietly. "What did you do?"

Talia told him about Andy speeding away. She finished by describing her call to Detective Prescott.

"So, the police must be looking for him," Scott said in a ragged voice. He slugged back a mouthful of steaming coffee. The glazed doughnut he'd taken from the bag still sat, untouched, on a napkin.

Talia gave him a look of sad resignation. "By now they've probably caught up with him. At least I hope they have," she added. "Scott, I'm sorry I had to do that to your friend, but I honestly had no choice. He scared me half to death."

Scott smiled and gave her hand a quick squeeze. "You did exactly the right thing, Talia. You had every right to protect yourself. Women have to be so careful, especially these days. There's a lot of nuts out there."

"Yeah, you said it," she agreed.

Scott looked thoughtful. "Of course it still doesn't prove Andy is guilty of anything. Other than acting like a pure idiot, that is." He smiled again, as if he were trying to convince himself.

"I'm sorry, Scott," Talia said, "but the more I think about it, the more it seems he's acting as guilty as sin." She glanced over at the table where she'd left the trash bag folded over the sketches. She realized she'd left her coffee mug over there, too.

"Well, then, shall we get started?" Scott said abruptly. He pulled out a small notepad from the pocket of his trousers. "I have another appointment at one. Do you have any ideas for what you want to do?"

Wow, that was a quick change of attitude, thought Talia. Where was the friendly, flirty contractor of only a few moments ago? Until now, he never mentioned having another appointment.

Feeling a bit unnerved, Talia swallowed. It didn't bode well that he wanted to wrap up their meeting so quickly. Her bombshell about his friend Andy had obviously shaken him more than she realized.

"Um, well, yes, actually I do," she said, explaining about the sketch Martha had drawn.

Scott looked at her and gave her a polite nod. When she kept staring at him, he grinned. "So, are you going to show me the sketch?"

Something about his amiable tone didn't ring true. He'd definitely been thrown off-kilter by her news about Andy. She sensed he was trying to adopt a professional manner for her sake. In truth, she wasn't as eager to discuss the renovations as she'd been before her scary encounter with Andy.

In the back of her mind, she kept wondering if the authorities had caught up with him yet. No doubt Scott's thinking was running along the same lines.

"Oh, of course—the sketch!" she blurted out, giving him a *duh* look. "It's in my purse. Let me get it."

She retrieved Martha's sketch from her purse and returned to their table, pushing aside the doughnut bag so she could spread it out. Scott had unbuttoned the left cuff of his white shirt and was folding it back over his sweater, all the way to the elbow. The temperature in the dining area now felt comfortable to Talia, but it was clearly a tad too warm for his liking.

Talia unfolded Martha's sketch of the kitchen and pushed it over in front of him. Her glance went automatically to the silly pirate on his left arm. She'd thought the tattoo cute when she first saw it, but now it seemed absurd—a grown man with a tattoo from a children's fantasy. She wondered if he'd ever thought about having it removed.

"I thought Martha did a spectacular job with these dimensions," Talia said, then realized how dopey that sounded. Dimensions were dimensions any way you looked at them. "But naturally I want your expert opinion on how doable all this is."

Still fussing with his cuff, Scott peered at the drawing. After a minute or so, he smiled. "Your Martha knows her stuff, doesn't she? I think she missed her calling. I'll need to retake all her measurements, but those look spot on to me."

She'd *had* a calling, Talia thought silently. But she sure as heck wasn't going to share Martha's history with Scott.

"Well, then. We're off to a good start," Talia said. "I guess my first question is, how far into the dining area could we actually build out to make the best use of space in the kitchen?"

Scott gave her a thoughtful frown and began unbuttoning the cuff on his right arm, folding it methodically over the sleeve of the blue sweater. He looked almost annoyed at the question. "As I said, I'd have to take my own measurements first. This place is a rental, right?"

Talia nodded, something tickling the back of her brain. "Um, yes, it is, so I'd have to get the landlord's . . . permission . . . first." Her last few words fell away to a low murmur. Scott had rolled up the sleeve on his right arm.

Every cell in her body froze. Before she could stop herself, she shot an involuntary glance at the table where she'd left the trash bag.

Scott followed her line of vision. When he realized what she was looking at, he gave out a laugh and tapped her hand. "I knew something was missing. You left your coffee mug over there. Let me grab it for you." He shot out of his chair.

"No, Scott, that's okay, don't bother! I really didn't—"

But by then it was too late. His fingers were already looped around her mug and he was pulling the trash bag forward, apparently with the intention of centering it on the table. He must have pulled it too far, because the edge of the bag slipped off one side and onto the tiled floor. Ria's sketches slid out.

"Scott, don't bother picking that up," Talia said. "It's just some stuff I was going to throw out later."

Ignoring her, he whipped the trash bag to the side and stared at the sketches. The Lucky Strike wrapper caught his eye, and he snatched it up. For a moment he seemed to be contemplating what to do, his eyes darting all around. Then he fastened his gaze on her, his face a mottled shade of red that made Talia's insides shudder. He snatched up the sketches and the cigarette wrapper.

Unable to keep her voice from trembling, Talia folded up Martha's sketch. "Scott, why don't we do this another time? I can tell you're upset about—"

In under a second he'd crossed over to her. With his free hand he squeezed his fingers around her forearm.

Talia tried to pull away, but his grip was like iron. "Ow! Stop it, Scott. You're hurting me. What's the matter with you?"

He shook the sketches at her. "Where did you get these?" His voice came out in a menacing hiss.

Her wrist felt ready to snap in two. "I . . . I . . ."

Scott shoved her arm, momentarily releasing his grip. "Never mind. It really doesn't matter anymore." His eyes had gone hard and distant. Even the color was off—an opaque brown with pinpoints of darkness that the strongest light wouldn't penetrate. "The question is what to do next?"

Not a question Talia wanted to contemplate at the moment.

Scott gawked for a second or two at the cigarette pack and then shoved it into his pocket. "So the little wench *was* telling the truth," he said, almost as an afterthought.

Wench. Was that supposed to be pirate talk? Talia looked at him with pure loathing. The tattoo on his right arm seemed to mock her, its jagged teeth belying the friendly expression it its oddly human eyes.

Not a dragon, as little Ria had thought. It was the wily croc from *Peter Pan*, the one that swallowed Captain Hook's hand. In a little girl's childlike eyes—and limited experience—it had looked like a dragon. That was how she always remembered it.

Somehow, some way, Ria must have witnessed him killing that young woman. She couldn't describe the tattoo so she drew it—over and over again until her mother got fed up and tried to destroy the sketches. But Ria was too clever. She'd brought them with her when they moved to Wrensdale, and found the perfect hiding spot in that dusty attic space.

"Scott, I'm afraid I don't know what you're talking about," Talia said, trying to slip an edge of impatience into her voice. "Why don't we plan on meeting next week sometime, when you're not as busy?" She scraped her chair back. "Let me get my appointment book and—"

"Sit down," he ordered, pushing her back into the chair. "Don't pretend you didn't figure it out, because it'll tick me off even more."

Talia looked at him and saw pure evil. How had she ever thought he was handsome?

She considered her options, none of which were good. Her cell was in her purse underneath the front counter. The eatery's land line was on the wall in the kitchen. Even if she tried to get to one of them, Scott would probably kill her first. He'd killed before—twice. Her only hope was to keep him occupied and pray she could think of a way to escape.

"I guess I'm baffled, Scott," she said. "Those childish drawings mean absolutely nothing to me."

He shook his head and smiled. "It's too bad, really," he said softly, and then dropped in the chair next to her. He leaned closer, his coffee breath gagging her. "I'd already kind of picked you for my Peter Pan." He stroked her arm with his forefinger, and she tried not to flinch. "This chick I'm dating now? She's young, and she's pretty enough. But she's too clingy, always calling to check up on me." His fist clenched. "She's not like you, Talia. You're cute as a kitten, and I'll bet you're just as cuddly, aren't you?"

What a scumbag, Talia thought, feeling her stomach turn

inside out. His notion that he could "pick" any woman he wanted made her want to slap him silly. Any moment, the bite of cinnamon doughnut she'd eaten was going to come spewing northward and out through her mouth.

She pulled her arms away and fisted her hands under the table.

His fake smile faded. "That day, at the fund-raiser, I helped Ria take her things back out to her car when she was ready to leave. When I rolled up my sleeves to help her pack up those stupid scarves, she must've seen the tat on my right arm. After I helped stash her display racks in her car, she turned and said to me, 'You're the dragon. You're the one who killed that girl.'"

Oh, Ria. Why did you do that? Aloud, Talia said, "Did you know what she meant?"

"There's only one thing it could have meant," he said. "Over the years I've thought a lot about that little girl. Wondered if she'd ever remember what she saw."

Talia swiveled her head toward the kitchen. "Do you mind if I grab a fresh cup of coffee, Scott?"

He barked out a laugh. "So you can throw it in my face?" His lip curled into a sneer. "If you want to hear the story, just zip it and listen."

Talia nodded and shrank into her chair.

"I was living in Agawam then. That year the summer was brutally hot, worse than usual. I'd picked up a pretty gal I knew. Her name was Lainie Johnson, and she'd just had a big ole tiff with her boyfriend. He'd dropped her off near her house and she was walking home, bawling her eyes out. Boo hoo," he mimicked, pretending to rub his eyes.

"She was feeling so low," he went on, "I figured we could have some fun, you know? Maybe it would cheer her up. She was more than happy to jump into my front seat and tell me all her troubles. I gave her lots of tea and sympathy, only the tea was really beer." He laughed at his cleverness. "I was a real looker then, Talia. I could have put any leading man in Hollywood to shame."

A faint rumble penetrated Talia's senses. Something outside. Something familiar and yet . . . different.

"I needed some Luckys, so I popped into the corner variety while she waited in the car. The parking lot was behind the store, and it was empty except for a big old jalopy parked a few spaces away. When I got back to my car, that sweet-looking Lainie was just sitting there, looking so sad and pretty and vulnerable. I scooped her into my arms and kissed her, hard. After that I couldn't stop myself. I made a move on her. My God, I was only nineteen! Next thing I know she starts going crazy on me, screaming at the top of her lungs. I told her to shut up but she . . ." He shook his head. "I grabbed her throat with my hands to stop that godawful shrieking. I didn't mean for her to die. I honestly didn't. When I realized she wasn't breathing, I shoved her under the glove box."

Talia's insides felt like ice cubes. "Ria was in the jalopy, wasn't she? She saw the whole thing."

Scott nodded. "I looked over and saw this little redheaded kid gawking at me from the front seat. I knew she must've seen everything. Nobody was around. Her window was rolled down, so I got out of my car and went over and leaned my arm on it. I said, *'You tell anyone what you saw and I'll kill you. You get me, you little witch?'* Only I used a slightly stronger word so she'd get the picture. I threatened to kill her mother, too."

That poor, terrified little girl, Talia thought, her heart aching for Ria.

"She must have noticed my tattoo that night, but at the time I never even thought about it."

Talia pulled in a shaky breath. "When Ria confronted you at the fund-raiser with what she saw that night, did you deny it?"

Scott looked at her with disgust. "Do I look stupid to you? Of course I denied it!" He pressed the fingers of one hand over his forehead. "But then she told me she kept the cigarette pack I'd tossed on the ground, even mentioned that they were Luckys. I didn't remember throwing away an empty pack that night, but she knew the brand, so I guess I did. The brat must have gotten out and picked it up after I tore out of that lot. She also said she drew pictures of my tattoo, and that she'd kept them all these years. I knew then that I was screwed."

Ria must have remembered where she'd left those childhood sketches, Talia surmised. Was she thinking about retrieving them from the old apartment?

Talia blinked away tears and looked around at her eatery. She loved this place more than she ever imagined she would. Was this the last time she would ever see it?

"At that point I kind of panicked," Scott admitted. "I asked her if we could go somewhere and talk quietly about it, so I could convince her she was wrong. I told her I knew who the real killer was, but that I needed her help before I went to the police."

"And she fell for it?"

"She looked confused at first, but then I gave her one of my most sincere smiles. I'm such a pro at that." Scott laughed. "You know that yourself, right?"

Ugh, what a narcissist, Talia thought.

When Talia didn't respond, his face darkened. "I could tell

she was going for it. She *wanted* to believe me. I told her I'd
volunteered to dismantle Santa's village after everyone cleared
out, so maybe we could talk there. Amazingly, she agreed.
She told me she'd pack up the rest of her things and meet me
in Santa's village in fifteen minutes. After that she raced into
the building ahead of me."

Because she thought she'd be safe there, Talia thought
grimly. *Oh, Ria, how could you have been so trusting? How
did you let him trick you so easily?*

"I followed her back inside. I wanted to keep an eye on
her so she wouldn't do anything dumb. I noticed her talking
to an older woman and figured it was her mother. Luckily,
the dame didn't hang around long. Then I saw Ria pack up
the rest of her junk, so I wasn't too worried."

Talia thought back. She remembered seeing Ria stuff the
rest of her things into her wheeled suitcase and storm off.
"But I saw her leave!"

"She didn't *really* leave. She brought that suitcase out to
her car, but then she came back inside and waited for me."

Somehow Talia had missed that, probably because she
was busy packing up her own things.

"So after I helped you pack up and you finally left," Scott
went on, "I went back inside the building. By then the gym
was empty. Andy had vanished inside his office. Sure enough,
Ria was sitting in Santa's chair, waiting for me, like the dumb
cluck she was."

"How did you lure her into that supply closet?"

Scott grabbed his coffee mug and slugged back the cool-
ing liquid. "I pulled her in there so fast she didn't know
what hit her. I sure was glad she had that blue scarf around
her neck." He laughed cruelly. "Ditzy chick made it so easy
for me."

"That was my grandmother's scarf!" Talia cried. "You are despicable." A lightbulb snapped to life in her head. "You're the one who broke into Anita's duplex, aren't you? You knew that if the authorities searched her room and found those drawings, someone might recognize the crocodile tat on your arm."

He shrugged. "Couple of the local cops are on my softball team. They're not the brightest bulbs in the pack, but if Ria's mother ever found the drawings and turned them in, even they might notice the similarity. I didn't want to take the risk." His gaze turned granite hard, and his nostrils flared. "But wherever she hid those things, I couldn't find them. I looked *everywhere*." He pounded his fist on the table. "Where did you get them?"

Another low grumble off in the distance made Talia's ears perk. Whatever it was, Scott didn't seem to notice. Ignoring his question, she said, "Andy saw you that day, didn't he?" Her voice shook, but she went on. "That's why you were so desperate to find him. He was the one witness who could pin you at the scene."

"Yeah, the poor SOB." Scott twisted his mouth into a malicious smirk. "After I took care of Ria, I shoved aside the Santa's village crap and pushed the divider wall in front of the door. I didn't know a piece of that scarf was sticking out from underneath. Anyway, Andy must've walked past the gym to use the men's room. He saw me moving that divider wall. I knew the light would dawn on him later, after Ria's body was found. Funny thing was, I was sure he'd get blamed for killing her. I was counting on it, in fact."

Talia shivered. "You were going to kill him, too, weren't you?"

"Yeah, I was going to take care of him the moment I

realized he saw me. I had an idea for making it look like a suicide. Then you came trotting back in for some stupid thing you left in the kitchen, and I lost my chance." He glared at her, and in that moment she saw pure reptilian eyes. "You're just like all the other broads, aren't you? Disorganized. Messy. Brainless."

A wormlike thread of fear wrapped around Talia's insides. She was none of those things, but it was obvious he'd painted all women with the same brush. Scott wasn't only a sociopath—he was a misogynist.

"You know, Scott, you really have no choice," she said to him. "Turn yourself in and beg for lenience. You didn't plan to kill Ria . . . or the other woman. Maybe the DA will go easy on you. You have rage issues. You need help."

She knew it was a useless plea, but she was stalling for time. He shot his hand out and grasped the folds of her ladybug scarf, jerking her toward him. "Do you remember what they called the crocodile in *Peter Pan*?"

Paralyzed by fear, Talia shook her head. She felt the scarf tighten around her neck.

"Tick-tock," Scott said, and gave a bone-chilling laugh. "It's fitting, don't you think? Because you, my little pixie, don't have much time left. And I guess I'm even smarter than I thought, because I parked in the alley behind your kitchen."

"Only delivery vehicles are supposed to park there," Talia said, wanting to spit in his face.

"Yeah, that's your worst problem right now. Get up."

Her heart pounding so hard she was sure he could hear it, she rose slowly. Scott pulled her arms roughly behind her, holding her wrists in a viselike grip with one large hand. From the cobblestone plaza came a loud noise, a beastlike roll of thunder. Talia screamed as loud as she could, but Scott slapped his hand over her mouth. He jammed his knee into the small of her back and then shoved her toward the kitchen.

Think think think.

An article she'd read recently in a women's magazine suddenly popped into her head—quick self-defense tips for women. What were they? *Think.*

Jab your fingers in his eyes!

She couldn't. Not with her hands held fast behind her.

Box his ears! Give him a karate chop to the throat!

Also not an option. *Come on, think. There was something else . . .*

Scott's hand was still clamped over her mouth. Her head swam, and her breathing grew labored. What was that other self-defense tip?

Stomp on the foot.

Oh, Lord, why had she changed into her soft-soled Keds? But it was too late for regrets. Using every ounce of power she could summon, she lifted her right knee and brought her foot down hard on Scott's suede loafer.

Scott cursed viciously. He pulled his hand away from her mouth and cuffed her on the back of the head.

It was a tiny window of opportunity, but Talia took it. She sucked in a deep breath, and then gave out a scream so ear-splitting it was a miracle the lights didn't shatter.

"You stupid little bi—"

The door to the dining area flew open with a bang, and Talia issued another deafening scream. She managed to twist her head around, just in time to see Lucas stumble around one of the captain's chairs and crash to the floor on his skateboard. A bubble of hysteria burst from Talia. His new skateboard wheels were the size of platters!

Instantaneous panic rode Scott's features. Fight or flee?

She could see the decision wavering in his eyes as his gaze skittered all around the kitchen.

Recovering quickly, Lucas popped up his skateboard with one sneakered foot and snatched it in both hands. Scott shoved Talia hard toward the fryers and then turned and fled in the direction of the back door.

"No way, dude," Lucas said. "No one hurts my boss and gets away with it."

Blond tufts sticking out from his head at all angles, Lucas slammed Scott in the back with his skateboard. Scott hit the floor with a thump, smacking his forehead on the tile. He groaned and tried to crawl away, but Lucas plunked the skateboard on his back and sat on it.

Scott realized he was trapped. He began spewing obscenities as he tried to wriggle out from under the skateboard. He might have been strong, but Lucas was younger and far taller. No amount of cursing and jiggling could dislodge her employee.

"Are you all right, Ms. Marby?" Lucas said, concern written all over his face.

"I'm fine, Lucas," she said, choking back tears. She reached for the land line.

"Good. Oh, um, I already called nine-one-one," he said, patting the cell phone in his zippered shirt pocket. He looked down at Scott's struggling form and chuckled. "I guess maybe we should tie him up till the cops get here."

Talia scurried over to the back door and whipped Martha's scarf off the hook. "I have the perfect thing!"

Lucas kept Scott pinned to the floor while Talia secured his ankles with the smelly scarf. Less than a minute later, the cavalry arrived, Sergeant Liam O'Donnell of the Massachusetts State Police leading the charge. Detective Patti Prescott was right on his heels.

"I see you didn't have the patience to wait for us," Prescott said curtly. She waved Talia and Lucas into adjoining chairs, and they both quickly obeyed.

"Actually," Prescott said in a softer tone, "are you okay? Right now you're looking a little worse for the wear."

Talia choked out a giggle of sheer relief. "I'm okay. We both are." She beamed at Lucas. "My knight on shining skateboard wheels here came to my rescue. What more could a boss—no, a friend—ask for?"

Lucas grinned. "I spent half the night putting those wheels on. I'm glad I did. When I heard Ms. Marby scream, I practically flew over the cobblestone."

Two uniformed officers hauled a dazed Scott to his feet and pushed him toward the door. Scott looked at Talia with hatred in his eyes. If his hands weren't in cuffs, she was sure he would try to strangle her, too.

"By the way, Scott," Talia said, "Lucas is nineteen—the same age you were when you killed Lainie Johnson. You could take lessons from him on how *real* men treat women."

Lucas blushed bright red to the tips of his ears. "Yeah, dude. It's not cool to hurt a lady. Not cool at all."

Prescott frowned. "Who's Lainie Johnson?"

Talia sighed. She was in for a long day.

After what seemed like hours of questioning, Talia and Lucas were finally allowed to leave. Lucas's mom had arrived to collect him, tears springing in her eyes. "My brave little boy," she kept saying, much to her son's chagrin.

Hands crossed over his chest, Sergeant O'Donnell strode over to Talia. "Well, it seems you cracked the case again, Ms. Marby. But the next time, may I suggest—"

"—that I leave the investigating to the police," she said, finishing the sentence for him. "And to that I say . . . gladly."

With a doubtful look, O'Donnell tipped his hat and left.

Detective Prescott dropped into one of the captain's chairs. She looked tired. Her gaze roamed the room appreciatively, and then she smiled at Talia. "So, anyone for fish and chips?" she said, mischief twinkling in her nutmeg-colored eyes.

Talia laughed. "All in good time, Detective *Patience* Prescott. All in good time."

The detective winked at her. "Touché. Now, since I'm officially off duty, let's whip up some grub."

20

Exactly one week later, Talia removed an experimental batch of batter-coated Brussels sprouts from the fryer. She'd already set the deep-fried broccoli florets on a platter, and her aunts were happily doing the official taste testing.

Instead of a peanut sauce for the sprouts, she'd come up with a creamy garlic dip recipe she was reasonably happy with. Laced with finely minced garlic, the buttermilk-based mixture turned out even better than she'd hoped.

"Here you go!" Talia said, delivering the fried goodies to their table.

Aunt Josie, one perfectly styled brunette strand bobbing in her face, tried the broccoli first, and then moved on to the Brussels sprout. She wrinkled her nose. "Okay, the broccoli is a *yes* and the Brussels sprouts are a *no*," she said. She dropped the offensive fried sprout onto her plate.

Her sister, Jennie, snatched it up and popped it into her

mouth. "You're such a fussbudget, Josie. These are scrumptious!"

Talia leaned over their chairs from behind and hugged
both her aunts. They were so different, and yet so madden-
ingly the same, she thought. Josie with her stunning makeup
and dazzling manicure looked ready for a night on the town.
Jennie, her graying hair framing her freshly scrubbed face,
reminded Talia of a youngish Miss Marple.

The aunts had arrived as planned that prior Sunday evening, just in time to hear all the hullaballoo about Talia and
Lucas's triumphant encounter with a killer. Since Talia was
now a restaurateur, she couldn't afford to close for more than
a day or so. She'd opened the following morning to a waiting
crowd.

Talia had also scrambled to put up some seasonal decorations in the eatery. Garlands of faux evergreen festooned the
walls along the ceiling. Holding them in place were bright
red velvet bows. A fake blue spruce about four feet tall sat
in the far corner of the dining room. Among the cream-
colored papier-mâché snowflakes that hung from its branches
were the six gold and blue vintage angels someone had left
in a bag near the restroom.

Three days after Scott's arrest, Vivian Lavoie had come
into the eatery. "I feel so awful for stealing those ornaments,"
she'd told Talia, a guilty expression on her plump face. "But
I never intended to keep them. I was going to sneak them
back to that redheaded girl after the fund-raiser was over.
And then—" Tears flooded her eyes, and she swiped a hankie
over them. "And then she was murdered so horribly . . ."

Talia had let her cry, and then said gently, "You were
afraid they were prettier than yours, weren't you?"

"Yes," Vivian blubbered, "and I had so much competition

already. Everyone had made such lovely things. I was afraid no one would buy mine. I left them near your restroom that day. I figured if someone found them and turned them in, you'd know what to do."

Talia had tried to return the ornaments to Anita Butterforth, but the woman had insisted Talia keep them. Anita had also come to the realization that owning a cat was not for her. She'd looked hugely relieved when Talia and Kelsey stopped by to pick up Princess. She had even given Kelsey an awkward hug. Kelsey and her mom spent the next few days buying up a whirlwind of accessories for their darling new kitty.

Over the past week, the eatery's customer base had blossomed. The sign was up—FRY ME A SLIVER—but everyone seemed to be calling it Fry Me. That was fine with Talia. She had to admit, she sort of liked the shortened moniker.

Lucas had been excited to learn that he was now the eatery's official delivery person between the hours of eleven thirty and one thirty, but only to downtown addresses within a half-mile radius or so of Fry Me. In between classes at the community college and his part-time job at the eatery, he was honing his skateboarding skills with his new oversized wheels. "Those new wheels cream the cobblestone!" he'd told her, his blue eyes dancing with sheepish pride.

The desserts were next. Talia headed back into the kitchen. She'd already cut up squares of fruitcake, along with slivers of orange pound cake from Peggy's Bakery. There were so many more things she wanted to experiment with. She found herself awakening each morning with ideas for new deep-fry recipes hopping around like frogs in her brain.

The kitchen was still too small, but for now she and Martha were learning to live with it. Renovations would come later, probably sometime in the spring. When the time was right, Talia planned to talk to Will Claiborne about setting out some weatherproof benches and tables on the plaza. That way, people could enjoy nibbling at their fried goodies and watch the downtown goings-on at the same time.

Liliana, Talia had learned, had agreed not to fight the divorce any longer. No doubt Will had been relieved to hear that, but moving past his insurmountable loss was not going to be easy. It still broke Talia's heart to think of how much he'd loved Ria.

The door opened and someone called, "Knock knock." Ryan stepped inside, his arm looped through that of a tall, gray-haired man with whose resemblance to Ryan was startling. He grinned. "Are we too early?"

"Never," Talia said, accepting a warm but brief hug from Ryan. She wanted a bigger hug, but with her lovably nosy aunts watching, she was happy to settle for a tiny one. For now.

"Talia, my dear," Arthur Collins said, "I am so pleased to see you." He wagged a finger at her. "You scared me, you know, confronting another killer the way you did. I must caution you against ever doing so again." The kindness in his tone belied his sternness.

What a sweet man he was, Talia thought. Arthur's diagnosis of early-onset Alzheimer's had been a blow to Ryan, but lately Arthur seemed to be enjoying more good days than bad. Ryan gave her a meaningful look. *Today is a good one*, it said.

"I will try never to do it again, Arthur," Talia promised. She kissed his cheek lightly and then squeezed his hand. "Now come in and meet my two favorite aunts."

Josie zoomed off her chair and grabbed the elderly man's other hand. "Pay no attention to that favorite aunt stuff," she piped in. "We're her *only* aunts so she has no choice but to worship us."

Jennie rolled her eyes, while Ryan and Arthur sat down between the aunts. It was a sight that made Talia's heart swell. They made their own introductions, and Talia excused herself and returned to the kitchen.

She noted with amusement that Aunt Jennie was studying Ryan with a sharp eye. Of the two aunts, Jennie was the practical one. Smart and analytical, she was no doubt sizing up Ryan for potential entrance into the family. Talia couldn't help grinning when saw her Aunt Jennie reach over and squeeze Ryan's wrist. He'd obviously passed one of her initial tests.

During the early hours of Saturday morning, the first snow of the season had fallen in the Berkshires, coating the ski slopes with eight inches of powder. The streets were messy, and a few fender-benders had been reported. Talia had grumbled about scraping snow off her Fiat, but in truth she'd been thrilled to see the white stuff.

"Are your mom and dad coming, Talia?" Ryan called to her in the kitchen.

Talia slid the deep-fried pound cake slivers onto a lined platter. "Nope. The siren song of the slopes was calling to them. They're spending the afternoon at Jiminy Peak." She plunked the orange sauce she'd made earlier into the microwave and warmed it for several seconds.

Lucas and his folks had been invited, but they'd already committed to visiting family in Vermont.

Talia had also invited Rachel and Derek to join them, but they'd already made plans to visit Derek's dad in Florida for an extended weekend. There was one other person Talia had asked to join them, but so far she was a "no show."

Talia delivered the snacks to the table, along with a

simmering pot of spiced tea. Everyone helped themselves. The chatter eventually turned to Scott Pollard.

Arthur gave a slight shudder. "I simply do not understand the darkness that courses through the hearts of some people. What horror lives in that man's soul that compelled him to commit such atrocities?"

"At least he confessed to both murders," Ryan pointed out, his jaw tightening. "He's probably angling for a lighter sentence, the lowlife."

Talia nodded. "I guess Andy Nash is off the hook, although I still think he's a stalker. He saw Scott coming out of the supply closet that day. He was terrified to go to the police, so he begged me to solve the crime!"

"Well, dear niece, you did solve a murder a few months ago," Aunt Josie pointed out. "And now you've solved a second one. Seems to me he picked the right woman for the job."

"Oh, no." Talia shook her head firmly. "I am a fry cook, not a detective, and I intend to stay that way."

Ryan beamed at her and raised his cupful of tea. "I second that motion."

Talia grinned. "Oh, I forgot to tell you all! Yesterday I received the nicest letter from Lainie Johnson's mother. She's living in Arizona with her son now, but if she ever comes back to Massachusetts for a visit, she's going to stop by and meet me. She said it was strange, but she could never picture Lainie's boyfriend killing her. He was always a bit wild and impulsive, but never nasty or mean. She always had doubts about his guilt."

A soft knock at the door made everyone turn. The door opened, and Martha Hoelscher stepped inside. Sans the smelly scarf, she wore her usual peacoat, along with sensible black rubber boots.

"Martha, you made it!" Talia slipped off her chair and hugged her employee. "Come in, I want you to meet everyone."

Martha nodded at the group. "Hope I'm not late. Mass just ended, and I had to walk all the way from Saint Agatha's."

Talia had figured out why Martha complained about the long walk to work every day. She'd spotted her one morning leaving the church, where she apparently attended the early Mass every morning. From where Martha parked in the town lot, the church was in the opposite direction from the eatery. The walk back added just enough extra steps to make her start off her mornings a bit grumpy.

Martha peeled off her coat and slung it over a nearby captain's chair. Talia made the round of introductions, and everyone greeted her warmly.

"By the way," Martha said, accepting an offer of tea from Talia, "Father Francese gave you quite a plug in his sermon today. He praised you for slaying demons and for making the best fish and chips in the Berkshires."

Arthur grinned. "I couldn't have said it better."

Talia felt her cheeks redden. She hadn't been to Mass in so long that a wave of guilt washed over her. "That was sweet of him," she said, hopping off her chair. She went over to the tree and reached behind it for a foil-wrapped box. "Martha, since you won't be with us for Christmas, I wanted to give this to you now."

Martha glared at the box. "We're doing gifts? Why didn't you tell me?"

"No, no, we're not," Talia said quickly. "But this is something I want you to have, especially since I . . . kind of ruined yours."

Ryan set his mug down. "Okay, now I'm officially curious."

Martha tore off the blue foil wrapping and opened the white box. Her eyes widened. With a wry chuckle, she pulled out the plush knitted scarf Talia had found at the Coat d'Azure. "Oh, boy, do I need this," she said. "And it's my favorite color—beige."

Talia laughed. Martha's smelly old scarf had served a noble purpose—tying the ankles of a killer until the police got there. The scarf was now retired, having been tossed out by the cops after they arrested Scott for murder.

Martha swallowed. "I am honored and proud to be a part of this eatery," she said in a quiet voice. "Thank you."

"You're also a part of this family," Talia said. "And don't you forget it."

At that moment, Talia's ears caught the tinkle of a familiar sound. She splayed her hands over the table. "Listen, everyone. Do you hear it?"

From somewhere outside, the sound of harmonious voices filled the air. Bells chimed as the singing grew closer.

Aunt Jennie turned sharply toward the sound. "It's the carolers. I haven't heard them in years!"

Every year, on the Sunday before Christmas, a dedicated group of carolers strolled the sidewalks of downtown Wrensdale. Over the years the faces had changed, but the voices were always the same.

"Sounds like they're right in front of the arcade," Talia said, rising from her chair. "I have to take a peek!"

No one else wanted to brave the chill, so Talia slipped outside alone. Hugging herself for warmth, she gazed out across the cobblestone. Dotted with clumps of snow, its rounded stones gleamed under the pale December sun. If not for the cars passing along the busy main drag, it could have been a scene from Dickens.

Swathed in their forest green capes and sporting bright red earmuffs, the carolers ambled closer. Nine in all, they stood in a cluster at the entrance to the arcade. Their voices carried over the crisp air, sweet and trilling.

Talia heard the door to Fry Me open, and then a pair of muscular arms slipped around her.

"I wish it could be like this forever," Ryan whispered, hugging her close.

Maybe it can be. Talia couldn't make herself say the words aloud.

For now, this was perfect. The rest, if it was meant to be, would happen soon enough.

21

"Get out of here," Talia told Martha. "I warned you we were closing at four on New Year's Eve, and I meant it. Now scoot."

A rare twinkle shone in Martha's eyes. She untied her blue apron and tossed it into the bin near the door. Talia had recently contracted with a service to launder the linens and towels. The cost was reasonable, and it left her more time to focus on the task she loved most—trying out new deep-fry recipes.

"I hear you, boss lady. You don't have to tell me twice." Martha tucked her new beige scarf around her neck. Wearing her old peacoat and black rubber boots, she ambled to the doorway with more spring in her step than usual. Talia knew she was looking forward to her evening at the women's shelter in Pittsfield. She'd started doing volunteer work there and loved it. This evening she was gearing up for a night of "deep fry" and storytelling, with Martha preparing snacks and then reading aloud stories by some of her favorite authors.

In a wry twist of fate, one of the raffle tickets Bea had bought her at Suzy's shop turned out to be a winner. Martha, who insisted she had no use for bath and body luxuries, was going to donate the basket to the residents at the shelter.

"It's snowing," Martha said, pausing in the open doorway.

Talia glanced past Martha onto the cobblestone arcade. Tiny flakes were drifting to the ground. Three inches were predicted by morning. "At least you've got new snow tires," Talia said, grateful she'd been able to hand out sizeable holiday bonuses to her two employees. "But be extra careful, okay?" She'd been relieved to know Martha was spending the night at the shelter and wouldn't have to drive home late on New Year's Eve.

Martha frowned. "Aren't you leaving?"

"I am," Talia said. "I want to give the restroom a quick once-over, and then I'll be out of here."

Martha hesitated and then said, "Talia, thank you for everything. I wasn't sure I was going to like living here, but now I feel as if it's my home."

Talia hugged Martha and pushed her out the door, locking it behind her.

Barely two minutes later she heard the door handle jiggle. No doubt it was someone who didn't know about the early closing time, even though she'd put an announcement in the local paper.

Talia wavered for a moment, and then unlocked the door. A frail, haggard-looking man stood in the cold, his hands shoved deep into the pockets of his thin jacket.

"I'm awfully sorry, sir, but we closed at four for New Year's Eve. Try us another time?"

"I . . . I was actually looking for someone. Do you know if a, um, Talia Marby works here?" His voice was so soft Talia could barely hear him.

"I'm Talia Marby," she said, her heart going out to this sad-looking soul. "Can I help you?"

The man's Adam's apple bobbed in his throat. "My name is Kyle Feeley, and I didn't come here to eat. I only wanted to thank Miss Marby for everything she did."

Kyle Feeley. What did that name jingle a bell?

And then it came to her. He was the man who'd spent over thirty years in prison for the murder of Lainie Johnson.

Talia opened the door. "Mr. Feeley, please come in. Can I make some coffee for you?"

He stepped inside and Talia closed the door. His sneakers, which looked new, were damp from the snow. "No, you said you were closed. I don't want you to go to any trouble."

"Please, have a seat." She pulled out a nearby chair and waved at him to sit. If she had to guess, she'd peg him in his late fifties, but he wore the world-weary look of a far older man.

"Are . . . are you sure? You said you were closed, and I only came to thank you, Miss Marby." His faded blue eyes filled with tears and he sat down. "You gave me the rest of my life back, for whatever it's worth."

Talia swallowed back her own tears. "I'm going to make us both some coffee, okay? Give me a minute."

She put on the coffee and returned to the table. "Mr. Feeley, I am so sorry for everything you've suffered. The system failed you, big-time. I can only hope they're going to make amends."

He shrugged. "I have a lawyer now, and she's working on that. Whatever happens, it won't be real quick." He gave her a crooked smile, displaying graying teeth. "The system doesn't work that fast, does it?"

Talia smiled. "No, I guess it doesn't."

"Miss Marby, I want you to know that I never would've hurt Lainie. I loved her."

"I'm sure you did," Talia said softly.

"Oh, don't get me wrong. I had my faults. Back then I had a hair-trigger temper on me. But I never, *ever* laid a mean hand on Lainie. She was my life. I wanted to marry her."

Talia looked at his hands. They were calloused and dry. No doubt they were icy cold. She wished she had a pair of gloves to give him.

Kyle slid a glance toward the kitchen. "Your coffee does smell good. Not like the swill we drank in the joint. Maybe . . . I mean, could I have a cup to go?"

"You can have it to go or here," Talia said. "Mr. Feeley, do you like fish and chips?"

His eyes brightened. "It's one of my favorite meals, but I haven't had the good kind in thirty years. In prison we only got the frozen stuff. It tasted like cardboard."

In her head, Talia whizzed through her plans for the evening. Ryan was picking her up at six thirty. They were celebrating New Year's Eve at the Wrensdale Pines with Arthur. The facility had hired a piano player to entertain the residents and their families. Arthur hadn't stopped talking about it for days.

"I have a few chores to finish up in the kitchen," she said, fibbing a little. In preparation for an early closing, she'd already completed her usual tasks. "If you give me ten minutes, I'll whip up some fish and chips for you."

Talia could tell he was torn. His eyes filled again. "Miss

Marby, that would be the best gift anyone's given me in a very long time. Thank you."

She turned on the fryer and gave him coffee while he waited. Normally at the end of the day she tossed away any unused batter. But today, anxious to close early, she'd shoved the bowl into the fridge, figuring she'd throw it out tomorrow. Now she gave a silent nod of thanks to whatever sixth sense made her save that batter.

Sensing he hadn't had a decent meal in ages, she added an extra slab of haddock to his meal.

Before he ate, he crossed himself and murmured a quiet prayer of thanks. She made herself a half cup of coffee and sat down with him.

Kyle raised his mug. "To freedom," he said. "And to the woman who gave it to me."

Talia lifted her mug to his. "To freedom," she repeated. "And to a fresh start for the New Year. Cheers, Mr. Feeley."

RECIPES

When Talia began experimenting with deep-fried snacks, she discovered she could use the same basic batter as a base and add sweet or savory touches as needed. The batter for her deep-fried meatballs contains Parmesan cheese and crushed basil for a little "zip." The sugar and vanilla added to the deep-fried marble cake batter make it work well as a sweet batter.

Please be sure to take great caution at the stove when making deep-fried treats at home. A good policy is to keep children and pets a safe distance from the hot oil while you're in the preparation stage.

TALIA'S DEEP-FRIED MEATBALLS

*Talia spent her childhood at her nana's elbow watching
her make homemade meatballs. She knew that Nana
tweaked the recipe depending on whom she was feeding.
Ingredients such as fresh garlic, Parmesan cheese, and
herbs can be adjusted to suit your taste.*

*If you'd like to cut down on preparation time for the
deep-fried meatballs, there are many frozen brands that
are quite good.*

Meatballs

¾ pound hamburger

1 tablespoon finely minced onion

1 teaspoon crushed garlic (more if you're a garlic lover!)

¼ cup Parmesan cheese

⅛ teaspoon coarse black pepper

1 egg

¼ teaspoon crushed basil

⅛ teaspoon crushed oregano

1 cup panko crumbs

5 tablespoons high-quality marinara sauce

Mix all of the above ingredients with a fork until well
blended. Form into small- or medium-sized meatballs (about
1½-inch diameter works well, but you can make them
smaller if you'd like).

Roast in preheated oven at 425 degrees in a roasting pan
coated with nonstick spray for 10 to 12 minutes. The meatballs should be browned but not overdone. Chill in the

fridge for at least a few hours or preferably overnight. They can also be frozen ahead of time.

Batter

½ cup flour

¼ cup cornstarch

1 teaspoon baking powder

¼ teaspoon salt

2 teaspoons grated Parmesan cheese

½ teaspoon finely crushed basil

½ cup plus 1 tablespoon water

1 tablespoon beaten egg

1 tablespoon vegetable oil

Combine together in a mixing bowl the flour, cornstarch, baking powder, salt, Parmesan, and basil. In a separate bowl, combine the water, egg, and oil. Add the wet ingredients to the dry ingredients and whisk until well blended.

In a deep fryer or heavy pan, heat additional vegetable oil to 350 to 375 degrees, using just enough oil to cover the meatballs. A candy/deep-fry thermometer will help gauge the oil temperature. One by one, coat the chilled meatballs in the batter. Using tongs, remove each meatball from the batter and lower each one slowly into the oil, but avoid crowding the pan. Fry until golden brown, about 3 minutes, then remove and drain on paper towels. Don't worry if your deep-fried meatballs end up with little batter "tails." They're crispy and delicious! Serve immediately with warm marinara sauce.

TALIA'S DEEP-FRIED MARBLE CAKE

Talia buys her marble cake at Peggy's Bakery, but there are some packaged marble cake mixes that would work nicely for this luscious treat and cut down on your preparation time. However, if you'd like to bake your own marble cake, here is a basic recipe that can be whipped up with ease:

Marble cake
    2 cups flour
    1 teaspoon baking powder
    ½ teaspoon salt
    1 cup white sugar
    ½ cup (1 stick) softened butter
    2 eggs
    1 teaspoon vanilla extract
    1 cup milk
    1½ tablespoons unsweetened cocoa

Preheat oven to 350 degrees, and grease or coat an 8-inch square cake pan.

Place all the ingredients *except for* the unsweetened cocoa into a mixing bowl. Beat on medium until smooth, about 2 minutes. Set aside about one-third of the batter and pour the remainder into the prepared cake pan. Add the unsweetened cocoa to the reserved batter and stir until thoroughly blended. Drop the cocoa batter by spoonfuls over the white batter. Using a butter knife, drag the cocoa batter through the white batter, making a swirly effect.

Bake for 30 to 35 minutes until a toothpick inserted into the center comes out clean. Cool thoroughly and freeze.

Sweet batter

½ cup flour
¼ cup cornstarch
1 teaspoon baking powder
¼ teaspoon salt
2 tablespoons white sugar
½ cup plus 1 tablespoon water
1 teaspoon vanilla extract
1 tablespoon beaten egg
1 tablespoon vegetable oil

Combine together in a mixing bowl the flour, cornstarch, baking powder, salt, and white sugar. In a separate bowl, combine the water, vanilla extract, egg, and oil. Add the wet ingredients to the dry ingredients and whisk until blended.

In a deep fryer or heavy pan, heat additional vegetable oil to 350 to 375 degrees, using just enough oil to cover the cake chunks. A candy/deep-fry thermometer will help gauge the oil temperature.

Keep the marble cake as close to frozen as possible before frying. Using a heavy knife, carve the mostly frozen marble cake into workable chunks, about 1½- to 2-inch squares. (You can also carve the cake into chunks prior to freezing.) Be careful not to let them thaw all the way through, as you'll end up with mush when you try to coat them. One by one, coat the cake chunks in the sweet batter. Lower each battered chunk slowly into the oil, leaving plenty of room between them. Fry until golden brown, about 3 minutes, then remove and drain on paper towels.

They're delicious to eat "as is," but Talia usually serves hers with a simple dusting of powdered sugar. If you'd like to add a swirl of raspberry sauce as a garnish (the way Talia did at the annual Santa fund-raiser), you can find quality brands either from gourmet food shops or online.

Serve warm and enjoy!

Feel free to experiment with different types of cake, such as pound cake or lemon cake or even fruitcake during the holidays. Any of your favorite cakes would make a scrumptious deep-fried snack!